I Faced the Wind:
A Frontier Woman's Courage

By Joy Newbold

(Historical Fiction)

Other books by Joy Newbold:

Where the Dragon Soars
The Dragon Kings, Book One

Ghosts in the Attic:
Warlocks, Witches, and Ghost
Heir of Devaknar, Book One

Shai: The Lamb that Jesus Loved
Legend of the Lambs, Book One

I Faced the Wind
A Frontier Woman's Courage

ISBN# 978-0692368619
© 2015 by L. J. Book and Audio
West Jordan, Utah
ljoynewbold@gmail.com
Cover: Zion Canyon
Shutterstock Photos

Biography of Main Characters

Although fictionalized, *I Faced the Wind,* tells the story of real men and women who faced danger and adversity to leave their footprints in the red sands of Utah's frontier.

Isaac Behunin (1803–1881)
Credited with naming Zion Canyon

Born in Richland, New York, Isaac was an early convert to the Mormon religion and served as a body guard to Joseph Smith. After being driven by angry mobs from their Nauvoo home, the Behunin family crossed the plains to the Utah Territory, where they were among the first settlers of Ephraim and Springville.

In 1861 Isaac and his family migrated to the Virgin River area, being among the first settlers of Springdale and Rockville. In 1863 he and his sons built a cabin, cleared land and farmed in **Zion Canyon** near the present site of Zion Canyon Lodge.

Elmina Tyler Behunin (1811–1883)
Wife of Isaac Behunin

An early convert to the Church of Jesus Christ of Latter-day Saints (the Mormons), Elmina Tyler first met Isaac and Meribah Behunin in Kirtland, Ohio. Meribah died in Kirtland leaving Isaac with three little boys. Elmina married Isaac in 1834 and raised Isaac's little

boys as her own along with the nine children that followed.
Driven from her Nauvoo home by mobs, she crossed the plains to the Utah Territory where the family moved from one new settlement to another. She experienced all the hardships of frontier life, from rattlesnakes to Indians, and settled with Isaac in **Zion Canyon** before there was a road wide enough to get a wagon through.

Stephen Mosiah Behunin (1842–1908)
Frontiersman, missionary, friend to the Indians

The seventh of Isaac Behunin's twelve children, Mosiah lived in Indian territory all his life and spoke both Ute and Paiute fluently.

In 1873 he was asked by Joseph Young to help negotiate a treaty that would end the Black Hawk War. Soon after, he was called by Brigham Young to serve a peacekeeping mission to the Indian people. He and his wife, Caroline, left their home in Richfield to spend fourteen years living among the Indians with their nine children.

Caroline Hill Behunin (1854–1914)
Wife of Stephen Mosiah Behunin

Caroline was not quite fifteen years old when she married Mosiah Behunin, a rugged frontiersman, who was friendly with the Indians and spoke their languages.

Like most white women at the time, Caroline was completely terrified of the Indians. But when

Mosiah and Caroline were asked by Brigham Young to abandon their homestead in Richfield and live among the Indians, Caroline conquered her fears and went with him to serve by his side on a fourteen-year mission, raising nine of her eleven children among the Indian people. *I Faced the Wind,* is written from her point of view.

Elijah Cutler Behunin (1847–1933):
First settler of Cainsville and Capital Reef

The ninth of Isaac Behunin's children, Cutler was a pioneer and a prospector. As did many of the settlers of that time, he served in the Utah militia during the Black Hawk War.

Cutler and his wife, Jane, raised fourteen children while living in early settlements in Sanpete, Emery, and Wayne counties. He was the first settler of the area that became Cainsville and later moved to nearby Notom. While in the **Capital Reef** area he devised a system of irrigation canals to help control the frequent flooding experienced in the area.

Tabatha Jane Earl Behunin (1853-1934)
Wife of Elijah Cutler Behunin

Jane Earl married Cutler Behunin in Rockville, Utah in 1868. Cutler was a frontiersman and prospector at heart. The couple moved from one newly formed community to another, building five homes in Wayne County, including one near Zion Canyon and one in St.

George, as well as the first cabin to be built in what was to become Cainsville. The family spent many years in the **Capital Reef** area, building homes in Cainsville, Notom, and Fruita.

Mosiah and Cutler were very close, and when the families lived near one another in the Fremont River Valley they shared many of the same experiences. Caroline and Jane were the best of friends.

Caroline and Stephen Mosiah family, ca. 1898
(Back row l–r: George, Joseph, Caroline, Brigham, David
Front row: l–r: Mosiah, with Robert on lap, Cynthia, Isaac, Elijah,
John, Mary Jane, Caroline)

Author's note:

I Faced the Wind is a work of fiction. Although many of the main events have been taken from Caroline Hill's journal and other family sources, they have been substantially fictionalized by the author. In some cases, the timeline has been intentionally altered. Chapter notes and a bibliography can assist in determining which parts of *I Faced the Wind are* true and which ones are the imagination of the author. All portraits seen here are available for free at www.FamilySearch.org.

Dedication

To Stephen Mosiah and Caroline Behunin, the Native American people they loved, and the posterity of each.

May we live together with respect and understanding.

Chapter One

St. George, Utah Territory
November 1869

I was fourteen going on fifteen the day my husband slipped a gold ring onto my finger. Old enough to fall head over heels in love, and young enough not to know what I was getting myself into.

I loved him—that was the short and the tall of it. Nonetheless, marrying the way I did was a mite like learning to swim by being chucked headfirst into the nearest swimming hole. Life with Stephen Mosiah Behunin was anything but easy—and I was awful young.

We met at one of those Saturday night dances down in St. George. Settlers for miles around used to come to those shindigs, and what a time we would have! St. George was a brand-new settlement then. A rugged land filled with rugged people.

Ma and I had left Salt Lake City to settle in St. George in '84. My mother to get away from a less than happy marriage. And me? Well, I didn't have any choice in the matter, and I didn't like it much. This desert land was hot as a branding iron and dry as a cracker.

Mosiah, though, was raised on the frontier, so it all came natural to him. He was near to thirty years old when I met him. Strong and free as the wind that sweeps the red desert sand. One look at him took my breath away, and I never recovered.

My ma, though, was not a bit happy.

***

"I'll not have it, Caroline! You hear?" Ma's glare bore deep into my soul, her dark eyes snapping.

1

I looked her right back. Square in the eye. I wanted her to see me as mature and determined, but it seemed all I could do was rile her.

"More Indian than white that one is," Ma almost spat the words at me as she plunged her fist into a pan of bread dough. Flour poofed into the air as she punched and prodded the white lump, wrestling with it like it was a living thing.

I bit my lip as I watched her. *I'm not bread dough, Ma. You can't pound me into doing things your way.*

"You marry that man, and you'll spend your life in some lonesome valley where white folks never go. Your children will grow up like little savages!"

I rolled my eyes and crossed my arms in front of me. "You're making things out to be worse than they are, Ma. And you know it!"

"Am I?" She snorted, jabbing a flour-and-dough-covered finger in my direction. "I've heard plenty about that young man and his Indian-loving ways. Folks say he's spent so much time around them savages, he talks their language better than he does English."

"Ma!"

"It's the truth, and you'd just as well hear it. You've got so many stars in your eyes you can't see what's right in front of your face. You'll be figuring it out fast enough, though, when you find yourself stuck down in that wild canyon month after month."

"Doesn't sound so bad to me," I murmured without looking up until I felt Ma's hot glare burning a hole in the top of my head.

"Doesn't, huh? You, Mosiah, the coyotes, and the in-laws. Right cozy I guess 'til you realize there's no way out. The road's so steep a wagon can't make it. Ask Ma Behunin, she knows. Folks say her washtub's nothing but a hollowed-out log. You want to live like that, Caroline? All the days of your life?"

"No, and I won't be needing to," I answered, leaning forward, my hands planted on my hips and my eyes boring into Ma's angry glare. "You know his family only stays in Zion Canyon in the summer, while they're farming."

"Yes, and in the winter they live in Rockville." Ma stripped the bread dough from her fingers and gave the ball of dough a slap as she glowered at me over the top of her spectacles. "They call that place Rockville for a good reason, you know."

"Well, we won't be living there for long. Mosiah and I talked it through already." I lifted my chin, tilting my head a bit as I threw my mother a smug smile. "He's up Richfield way right now, claiming some land for us."

"Richfield!" Ma rolled her eyes with disgust. "I should have known."

"Richfield is growing fast," I snapped back at her. "It'll be a proper town soon. It'll have stores and a chapel and a school, maybe even a doctor. I told him that's what a family has got to have, and he agrees with me." My eyes flashed a triumphant glance in Ma's direction.

"Yes, well, that's what he's saying today!" she grumbled.

"He's a good man, Ma." I took a step closer and reached for her hand, my eyes pleading with her to understand the depth of my commitment. "He'll take care of me. You'll see."

Ma snatched her hand away and glared back into my eyes. "He's twice your age, Caroline. You might not think that's a problem, but it will be. And that's coming from someone who knows."

"I love him, Ma. And I'm going to marry him!" Tears burned my eyes, and I could feel my fists ball up at my sides. Standing up against Ma's anger was about as easy as holding back a roaring river.

"You're a willful child, Caroline. Always have been. Seems like I've been running behind you, getting you out of one mess after another, since the day you learned to walk. Well, this here is one mess I'll not be getting you out of. Do as you please. You will anyway. But don't expect me to dance at your wedding!" Ma gave me one last hard look, wiped her hands on the dish-rag, whipped around, and was gone.

I stood staring at the staircase she had mounted moments before, and my lips began to tremble. Ma had never been one to let any softness show, but I knew that in the upstairs bedroom, my ma was crying.

I turned and began to knead the dough Ma had abandoned. Hurting my ma was the hardest thing in the world for me to do.

I shot a glance in the direction of the upstairs bedroom. "Durn it, Ma! Why do you have to make everything so hard?" I muttered to myself as I gave the dough a punch of my own. "This should be the happiest time of my life. Any other girl's mother would be pleased."

I slapped the dough into a ball, dropped it into the pan, and tossed a cloth over it. "Well, don't be thinking I'm going to let you ruin my wedding!"

I stomped over to the washbowl, gave my hands a quick rinse, and dried the residue on my apron. Then I marched out the back door, letting it slam behind me with a bang. My feet hit the back path, and I just kept on going, my skirts swishing around my legs as I strode forward, all the while muttering words I was glad my ma couldn't hear.

I was halfway down the path before I stopped to wipe away an angry tear and found that I had been followed. The black-and-white face of my border collie, Scooter, looked up at me, his head tilted to one side and his one white ear pricked straight up. Somewhere in the depths in his brown eyes, I found the unconditional love I craved.

I dropped to my knees, wrapped my arms around his white ruff, and buried my face in his fur. Then I let the sobs come. I hadn't wanted Ma to see them. Wouldn't, for all the world, let her know that deep inside I was just a frightened child. A girl who needed her mother to smile at her just once, and say, "Ya done good."

***

I knelt beside the battered wooden trunk and drew my hand across its worn surface. The delicate roses carved long ago by the hand of some forgotten ancestor were still visible. I didn't know how many generations of women had passed this trunk along to their eldest daughters on their wedding days, but I did know that my grandmother had treasured it enough to find room for it in her cramped wagon and had brought it all the way across the plains. Then, as a line of mothers before her had done, Grandma had given it to my ma when she married Pa. And now, it would be mine.

For Ma, though, the wedding trunk held only bitter memories. She must have stroked its surface once, as I did now. She must have watched over it with care as she and her mother made their long journey west. And her anticipation must have been similar to mine as she waited for the day this trunk would be hers.

4

Ma was seventeen when she crossed the plains with her mother and her sister. I could hardly imagine her as a young girl, shy and in love; but she had been. Very much in love. At least that's how Aunt Mary told the story.

A young man named Durk was in the same company for the trek west. As harsh and difficult as that journey was, somehow the couple found each other and love blossomed. They had promised to marry as soon as the wagons made it to the Great Salt Lake Valley.

Such happiness, however, would never be.

One night, in a thunderstorm, Durk rode out with the other young men to head off a restless herd. When a bolt of lightning hit the ground, Durk's horse reared and went over backwards. When the lightening cleared, Durk was dead.

"Your ma was inconsolable," Aunt Mary said. "A light went out inside of her that day, and she never seemed to take much joy in life afterwards."

I sighed as I lifted the heavy lid from the trunk. It wasn't really Mosiah that Ma was objecting to, or my age, either. Love had never smiled on my ma, so she had turned her back on it.

I knew it wasn't fair that life had gone so wrong for Ma, but it still wasn't right for her to begrudge me love and happiness.

I felt it before I saw it. Made of fabric as soft as a baby's skin, the yellow dress made me smile the moment I touched it. Lifting it carefully from the trunk, I unfolded the delicate fabric and held it to my cheek. Pa had given it to me when he came to visit last spring. The prettiest dress I'd ever seen; and I'd never worn it! I hadn't dared! So, I'd tucked it inside in the trunk, away from Ma's angry eyes, waiting for—who knows what? And now, I knew what. It would be my wedding dress.

Thank you, Pa! How could you have known?

I felt sure Aunt Mary had helped Pa pick it out. The yellow reflected her sunny outlook on life; the lace collar and big puffed sleeves, her softness and warmth.

How could she and my ma have been sisters? Had my mother's tragedy hardened her so much, or had they always been different? They were a year apart in age, but eons apart in nature.

I stood and held the dress against me as I waltzed around the room. There would be dancing at my wedding—

that was for sure. Mosiah and I loved to dance! I paused to look at my reflection in the mirror. My eyes were brown like my Pa's.

Oh, Pa, I wish you were here now!

Pa would have danced at my wedding. He would have liked Mosiah too. I could imagine him putting his arm around Mosiah's shoulder and telling him that he would be real proud to have him for a son. But St. George was a mighty long way from Salt Lake City, and Pa was busy, being bishop and all.

What had possessed Ma to up and leave him like she did? One day she had just packed everything and joined a group of settlers headed for St. George to live with her mother and stepfather. I hadn't understood why then, and I still couldn't figure it out. But I sure did miss my pa!

Chapter Two

Scooter heard him before I did. One minute the little dog was chasing the chickens while I threw scratch, and an instant later, he was gone. Nothing but a black-and-white streak heading for the lane. I set the scratch pan on an over-turned barrel and smoothed down my skirts with trembling hands. I'd put on my favorite dress that morning, the blue one with the tiny white buttons down the front, and tied a white ribbon in my hair. Mosiah was sure to make it by noon, and I wanted to look my best, even if I did have chores to do.

I rounded the chicken coop and hurried to the lane just in time to see him jump lightly from his wagon and tie up the team. Scooter greeted him with yips and wags, then jumped up and landed mud-covered paws squarely in the middle of Mosiah's clean shirt.

"Durn it all, Scooter, look what you did! I put this shirt on clean, just this morning, so I could impress Caroline with what a fine-looking man I am!" His laughter boomed across the yard as he went down on one knee and proceeded to give Scooter's ears a good rub. When he saw me coming, he jumped to his feet and spread that grin I loved all over his handsome face.

"Well? What did she say?" he asked. I could tell by the way he stuck his hands in his pockets and tilted back on his heels that he was nervous.

"About what?" I asked as I looked up into his eyes with all the pretended innocence I could muster.

Mosiah took me by the shoulders and pulled me close, mischief twitching at the corners of his mouth and sparkling in his eyes, "You know very well what I mean, Miss Caroline Hill. I've been as nervous as a hog on butchering day, all the way from Richfield, wondering what your mama would say about you marrying a polecat like me."

"Well . . ." I pushed myself away from him and wandered off a bit, pretending to forget the subject of our conversation.

He followed me like a lost puppy. "What did she say?" he begged impatiently, grabbing me by the waist and wrapping his arms around me.

I turned and looked up into his eyes, watching the way the light turned his hair to gold. "She said yes," I whispered and watched his face light up like the early-morning sun.

Mosiah let out a war whoop, yanked his hat off his head, and threw it into the air; then he came for me with a look in his eye that made me giggle. The kiss that came next was so swift and so strong, I thought my bones would melt and they would have to scrape me up off the ground.

I planted both my hands on his chest and shoved. "Mosiah!" Nobody had ever kissed me like that before. I could hardly catch my breath.

"Well, we're engaged now, aren't we?" Mosiah's blue eyes twinkled, and he smiled so wide, he could have swallowed the whole Salt Lake.

I reached up and cradled his face in my hands, touching his cheeks, his hair, his lips. "I guess we are, at that," I whispered.

Then he gathered me softly and kissed me so gently you might have thought you could hear the angels sing. I melted into his arms, oblivious of anything in the universe but him. That is until we heard the door slam behind us and we jumped apart like two kids caught raiding the cookie jar.

***

Ma stood on the porch, her arms folded across her chest and her eyes cold as a January blizzard.

Mosiah retrieved his hat from Scooter. The dog had snatched the flying object mid-air and was now prancing around the yard with it in his mouth. After a few minutes of tug-of-war with the dog, Mosiah started towards Ma.

In his hand, he held the crumbled hat. But a hopeful grin spread ear to ear across his handsome face. "Sister Hill, I can't tell you how proud and happy I am—" Mosiah began as his huge stride ate up the distance between himself and Ma. That was the last word he got out, though, because she took one look at him, whipped around, and slammed the door behind her.

Mosiah stood there for a minute, his eyes glued to the spot where Ma had been seconds earlier, before he turned to face me, an incredulous expression replacing his confident grin. "I thought she said yes," he murmured as his questioning gaze met mine.

I picked up my skirts and hurried to his side. Mosiah stood rooted to the ground, confusion and hurt clouding the blue of his eyes.

"She did," I whispered apologetically, "but she's none too happy about it."

As comprehension dawned, his body sagged like someone had knocked the air out of him. "If she's thinking you're too young, we could wait a while."

"It's more like she's thinking you're too old."

"Oh," Mosiah shook his head and slapped his hat against his leg. "Well, there's not much we can do about that, is there?" he said, turning toward the house. "Guess I'll just have to go talk to her."

"Wait, Mosiah," I said, stopping him before he could leave. "The way Ma's feeling right now isn't just about you and me. Things are a lot more complicated than that. Come and help me finish my chores, and we can talk a while."

Reluctantly, he followed me as I turned and headed toward the chicken coop and the scratch pan I'd left behind.

Scooter ran before us, skillfully rounding up the chickens and herding them into a corner.

"Will this sorry excuse for a herd dog be coming along to Richfield too?" Mosiah questioned, his laugh easing some of the tension we were both feeling.

"I reckon not," I answered. "Ma and the kids will need him when I'm gone. The chickens would be more than glad to see him go, but he does come in handy when my brothers head out to bring in the cows."

"Those chickens lay any eggs with him around?" Mosiah chuckled at the sight of the chickens, all herded into a corner.

"Oh, they're pretty used to it," I said as I picked up the pan and started to throw the scratch, fanning the grain out with my fingers in the direction of the cornered chickens. "Let them go now, Scooter."

Scooter gave the chickens one last, longing look and trotted to my side, his tongue lolling out. Very soon, however, he abandoned us and darted across the yard to run after my youngest two siblings as they chased each other about.

"Your ma had all of you real close together, didn't she?" Mosiah asked, nodding toward the pair of youngsters who filled the air with their laughter.

"Real close," I agreed as Cynthia dodged her brother and the little black dog with her petticoats flying. "We're all about a year apart. I think that was some of the trouble between her and my pa." I set the scratch pan down and hitched myself onto the top rail of the fence.

Mosiah jumped up beside me and wrapped his arm around my waist. "I wondered," he said. "Folk's say your pa's a real good man. I heard he's a bishop in Salt Lake."

"He's wonderful," I answered, chewing a bit on the inside of my lip. "He tried to be good to Ma and take care of us kids, but he could never be the man she fell in love with—and that made it hard."

"Your ma loved another man, but she married your pa?"

I sighed and studied my hands for a minute. "She couldn't marry the man she loved, because he was dead."

"He was what?"

"He died in an accident crossing the plains. I think she's still grieving for him, even after all these years. But she was afraid to be alone, so she married my pa."

"That's not a very good reason to get married."

"I know, but Pa's a good man—she knew he'd take care of her." I turned to look into Mosiah's eyes, hoping he could understand what I couldn't quite understand myself. "I don't really blame her. Grandpa died in Nauvoo and left Grandma and her girls to face the mobs and cross the plains alone. She learned firsthand how hard it is for a woman without a man."

"And what about your pa?"

"I don't think he really loved Ma either. He was almost sixty years old and had been married twice before. His second wife died on the plains, leaving him with a family to take care of. He needed a wife. It was a marriage of convenience for both of them."

Mosiah frowned. "Well, that happens a lot, but people usually work it out. My folks got married in a lot the same way—guess you do what you have to do."

10

"Really?" I asked, surprised to hear that our parents had similar stories. "Are they happy?"

"You bet they are," Mosiah answered. "I don't know what they would do without each other. But I don't think my dad will ever get over missing his first wife, and my mother knows it."

"Pa's married to my aunt Mary now, and they're real happy. I'm glad for them, but I sure do wish it could have been different with him and my ma. I miss being a family."

Mosiah tucked a stray strand of hair behind my ear and wiped a tear from my cheek.

"Anyway," I turned to Mosiah smiling through my tears, "I think that's why she's giving us a hard time. She hated being married to an older man, and she's bitter about marriage in general." I took his hand in mine and looked into his eyes, drinking in the love that I saw there. "I'm sad for Ma; I really am. But I've learned from watching her how important it is to marry someone you love. That's why nothing—not my mother, or anything else—will stop me from marrying the man I love. I'm yours forever, Stephen Mosiah Behunin. I'll never let you go—and that's a fact!"

Mosiah threw both hands above his head and laughed, "You've got me, darlin'. I'm yours 'til the rivers all run dry." Then he reached over and pulled me to him, his lips brushing mine and his eyes reaching into my very soul as he whispered, "I will be yours until there are no more tomorrows and the scrolls of time fold up."

We clung to each other in a desperate kiss, my hands buried deep in his hair and his arms almost crushing me in the strength of his embrace. He was the sun and the moon for me. My earth and sky, my day and my night. He was every breath I would ever take and every dream I would ever dream. He was my life, my universe, my eternity.

When, at last we drew apart, my heart still pounding with the strength of our love for each other, we wandered hand in hand toward the barn. I still had chores to do.

11

Chapter Three

Cynthia pulled open the barn door, the resulting burst of light interrupting another kiss I'm sure Ma would not have approved of. I, however, was thoroughly enjoying the passionate moment filled with the promise of sweet things to come.

"Don't go, Caroline! Please, don't go!" My little sister's brown eyes swam with tears, and her lower lip trembled.

Reluctantly, I pulled away from Mosiah's embrace and turned to face the ten-year-old girl who hurtled herself toward me, all arms and legs and petticoats. I caught her in my arms and drew her to sit with me on a bale of hay.

"Oh, sweetie, I'm getting married. I have to go." My hands cradled her freckled face as I bushed rivulets of tears from her cheeks with my fingers.

"It's all because of him." Cynthia's black glance spewed daggers of venom as she turned to face Mosiah, who crouched beside us, his arm across my shoulders. I wrapped my arms around her and whispered as I drew her close.

"I know it's hard to understand now, but someday you'll find someone special and want to get married. Then you'll understand."

Cynthia pulled back and looked at me. Her eyes, round as saucers, were still swimming with tears. "Ain't I special?"

"Aren't you special? Cynthia, you are the only sister I will ever have, and it rips my heart out to leave you."

"Then don't go!"

Mosiah and I exchanged glances, and I bit my lip. With trembling hands, I unfastened a golden chain from around my neck, caught the filigreed heart in my hand, and held it tenderly one last time before I fastened the chain around my sister's neck. "Pa gave me this necklace on my eighth birthday. I want you to have it, so you remember that you are always in my heart."

Cynthia pressed the delicate locket to her throat with the palm of her hand, her eyes filled with questions and wonder.

"I think Pa knew when he gave it to me that Ma was getting ready to leave and take us kids. I think he knew I would have to live my life without him. I could see the pain in his eyes when he told me how much he loved me."

Cynthia sniffed and looked up, her lips trembling and her eyes pooled with tears.

"He said if we were ever apart, this locket would remind me that I wasn't alone—that I would always be in his heart."

"And did it?"

"Indeed, it did. I've felt alone so many times since then, honey, but whenever I'm feeling sad, I just hold this locket close, and then I know that I'm never really alone."

"Won't Pa feel sad if you give it to me? And won't you miss it?" Cynthia asked.

"No. Pa loves us both, and you're the one who needs it now. He'd understand. I have my Mosiah."

Cynthia nodded solemnly and smiled through her tears. "I'll take real good care of it," she said, "and I'll give it back to you when I get married."

"When you find someone special of your own, I'd love to have it back. But until then, I want you to wear it and remember that Pa loves you and so do I." I tweaked her nose and whispered, "And Ma loves you too. She just doesn't know how to show it."

"I know. I love you too, Caroline." Cynthia smiled like a ray of sunshine breaking through the clouds after a storm. Then she threw her arms around me and hugged me as tight as her spindly arms could hug.

We hugged long and hard until Cynthia was finally ready to let me go. Mosiah put his hand on her shoulder and asked, "Do you think you could do us a favor?"

Cynthia nodded eagerly.

"Could you run to the house and tell your Ma that we're coming in now? Tell her we'd like to talk with her, if it's all right."

Cynthia flashed us a quick smile and a nod, then she turned and was off, pigtails bouncing against her back as her bare feet carried her toward the house.

Mosiah and I sighed. I picked up the milk pail, and we headed for the house, hand in hand.

***

Ma sat in the parlor, her rocker barely moving as she stared at the wall. I was sure she had heard us come in, but she didn't turn her head. Not even when Mosiah cleared his throat.

"Sister Hill, we'd like to have a word with you," Mosiah began.

At last she turned toward us—her body drawn stiff and tall and her face like chiseled granite. "So, you've come to take my daughter, have you? I don't approve, and she well knows it. But I'll not stand in your way, so you'd best take her and be done with it." With that, she turned back to face the wall and began to rock at a furious pace, her jaw set hard and her chin stretched high.

"I love your daughter, Sister Hill," Mosiah tried again, taking my hand in his and looking deeply into my eyes. "I love her with all my heart, and I give you my word that I will take care of her."

"Well, you'd best do that, young man—you hear?" Ma's rocking stopped, and she turned to face us, her eyes full of fury. "I'll not have you taking her off to some God-forsaken corner of nowhere and raising my grandchildren where there's no schools nor nothin' but savages!"

I could feel Mosiah draw himself up with stunned indignation. "Sister Hill, I promised you that I would take care of Caroline, and I will. I've already filed a claim in Richfield, and as soon as I can build a house and clear the land, we'll be—"

"I've heard plenty about you and your folks!" Ma interrupted impatiently. Obviously she was making no effort to hear Mosiah out. "Living the way they do, down in that canyon where even the savages are afeared to go. I'll not have my grandchildren—"

I saw something snap inside of Mosiah. He took a few steps toward my Ma, then he looked down at her, indignation written all over his face and his fists clinched at his sides. Their eyes locked—neither one backing down. But Mosiah continued with controlled consternation.

"Sister Hill, you well know that Brigham Young called my father to help settle Utah's Dixie. My family did

14

what was asked of us because we were called by a prophet to do it; just like lots of other folks around these parts."

"And if you get a call to do some fool thing like that?" Ma's piercing dark eyes bore into his.

"Where the Lord calls us, we will go." Mosiah looked at me, and I stepped quickly to his side, lacing my arm through his. "And your daughter, Sister Hill, will be there by my side."

Ma looked unflinchingly back into Mosiah's eyes and answered with measured words, "Now that there's the rub, ain't it?"

"I've not found the Lord to lead me wrong yet, and I don't reckon I ever will," Mosiah answered unwaveringly.

Ma looked up into his eyes, searching them deeply. I guess she felt somehow satisfied by what she found there, because her expression softened and a tight smile crept across her lips. "Well, see that you take care of her like you said you would."

I hurried forward then and knelt at her side, touching her lightly. "I've got my things near ready, Ma. I'll be going with him to Rockville in the morning and staying with his folks 'til we get married."

Ma's eyes shot to my face, an objection ready on her lips; but I hurried on, "Don't worry, Ma. Mosiah will stay at his brother's place until we get married. We'll be spending the winter in Rockville and heading to Richfield in the spring. I'll write."

"See that you do," she said.

***

I was almost finished with my packing when my bedroom door quietly opened, and there, in the doorframe, stood my ma. Something soft and warm about her took me by surprise. Then she opened her hand to reveal the lovely cameo brooch I had seen her wear on special occasions.

"Caroline, this here brooch belonged to my mother. I want you to have it and wear it on your wedding day."

Sudden tears sprang to my eyes and choked my throat as I threw my arms around her. "Thank you, Ma, for everything!"
She patted me gently and turned to go. "Be happy, Caroline."

Chapter Four

Washington County, Utah Territory
November 1869

The ride was long and bumpy, but I managed to fall asleep, nestled close against Mosiah's side. That is until the left wheel hit a rock; then I came near to falling right out of the wagon. When I opened my eyes, I couldn't believe what I saw ahead of me. Instead of heading toward the snow-capped peaks of Zion Canyon, we were jostling and bouncing our way down a barely distinguishable trail through sagebrush and cactus.

"Mosiah, where are we going?" I asked as I tugged on his shirtsleeve.

The hint of a smile crept across his lips, and I could see crinkles forming around his eyes, but he just kept looking straight ahead, "Oh, I just thought that we'd pay a little visit to some friends," he said nonchalantly.

"Visit friends? Here?" I stared at the brush-covered foothills and then at the windy, dirt trail before us. "I can't imagine anyone living here except maybe . . ."

The wagon made a turn around a barren hill to expose an encampment previously hidden by the rough terrain, and I suddenly understood.

"Oh, no, Mosiah—not Indians!" I clutched his arm with icy fingers, terror rising within me like a spring flood.

He turned to look at me quizzically, laughing at my obvious discomfort. "Caroline, there's no reason to be scared. I know these Indians. They're Paiutes—they're friendly."

I stared into his face, knowing he had spoken the truth. Mosiah would never endanger me, but I couldn't control the panic creeping over my body. "No, Mosiah, please—I can't do this! Let's go back."

The look of amusement faded from his face and was replaced by puzzled irritation. "Caroline, I have an important reason for stopping here. You'll just have to trust me."

My body froze to the wagon seat, and I said no more. Mosiah was to be my husband, and it was my duty to obey him. Still, my muscles grew tighter and my breathing more erratic the closer we came to the Indian encampment.

After another minute, the village suddenly came to life—they had seen us coming. Several Indian boys, wearing no shoes and very little clothing, left the camp and ran toward our wagon. I could hear laughter and whooping from within the camp. Everyone seemed glad to see him. The moment Mosiah jumped down from the wagon, smiling Indians surrounded him, shaking his hand and patting him on the back.

I had just begun to relax a little, distracted from my apprehension by the surprising scene playing out before me, when they all turned to look me.

A young brave gestured toward me. Mosiah smiled, nodded, and answered with words I couldn't understand. Whatever he said caused quite a stir. They began to laugh and chatter to each other.

Suddenly Indian women surrounded me, climbing onto the wagon as they reached out to touch my hair, finger my clothing, and pat my face. If I had been any less frightened, I would have screamed and pushed them away; but as it was, all I could do was cower and plead with my eyes, hoping that Mosiah would come to my rescue.

I could see from the concerned look that clouded his features that Mosiah was as surprised as I was by their behavior. Still, his eyes silently admonished me to endure it.

As if in answer to my dilemma, a tiny, bent woman emerged from a brush-covered dwelling, carrying a bundle in her arms, and all eyes turned toward her.

Mosiah returned to my side, placed a gentle hand on my shoulder, and reached under the seat as he withdrew a bundle of his own. "Are you all right?" he whispered.

I nodded, surprised by the fact that I actually was.

He gave me a quick, knowing smile, and moved toward the old woman, carrying the bundle in his hands.

I was impressed by Mosiah's gentle, respectful manner as he conversed with this tiny, ancient woman in her own language. They exchanged bundles, and Mosiah returned to the wagon, climbing onto the seat beside me. He wrapped his arm protectively around my shoulders and flicked the reins across the horse's back. The wagon jerked into motion.

Neither of us said anything until we were well out of sight of the Indian village. Then he leaned close and gently whispered, "I'm sorry," and I began to cry.

"How could you let them touch me like that?" I stammered when my strength returned enough for me to speak.

"They didn't mean to frighten you, Caroline. They think you're pretty—and they're curious. I told them that we were getting married, and they were excited. They were only trying to be friendly."

"A bit too friendly if you ask me!' I snapped. "That was a terribly rude thing to do—someone should tell them that." I shot an icy glance in his direction.

"I'm afraid their idea of polite behavior is a little different from ours," Mosiah shrugged.

"I don't think they have any idea what it means to be polite," I answered indignantly, drawing myself up tall and wrapping my winter shawl tightly around me.

"That's not true, Caroline. The Indians have a strict set of rules when it comes to polite behavior. But their rules are different from ours. Maybe that's what causes some of the trouble between us. We just don't think alike."

An explanation like that wasn't enough for me. I was hurt and angry, and I wanted him to know it. "What I'd like to know," I shot at him, "is how you thought it would be a good idea to take me into that Indian camp. And what was so important that you had to do it—even when you knew how scared I would be?"

Mosiah gave me a long, hard look; then he pulled back on the reins and stopped the horses.

I hardly dared to look at him. He was probably real mad at me. Maybe he was even thinking of turning around and taking me back to St. George.

I ventured a little peek at him out of the corner of my eye and was surprised to see that he was looking at me with soft, warm eyes. He reached down and withdrew the bundle he had stowed under the wagon seat and held it in his hands.

He cleared his throat and began: "I'd intended this to be a wedding present for you; but I think, maybe, I'd like to give it to you now." He placed it in my lap and smiled at me tentatively. "Hope you like it."

I looked down at the bundle in my lap, then up into Mosiah's hopeful eyes, sudden understanding flooding into my consciousness.

"Oh, Mosiah," I whispered as a lump the size of a boulder forced its way into my throat and my eyes stung with tears. I felt petty and small. I had been so selfish.

"Well, see what it is," Mosiah urged me, and I untied the string. The cloth covering fell away to reveal a pair of leather moccasins, soft as a baby's skin and the warm color of sand.

"Mosiah, they're beautiful!" I fingered the soft fringe on the leggings that extended up to the knee. Touching the carefully crafted quill work, I caught my breath. "They're incredible. Did the old woman make them?"

Mosiah nodded.

"It must have taken her weeks to do this," I whispered as I held them up to admire their beauty and to touch the soft leather to my cheek.

"I'm sure it did. Yellow Leaf does the best leather work I've ever seen. She made those designs in the old way, from dyed porcupine quills. They have a sacred meaning about the happy life she wishes for you and me."

Suddenly I felt ashamed. "I'm sorry, Mosiah. I was wrong about those Indians. It's just that I've heard so many horrible stories about things Indians have done to settlers."

"We've all been wrong about the Indians, Caroline, and more afraid than we needed to be. I won't tell you that the stories you've heard about the Indians aren't true; lots of them are. My older brother, William, was killed by Indians in '55."

I gasped and pulled back, staring into his face with shock and horror.

"He was serving on a mission to the Indians at Elk Mountain, and there was an uprising. The missionaries were all killed."

"Oh, Mosiah!"

"Once, when I was about eight, my pa stepped out of our door to do the morning chores, and an arrow flew out of nowhere. It went right through the muscle of his arm. If that arrow had hit a few inches to the left, he would have been dead."

I stared at him in disbelief as he continued.

"Not long after that, angry Indians shot a flaming arrow into the wall of our cabin. Pa and me had to sneak around back so we could put the fire out before the cabin burned down with our whole family in it. We were real lucky we weren't all killed."

A cold chill ran through my body, and I was finding it hard to breathe. "But you don't hate them, Mosiah?"

"No, I don't. The truest friends I've ever had have been Indians. They've saved my life more times than I can tell."

"Really?"

"Yep. Once when I was nine, I was tending the cows up in the foothills when a band of hostile Indians came down on me. I jumped on my horse and tried to outrun them, but they chased me down an embankment and shot my horse out from under me. He rolled on me and broke my leg. I was lucky it wasn't worse than that, but I was in a sorry way."

I reached over and laid my hand on his knee. I knew he was real lucky to be alive, and that meant I was real lucky too. "What did you do?" I whispered.

"I played dead. After they took the cows and left, I dragged myself to the camp of some friendly Indians that I knew. They took real good care of me and got me back to my family."

"How bad was your leg?"

"Pa set it the best he could, but after a while, it got a big lump on it. Looked like blood poisoning was starting, and they thought they might have to cut off my leg. I sure didn't want that—so when I was alone, I got a knife from off the table and stabbed that lump, deep as I could. You should have seen it! Puss squirted clear up to the ceiling! Fixed it though. See?" He held out his leg and flexed the knee. "It's good as new."

I shook my head. "I don't understand how you can feel so friendly toward Indians. I know people who haven't had half as much happen, and they hate Indians so bad, they'd kill 'em all in a minute. And not feel a bit bad about it either. I've heard people say, 'The only good Indian is a dead Indian,'—and they mean it!" I searched his face for the vengeful feelings that I'd seen in others but found only deep sadness written there.

"They're dying, Caroline."

"What?'

"They're starving to death. I've seen children pick decaying flesh from dead carcasses and eat it because they were so hungry. I've seen them break old bones to eat the marrow."

My stomach sickened. I didn't want believe what he was telling me.

"Did you notice the children that met our wagon, or the little ones playing on the ground? They're not much more than skin and bones. They're near naked too, and winter's coming on. The desperation in their faces haunts me, Caroline. What would we do if they were our children and we had no way to feed them?"

"I think I'd do almost anything to get food for my children."

"That's what they're doing, Caroline. They're hungry, and they're desperate. And it's us that's made them that way."

"But can't they hunt? I thought Indians were good hunters."

"Sure, they're great hunters. But there just isn't much left to hunt. Settlers are homesteading on all their hunting grounds. And they don't want Indians roaming around nearby. Things are getting worse for them every day."

"Can't they learn to farm?" I asked.

"That's what my brother, William, was trying to do. Teach them. We all know that farming is the only way they're going to survive; but they're not real open to the idea. They've been hunting and living off the land for generations. It's all they know. It's a hard problem, Caroline; it truly is." Mosiah shook his head, deep sadness clouding his usually cheerful face. He flicked the reins, and the horse picked up his step. We were back on the road to Rockville where we would be getting married.

I didn't quite know what to say, or even how to feel, so I slid my body next to his and laid my head on his shoulder. "Thank you so much, Mosiah, for the lovely gift. I'll treasure it all my life."

Mosiah pulled back on the reins with a suddenness that took me by surprise; then he wrapped one arm around my waist while the other hand slipped under my hair to find the back of my neck, and he drew me to him in a hard kiss.

I caught my breath and melted into his embrace. Love was such a wonderful thing. It stirred within me emotions every shade of the rainbow. The warmth of a crimson-and-gold sunrise, the depth of a clear blue lake, the

21

cool softness of snow falling thick and fast, the green of spring and new life, and a red-hot desire whose flames leapt high, threatening to consume us. But Mosiah always kept his emotions within proper boundaries. I knew it took willpower and strength of conviction for him to release me and smile warmly into my eyes, but he did it.

"Best to keep a good ring of stones around a hot campfire," he said with a wink. "Seems to me it could burn out of control real easy like." Then he turned and clicked to the horses. "Get up."

I smiled contentedly to myself as I cuddled close to his strong shoulder. We would bank the embers of our love and keep them smoldering. I knew they would keep our cabin warm on many chilly nights to come.

Chapter Five

Rockville, Utah Territory
November 1869

Mama Behunin tucked me under her wing the moment Mosiah lifted me down from the wagon, clucking and fussing over me like I was one of her own. And I lapped up her love like a thirsty animal at a crystal spring.

She set me up comfortably in Percilla's old room. Mosiah packed up a few things and moved in with his brother Cutler. Everybody made a big show of chaperoning us since we wouldn't be married until after Thanksgiving, but we still found time to be alone together.

Two days after my arrival, Mosiah and I wandered down the lane to the old, abandoned Behunin cabin. "We lived in a dugout when we first came here," Mosiah explained as he gave the door a push and it creaked slowly open. "But when the flood of '62 washed us out, we built this cabin."

I stepped over the threshold and into the dim light of the cabin, an involuntary shudder running down my spine.

"It doesn't look like much, I know, but it was heaven on earth to us after living in a dugout for so long."

I turned slowly, looking around at what would be my future home. The late-afternoon sun streaming in through the one small window didn't provide much light, but it was enough to see what there was to see: four log walls, a rock fireplace, and a dirt floor. From the smell of it, I guessed numerous animals had occupied it since the Behunins moved out.

"Well," I said, forcing a smile and trying to look more enthusiastic than I really felt.

"We'll clean it up," Mosiah ventured. "It'll be a good place for us to start out in." I tried to think of something positive to say but found myself at a loss for words.

Mosiah seemed not to notice though. "My brothers and I helped Dad to build this cabin," he said, beaming with pride as he showed me how tightly the logs were chinked together and how strong the roof still was.

"And this here fireplace is one of a kind," he said as he patted the stones that extended all the way to the ceiling. "Cutler and me hauled all these rocks here, one by one. When the sun hits 'em, they kind of glisten. Cutler was sure they had flakes of gold in them. Said we'd discovered a fortune." Mosiah's eyes twinkled as if divulging a private joke. "That's Cutler for you—always checking every rock and stream for gold."

I put on a brave smile and moved toward him, but as I did, I felt my skirts brush the dirt floor, and I looked down. My petticoats were already edged with gray. I bit my lip and tried not to hear my mother's dire predictions as they echoed through the back of my mind.

"You want to live like that, Caroline? All the days of your life?"

I pushed my Ma's sour words out of my mind and smiled up at my husband-to-be. *It'll be all right. Soon as spring comes, we'll be going to Richfield,* I told myself. *We'll have our own little place and our own home. I can wait.*

"How do you manage to keep clean with a dirt floor like this?" I asked.

"A dirt floor isn't as bad as you might think, angel." Mosiah wrapped his arms around my waist and pulled me close to him as he spoke—his mind clearly not on the subject of cabin floors. "You just sprinkle them down with water every day or so and cover them up with pelts and rugs as much as you can. They get real hard."

Then his lips were on mine, and I wasn't thinking much about cabin floors either. When we pulled apart, he took my hand and led me toward the fireplace to examine Cutler's golden stones.

"It's real pretty," I said, "but I've never cooked over a fireplace before. How on earth do you bake bread?" I tried to stop myself from reflecting back to my St. George home with its cook stove, wood floors, and spacious rooms.

"Mama will teach you all about kettle cooking. She's a master at it," Mosiah beamed. "She can cook anything in a kettle—bread light as a feather, and dinners fit for a king."

I felt my heart do a little flip-flop, and I bit my lip as I looked down at the dusty floor beneath my feet. "I can't be like your mother, Mosiah."

24

It was silent for a moment—except for the call of the birds outside the window. Then I felt his fingers touch my chin and lift it 'til his eyes met mine. "You don't have to be anybody but who you are, darlin'. I love everything about you. From the freckles on your nose right down to your spitfire temper."

"I mean it, Mosiah—I'm real afraid I'm going to disappoint you. Especially now that I've met your mother and seen how wonderful she is—even with all she's had to go through. I could never be strong like that."

"Darlin', you aren't giving yourself your right deserves. There's strength in you to do whatever you have to do. You just don't know it yet."

I felt the weight of his hands on my shoulders, and I looked hesitantly into his intent gaze. "Do you really think so?" I asked.

"I know so. But I pray, with all my heart, you never have to do the things that made my mother who she is. No woman should have to go through things like that."

"I'll bet she left a nice home in Nauvoo, didn't she?"

Mosiah nodded. "My folks left everything they had when the mob drove them out of Nauvoo. I was just six years old, but I remember lying under the wagon at night, when she thought everybody was asleep, and listening to my mother cry."

I reached out to touch his cheek, feeling the stubble of his beard prick my fingers. "That must have been real hard for you too."

"I didn't understand all of what made her cry, but lots of times, I cried too—just from listening to her."

I bit my lip, and he gave me a squeeze before he went on.

"Every step of the way, she dreamed about what it would be like to live in Salt Lake City, but soon as we got to the valley, Brigham Young asked us to settle in Utah County instead. This cabin is a palace next to what we lived in there."

"Really?" I looked around me, wondering how much more rustic you could get.

"Well, it was October by the time we got there," he said. "Too late to build a cabin before winter. Some of the company tried to winter over in their wagon beds; but my dad was sure we'd need more shelter than that, so we all went to work and hollowed out a dugout. It was a good thing too. It snowed four feet that winter."

"And some of the people were trying to live through that in a wagon bed?"

"Most of them didn't make it. They were back in Salt Lake after the first snow. But we stayed." He wandered over to the window and looked out. I followed him, trying to see in my mind what he was seeing in his.

"Snowed so deep, we could hardly get out our door to tend the stock. Most of our cattle starved or froze that winter." He turned and looked at me—a faraway look in his eyes.

I felt a cold shiver run through me. "What did you do?"

"There was a band Utes camped close to us. And they were having an even harder time than we were, so when our cattle died, we drug them up to the top of the hill and left them there for the Indians. They were real grateful. I still remember that Ute chief sitting on his horse on the crest of the hill, surrounded by a half-dozen braves—thanking us in words of half broken English and half Ute. But we knew what he meant. He was majestic—and it was a sight I'll never forget." He shook his head and took my hand, giving it a little squeeze. Then his eyes brightened, and his contagious smile returned.

"We'd better get back; Mama will be wondering where we are."

I smiled back at him. He reached for the latch and opened the door. The smell of damp earth and fallen leaves filled the air as we started toward the house where his family spent their winters. We could see it, through the fields—not so nice as the one I'd left in St. George, but as strong and comfortable as Mama Behunin herself.

We wandered arm in arm, drinking in the fresh autumn air. The cottonwood and mulberry trees that lined the lane were golden in the late-afternoon sun. Nudged from the branches above by a gentle breeze, the straw-colored leaves swirled around us and cascaded to the ground. We stopped beneath a cottonwood to share a gentle lovers' kiss; then wandered on, stirring the golden piles of leaves with our feet as we went.

Chapter notes:

1. The story of Utah County settlers dragging their frozen cattle to the top of the hill for Chief Sanpitch's Ute tribe is recorded in Ruby Noyes Tippet's history of the Cutler Behunin family, *A Song in Her Heart.*

Chapter Six

"Hope you like it, honey," Mama Behunin smiled at me as she laid the patchwork top across the cotton batting and began sewing it to the frame. "Percilla, pull it nice and tight on your side now. And, Caroline, can you get the bottom?"

Mama Behunin was real particular when it came to setting up a quilt. First, the muslin was sewn snuggly to the quilting fame; then, a soft, white cloud of cotton was laid on top; finally, the quilt top was stitched in place, forming a wide fabric sandwich.

"It's all got to be pulled tight, or it won't fluff up nice when it's done," she explained.

"I love it, Mama Behunin," I said as I smiled at her across the quilt we were setting up for the quilting bee in my honor—a Rockville tradition for all brides-to-be.

I ran my hand across its multicolor surface thinking of the many hours it must have taken to piece it together. "I'd love to hear where all these squares came from."

Mama Behunin tugged slightly on the quilt top and continued to secure it to the frame as she replied. "Now, let me think. Cloth is dear you know—can't waste even a scrap. I sew a lot for this big family, and I keep all the pieces. When I have enough colors that look good together, I sew them into a quilt top. Sometimes I make a design, sometimes not; but no two are alike, and they're all real warm."

She nodded toward a blue floral square. "That calico came from a dress I made for Percilla when she was six. She looked right pretty in it. The dark green came from shirts I made for the boys, and the lavender, from Nancy Meriba's wedding dress." She paused, a wistful smile playing across her lips. "Oh, but she was such a lovely bride, her red hair falling all the way down her back to her waist. Hated to see her marry so young though." She shook her head, clucked her tongue, and glanced quickly at me.

I guessed that Nancy Meriba was probably about my age when she got married.

Old enough, I thought.

"Mama, do you think Sister Spencer will be coming today?" Percilla asked, rolling her eyes. "Every time she comes to quilt, we end up picking out all her stitches."

"Percilla, what a thing to say!" Mama Behunin's voice was indignant, but a smile tickled the corners of her mouth. "Sister Spencer's heart is in the right place. It's just that her eyes aren't quite what they used to be."

Percilla's mouth puckered, and her eyebrows lifted. "Just asking."

The dogs began to bark in the yard, and I turned to look out the window. "That'll be Jane," Mama Behunin said and hurried toward the door. "She promised to come early and bring a couple of pies."

The door opened, and a young woman with dark brown hair whisked through it, handing pies to Mama Behunin and Percilla as she came.

"We'll get these pies out on the table, Jane," Mama Behunin called back over her shoulder as she bustled toward the kitchen. "I want you to meet Mosiah's Caroline. I know you two are going to be great friends."

And we were! Jane didn't wait for an introduction. Just scurried right over and threw her arms around me, squealing like a spring pig about how excited she was to meet me and how wonderful it was that Mosiah was *finally* getting married.

"Cutler and Mosiah are as thick as thieves. And you and I are going to be really good friends too, aren't we?" Jane exclaimed. Then she held me out at arm's length, her eyes smiling into mine.

I couldn't help but feel a warm glow light up within me the moment I saw Jane. I felt like I'd known her all my life. "Yes, we will be," I answered resolutely, "You must be Cutler's wife."

"Yes, I am!" she exclaimed. "I was so excited I forgot to introduce myself. I'm Jane Behunin—soon to be your sister-in-law." Jane beamed as she gave me another enthusiastic hug. "I'm so glad we're having this quilting bee—we'll have all day to talk and get acquainted. And you can meet the other women that live around here too."

As if on cue, the door opened to admit three more women. Sister Spencer was a tiny, bent little woman who looked to be in her seventies. She wandered around a bit before finally choosing a place to quilt beside me. Her daughter, Sarah, a forty-ish woman with a no-nonsense look about her, marched straight over to the quilt and picked up a needle across from us. Sister Spencer's granddaughter, Elizabeth, looked just a bit older than me. Jane motioned her toward us, and she took a place on the other side of Jane.

Every few minutes another group of sisters would join us. Before long, the quilt was surrounded by laughing women and my head was swimming, trying to remember all their names.

Jane chattered away at my elbow, her eyes dancing as she recited story after story about Mosiah and Cutler's youthful escapades. "They were a couple years apart, but that didn't keep them from being the best of friends."

"It didn't keep them from getting into a whole passel of trouble either," Mama Behunin said, rolling her eyes and shaking her head as her needle moved in and out of the fabric, her tiny stitches barely visible as she went.

Sister Spencer, to the left of me, was making a valiant effort, her nose almost touching the fabric in her effort to see what she was doing. But I could see why Percilla said what she did. No doubt, there would be stitches to pull out.

"Where will you and Mosiah set up house?" Sarah asked me as her needle moved deftly in and out around a light-blue square.

I explained about the old Behunin cabin down the lane, trying to sound appropriately appreciative. "But when spring comes, we'll be going to Richfield," I added. "Mosiah claimed some land there."

"I hope you appreciate how fortunate you are to have a sturdy roof over your head," Sarah stated as she peered at me over the top of her spectacles. "That cabin is a hundred times better than the dugouts most of us started out in."

"We made do pretty well in those dugouts, though, didn't we?" said a woman with a tight bun and piercing black eyes that the other women called Naomi. "At least until that terrible flash flood came." Several of the older sisters nodded as she spoke.

"Better to live in a dugout than a wagon bed," she continued, turning to me. "One poor woman, trying to live in a wagon bed like that, started to have her baby just as the terrible flood hit. The poor dear almost got washed down the Virgin River."

"Indeed she did!" a tall thin woman named Cora Lee replied, her lips pinched tight. "Mercy me, if that wasn't a time! All the men waded into that roiling river, trying to save her."

"Yes, and all the while, we women folk were having a tizzy fit on the shore, scared half out of our wits that they'd all get washed downriver with her."

"They made back it all right, though," Mama Behunin said, with a shake of her head. "Picked that wagon bed up and carried it to higher ground, just as the baby was being born."

"Really?" I asked. And everyone began to talk at once.

"They named that baby Terrible Flood Tenny, would you believe it?" asked a small round woman with rosy cheeks.

"A dugout is cool in the summer and warm in the winter," Mama Behunin said, moving the conversation back on track. "And it gave us a place to live while we were building our cabins and clearing the land. You learn to make do better than you ever thought you could. But that year in Spring City when the rattlesnakes came—well, that was too much!"

Percilla shuddered, "Oh, Mama, don't talk about it. It's a wonder I'm alive!"

Mama Behunin raised one eyebrow and shook her needle at us. "We had no idea we had built our dugout in a bed of hibernating rattlesnakes. Did we ever have a surprise when spring came and those rattlers woke up!"

"Elmina, you didn't actually have rattlesnakes in your dugout, did you?" Sarah asked, going pale. Every needle around the quilt froze as the women gave a collective shudder.

"Oh, yes! One day I went to get Percilla out of her cradle and found a fat old rattler, all curled up in bed with her."

Percilla squealed and began to dance, shaking her hands and hopping from foot to foot as if she was standing in a bed of red ants.

"I screamed for Isaac, and he snuck over and tipped her cradle to the side so the old snake could slither out. It hissed and zipped like lightning under our bed. I near to fainted dead on the spot! Percilla was all right though—obviously, since she's here today—but merciful heavens, what a fright I'd had!"

31

"There were rattlesnakes in all the dugouts that spring," Naomi said, raising her eyebrows over her flashing black eyes. "Had 'em in our cupboards and under our beds. We women took the children and climbed into the wagons while the men chased the snakes out with torches. Killed 'em all and burned 'em. Smell near to choked us, didn't it, Elmina? Killed hundreds of 'em in one day."

"What was worse, Elmina, the rattlesnakes or the Indians?" the round, little woman named Flora asked when the exclamations died down.

"I was terrified of them both, and that's a fact. But I think I was even more afraid of the Indians than I was of the snakes," Mama Behunin said as she reached for the scissors. "They liked to camp right close by us, you know, where they could smell our food cooking. Then they would come round and ask for some."

"Brother Brigham said we should feed the Indians and be friends with them," Cora Lee muttered, her eyes darting around the quilt. "But how could we be expected to feed the Indians all the time when we didn't even have enough to feed our own families?"

"They got real pushy too when you told them no," Flora said. "But what could we do? Indians kill people."

"Well, it scared me to death," Mama Behunin said. "And it worried Isaac so much that he hated to leave us, even to go to work in the fields—especially after Indians killed our son, William." Mama Behunin looked up from her quilting and glanced quickly about the room at the horrified eyes that met hers.

"He was one of the young men killed in the Elk Mountain Mission Massacre," she murmured. "After that I was even more afraid. And angry too. I couldn't look at an Indian without wanting to cry."

Every needle stopped, and all eyes focused on her. The group collectively held its breath until Flora blurted out, "I have no idea how you folks go on, still being kind to the Indians after such a thing as that."

"It was real hard for me. But Mosiah was fascinated by them—even when he was little." Mama Behunin glanced across the quilt and smiled at me. She knew I would be especially interested in hearing this part of the story.

"One of the squaws had a little boy about Mosiah's age. Usually, she would bring the boy with her when she came

32

for food. His name was Two Owls. While Two Owls's mother was busy getting food from me, he and Mosiah played together. Pretty soon Two Owls started showing up by himself. He and Mosiah would play together until someone from the village came to fetch him."

"Is that how Mosiah learned to speak the Indian language?" I asked.

"That was the beginning of it," Mama Behunin answered before returning her focus to her quilting.

Jane nudged me and asked under her breath if Mosiah had told me about the time he and his brothers snuck out at night and went to the Indian village.

"What?" Mama Behunin's piercing eyes took us both in. "The boys were under strict orders never to go to that camp unless Isaac was with them." Mama Behunin drew herself up tall, her hands on her hips. "The few times Mosiah disobeyed that order, there was heck to pay, let me tell you!" Throwing another stern glance in Jane's direction, she resumed her quilting, eyebrows knit into a frown.

Jane waited until an animated discussion drew in Mama Behunin, and then she whispered, "Make Mosiah tell you about it. And ask him about the raid too."

You could be sure I would be asking him. I was right curious now.

"Yes, dugout life was truly an adventure," I heard Mama Behunin say. "But a cabin is better, and this house, here in Rockville, is a blessing. I sure am glad to come back to it every fall after we get the crops in."

"Do you live in a cabin in the summer while you are farming in the canyon?" I asked.

"Sure do, honey. Not much different from the one you and Mosiah will be sharing after you're married." Mama paused to help Cora Lee roll the quilt on the far side so that they could reach the places where the quilt still needed stitching.

"Someone told me that your wash tub—" Flora began.

"—that my wash tub is a hollowed out log with a plug in the bottom?" Mama Behunin laughed and shook her head. "How does everybody know about that? It's surely a lot better than no tub at all," she answered. "The only way into that canyon is on horseback—can't get a wagon in. I would be a pretty sight trying to carry a metal wash tub on my horse, now wouldn't I?"

"Don't you get lonely down in that canyon?" Flora asked.

"Well, a few more folks live there now. But to tell you the truth, Flora, I think it was the solitude of the canyon that drew us there in the first place."

Several women lifted their heads up from their quilting, waiting for her to explain.

"We'd been driven out of Kirtland and Missouri by angry mobs, and it near to broke out hearts both times. When Isaac built our home in Nauvoo, we thought we were there to stay. He built us some beautiful pieces of furniture, and I fixed it up pretty with curtains and the like. Then things started to get bad again. We lived just a few houses down from Joseph and Emma. And Isaac was one of the Prophet's bodyguards. The mobs got more and more vicious until he was worried half to death about Joseph's safety.

"We were all scared half out of our wits, weren't we?" Naomi said, her mouth a tight line and her brows pulled close together over her dark eyes. "When I think about the burnings and the beating, I can hardly breathe to this day."

"But when they killed the Prophet and Brother Hyrum," Cora Lee whispered through thin colorless lips, "and we saw their dead bodies brought back to Nauvoo in a wagon—well a person can only take so much!"

Sister Spencer beside me had said very little all afternoon. But I noticed her hands stiffen and her fingers begin to shake so badly that she could hardly quilt. Then I noticed the other women giving her little sideways glances; but I was still unprepared for what happened next.

I had just poked my finger with the needle and was lifting my finger to my mouth to suck the red drop of blood away before it soiled the quilt when Sister Spencer's claw-like fingers jerked me around, her red-rimmed eyes boring into mine as she wailed and shrieked at me.

"They shot my Ira!" she screamed into my face as she shook me by the shoulder. "And Benny too! They were demons—demons from Hell!"

I tried to pull away, but she held me in an iron grip, her nails digging into my flesh.

"They had guns and knives, and they were screaming like the devil himself—." Her features contorted in a way that frightened me and I tried to step back.

Tiny and bent, Sister Spencer looked like a stiff wind could blow her over, but somewhere within her was amazing strength. She tilted even closer toward me, her eyes crazed and her spittle flecking my checks as she hissed. "Most of the men and boys were in the blacksmith shop and they wouldn't let none of 'em out. We women screamed, and cried, but they didn't listen. They didn't listen to none of us. Then they started shoot'n in through the doors and windows. We heard cries and screams from inside—but those demons just kept on shoot'n and shoot'n, even after everything was stone quiet."

Like a storm that rises in fury—black and destructive—then collapses into a deadly calm, Sister Spencer let go of my arms and dissolved into tears, hanging onto the quilting frame with hands that shook so badly that the quilt threatened to come down.

Sarah and Elizabeth gently pulled her away from my side. But she turned back to me, her eyes still stricken with horror, and whispered, "They killed them all, you know—even the young boys; and they abused us women in terrible ways."

Mama Behunin, who had scurried around the quilt when Sister Spencer began, surrounded her trembling friend with strong arms, her voice soft and soothing. "Take her into the back room, Sarah, dear. She'll pull out of it. Just give her a little time."

Sarah and Elizabeth led Sister Spencer away. The room was so quiet you could have heard a flea breathe. Then Mama Behunin looked at me with sorrow as deep as the ocean in her eyes. "She was at Haun's Mill. The mobbers killed her husband and her son."

"Oh," was all I could say. I knew about the horrors of Haun's Mill. Every Mormon did.

We stitched quietly for a time, each woman deep in her own thoughts.

At last, Mama Behunin broke the silence, her eyes circling the quilt, connecting with each sister in a way that words never could. "We were all touched by those awful things in our own way. As a church, it's made us strong, but for some, it was too much. Some people fell away, and some fell apart." She glanced toward the back room. "And can you blame them? Isaac and I retreated into that remote canyon—

where you could only enter on horseback, where even the Indians were afraid to go. We found solitude there. No more angry mobs to burn and kill and take away all we hold dear. No more fear, and no more pain.

"One evening as we watched the sun dip below the red rock cliffs, Isaac said to our new neighbor, 'Look at that! It looks like a great temple, doesn't it? To me this great canyon is Zion, the place of the pure in heart. It's a place of refuge and a place of peace.'"

"Mama Behunin, is that why he named it Zion?" I asked.

"It surely is, darlin'. And the great canyon has been called Zion Canyon ever since. He was the one that gave it that name."

———————————

Chapter notes:

1. The story of rattlesnakes coming out of hibernation in the dugouts of the settlers in Spring City is recorded in Ruby Noyes Tippet's history of the Cutler Behunin family, *A Song in Her Heart*, and in *The Story of Isaac Behunin* by Fenton E. Moss.

2. The events of the Haun's Mill Massacre are recorded in *Our Heritage: a Brief History of The Church of Jesus Christ of Latter-day Saints*, (pp. 47-49).

Chapter Seven

The spicy fragrance of pumpkin, apple, and berry pie wafted through the air, making our mouths water and our stomachs growl. It was the day before Thanksgiving, and we women were mighty busy. I'd never experienced the excitement of a big family gathering, and I was enjoying every noisy moment of it.

Wearing Mama Behunin's apron and wielding a butcher knife, I chopped up mounds of onions and celery for the turkey dressing. Percilla had just arrived to help, and we expected Jane any minute. Andrew's wife, Mary, and her six children were there too. It was a full house.

Mama Behunin bustled about, telling us all what to do, her face flushed with the enthusiasm of a sea captain about to embark on an ocean voyage.

"Can I help you kill the turkey, Uncle Mosiah?" Andrew's six-year-old son, Willy, asked. His blue eyes sparkled as he looked up into his uncle's eyes, his adoration obvious.

Since his father's death several months earlier, Willy had taken to shadowing his Uncle Mosiah like a little lost puppy.

"Sure you can, tadpole," Mosiah replied, swinging his young nephew onto his broad shoulders. "I'm going to need all the help I can get. That turkey's almost as fat as a pig. Think you're big enough to tackle the old bird if he starts running around after I cut off his head?"

Willy's eyes widened 'til they were as big as wagon wheels. "Do you think he will, Uncle Mosiah?"

"Well, you never know. Chickens do sometimes," Mosiah's eyes twinkled as he tossed a knowing glance over his shoulder at his tow-headed passenger.

"I bet he will, and when he does, I'll catch him for you!" Willy squealed, giving his uncle a nudge in the ribs. Mosiah yelped with pretended pain and trotted out the door while Willy shrieked and laughed. The boy buried both his hands into Mosiah's hair and held on.

Mama Behunin wiped her hands on her apron and laughed as she paused to watch them gallop out the door. But when she shut the door, I saw tears were running down her checks. I couldn't help thinking she was saddened because there would be another empty plate at the dinner table this Thanksgiving.

She shook her head and went back to work chopping potatoes, suet, and dried apples for the traditional pudding.

I watched her out of the corner of my eye and felt a lump rise in my throat. Putting down my knife, I walked to her side and wrapped my arms around her bent shoulders. "Mama Behunin, I'm so sorry," I said, wishing I could think of something reassuring to say.

That was the wrong thing to do, I guess. Or maybe, it was the right thing. Because it seemed to break through some invisible wall. In an instant, her composure shattered like glass dropped on a rock, and she sank into the chair beside her, sobbing into her hands, her body shaking like a rag doll.

Percilla dropped the peas she was shelling and hurried to her mother just as Jane came running from the other side.

I pulled my chair close to hers and held her hands. "Go right ahead and cry," I said. "You have a right to."

I didn't know Mosiah's brother Andrew, but I felt his family's sorrow deep in the wells of my soul. Death is never welcome, but it's especially hard when it comes to one so young. And when a father leaves a grieving wife and six young children, it's the most difficult thing in the world.

Nobody knew why Andrew died. He ate a hearty breakfast and headed out into the fields one morning, whistling as he went. Hours later, thirteen-year-old Mary discovered his body when she went to fetch him for dinner. He was lying peacefully between two rows of corn. The Lord had called him home.

Elmina rose to her feet, gathered all three of us into her arms, and we just let the tears flow. Somehow, it felt good.

Then, with a start, Elmina caught her breath and turned. Mary, Andrew's young widow, stood in the doorway. The color had drained from her face like water from a barrel, and her knuckles were jammed against her teeth.

Mary was a tall, thin woman and naturally quiet, according to Jane. But I'd barely heard her put two words together since she'd arrived with her children three days ago. And I'd seen Mama Behunin watching her with worried eyes.

"She's going to explode one of these days," I'd heard Mama Behunin say. "You can't lock sorrow away like that without creating a volcano deep inside of you."

And right before our eyes, she erupted.

Her keen started in low, like it came from down deep inside of her. But once she started to let go, I think she lost control. She began to wail as if everything inside of her was being wrenched out. She clenched her fingers into fists and shook them like a wild animal, desperate to escape a trap.

I stood rooted to the spot, but Mama Behunin and Jane ran to her side, dodging her flying limbs, and tried to envelope her in their arms. At last, she sank to her knees, sobbing and burying her face in her hands.

"No! No! No!"

I thought it would tear my heart out.

Mama Behunin knelt beside her, clasping Mary's trembling hands in her own and touching her forehead to the sobbing young woman's, as she whispered again and again, "Mary, darling, it's all right. It's all right."

"No, it's not all right! It will never be all right! Andrew is dead, and I want to die with him!" Her sobbing seemed to churn up from the depths of her tortured soul. "He's gone! Don't you understand? He's gone!"

"No, Mary, dear," Elmina cupped her daughter-in-law's chin in her hands and pierced the young widow's eyes with her own. "Andrew is not gone. He is only a breath away—just beyond a veil so thin you can almost reach out and touch him. You can't see him right now, but he sees you. He will walk beside you every step of this life. You were sealed together by God's power in His holy temple, and not even death can break that seal. You are bound together for eternity. He waits for you there."

It was silent for a moment, and we all felt Andrew there beside us, reaching out to the people he loved.

At last, Mary let us help her onto a chair. She was weak and maybe a little embarrassed, but she seemed to feel better. It all has to come out one way or another and, I think that was as good a way as any.

"Mama Behunin," I ventured when I thought the atmosphere had calmed enough for me to ask a question. "You were sealed in the Nauvoo temple, weren't you—just before the Saints were driven out?"

"Yes—and, oh, honey—that was the most beautiful day of my life! Or night, I guess I should say. It was three o'clock in the morning when our turn came."

"The temple was open at three in the morning?" I asked incredulously.

"Oh, yes, it was open all night long for quite a while. We worked day and night to get the temple finished before the mobs came to drive us out of Nauvoo. We didn't really know where we were going or what would happen to us—but we knew we would be all right, so long as our families were sealed together before we left."

"You were working to finish the temple even with the mobs at your throats?" Jane asked.

"Mm-hmm, and we knew we didn't have much time. I wish you could have seen it, honey. It was so beautiful! But the moment we were out, the mobs took it over—they even shot cannonballs at us from the top of our own temple."

I gasped. "How could they do such a thing?"

"Well, they did much worse than that. It broke my heart into a million pieces to see them desecrate our temple like that. But we were comforted just by knowing we were sealed. They couldn't take that away from us—not even if they killed us." Elmina gave Mary's hands a firm pat and stood up, her hands on her hips.

"Death is a hard thing—it truly is. But it's part of life, and that's a fact. At times like this, death might seem like the end. But it's not. Just a step along the way."

Mary looked up at her mother-in-law and smiled. "I wish I had your faith, Mama Behunin."

"Well, darling," she answered back, "Faith is a growing thing. You're welcome to borrow some of mine for right now if it will help you to make it through. But I think you'll find plenty of your own along the way if you just ask the Lord for it. Faith is a gift from Him, you know."

"Mama Behunin, would you tell us about how you joined the church?" I asked.

But before she could answer, a commotion in the yard brought all our heads up with a start. Above the frantic gobbling of a turkey came the barking of dogs and the excited squeals of children. Over it all, Mosiah's hearty laughter boomed across the yard.

Percilla scurried to the window, her baby over her shoulder. "What's all that ruckus about?"

"By the sounds of it," Mama Behunin laughed, "I think our Thanksgiving dinner is about to meet with his demise."

We were all headed toward the window to have a look when Papa Behunin's bewhiskered face and twinkling eyes poked inside. "Elmina, you've gotta see this," Isaac laughed. "Come on out."

The scene in the yard was certainly a sight to behold. Mosiah, who had straddled an old stump, was hee-hawing and slapping his knees so hard that I thought he would fall off. Willy was scrambling around the yard as fast as his young legs could carry him, swinging a lariat about in a futile attempt to lasso a large brown turkey.

Jake and Lucas, the Behunins' oversized dogs, had joined in the chase and were further terrorizing the poor bird, with Anthony and Andrew, the three-year-old twins, scampering along behind.

"Get him, boy!" Isaac called out between fits of laughter.

"Over there now," Mosiah hooted. "Swing that rope over your head, and let it go easy-like."

Willy's rope swung to where the turkey had been moments before, but by the time the loop landed, the fat old bird was yards away.

"That's all right—try again. You're getting the hang of it," Mosiah called out, riding the stump like a bronco.

Willy moved fast, but the turkey was faster. And the dogs weren't helping any either. Tripping over a rock, the little guy landed on his hands and knees but was up again in an instant. A few more attempts, and he was clearly out of wind.

"He'll never lasso that old bird," Mama Behunin laughed.

"That's all right, Elmina. It's good practice for him," Isaac chuckled. "But I think that turkey's going to be a few pounds lighter by the time we get him on the dinner table." Still laughing to himself, Isaac found a three-legged stool and sat down watch the proceedings more comfortably.

Willy stopped for a moment and threw his uncle a defeated look. Mosiah let out a war whoop, jumped off the stump, and ran toward his nephew. Then he swooped him up and tucked him under his arm. The chase was on!

That turkey was all over the yard with Mosiah right on his tail. Willy laughed with a bouncy little giggle while his uncle used his one free arm to toss the lasso again and again, only to have it land inches from the frantic bird.

In the blink of an eye, a miracle happened. The old bird ran right under the falling lasso, and Mosiah jerked back just in time to catch him by the leg. That's when the ruckus really began!

The big bird screamed and beat the ground with his wings, struggling to be free. Willy, who had been dropped to his feet, jumped up and down, hollering with excitement while the dogs raced around, barking fit to kill. The rest of us slapped our knees and laughed until our sides ached.

Mosiah let out a "ya-hoo!" that echoed off the red cliffs and back again. Our Thanksgiving turkey was caught, but the excitement wasn't over yet.

Mosiah—with Willy's help, of course—carried the flapping, struggling bird over to the old stump, next to which an ax had been strategically located. "Hold onto his legs now, Willy," he coached. "He'll kick, but don't let him go!"

Mosiah and Willy got the turkey across the stump, but he didn't cooperate—not by any means. I couldn't see how Mosiah was going to chop the old bird's head off with him flapping around like that, but with one well-placed whack, the head was gone.

"Oh, drat it all!" Mosiah gasped. The turkey's last flapping attempt to free himself spewed a large squirt of blood right into the face of his executioner. Mosiah jumped back, losing his grip on the turkey.

The little girls screamed and ran in the opposite direction while Willy struggled to hold onto the flapping bird by one leg.

"He's getting away, Uncle Mosiah!" Willy squealed as he lost his grip. In an instant, the turkey flopped off the stump and onto his feet, half-running, half-flapping about the yard while his head lay quietly beside the stump—a strange sight indeed.

"Get him, Willy!" Mosiah called out, and the chase was on again. The old bird flapped and ran in a zigzag pattern into the weeds with Willy, the twins, and both dogs in hot pursuit. There, he collapsed at last, the contest over.

Willy whooped with joy, and the twins jumped up and down, yelling, "We got him! We got him!" All the while, the dogs bounced around the boys, barking so proudly you'd have thought they did it all themselves.

"Guess I'd better get some water heating." Mama Behunin chuckled to herself as she headed back inside.

I wandered over to where Mosiah and Willy stood looking down at the big headless bird.

"He's a fine turkey," Mosiah said. "He'll make a right nice meal tomorrow, I reckon." Reaching down, he picked the bird up by his feet. "For now, though, I think we'd better hang him up in that tree yonder so he can bleed out."

"Eeww!" Willy quickly backed away with a disgusted expression on his face.

Mosiah wrapped a strong arm around my waist and drew me close. I glanced up at his blood-splattered face and laughed, "You've got freckles redder than your hair."

"I reckon I do, darlin'." He grinned back. "Tell you what, you just give me a little kiss, then I'll wash up and meet you in the house."

"Not on your life!" I struggled out of his arms and ran back in the direction of the house."

"Now, what do you suppose got into her?" Mosiah asked Willy innocently. "I just wanted a little kiss." Then with a laugh, he laid his hand on Willy's shoulder, and they started together toward the old cottonwood tree.

***

I could hear the Behunin family still chuckling as I entered the house. Jane hurried over to me and gave me a quick hug. "That was the best show I've seen in a long time—wouldn't have missed it for the world!"

"Can you believe Mosiah actually tried to kiss me with that turkey blood splattered all over his face?" I whispered as I rolled my eyes.

Jane shook her head and tried to look sympathetic, but the twitches at the corners of her lips gave her away.

When we heard giggles behind us, I blushed and turned around. Not one person met my eye. They all seemed very busy with food preparation. Then, to my horror, Jane laughed out loud, and everyone else joined in.

"It's all right, Caroline," Isaac chuckled. "We were young and in love once too." His blue eyes twinkled as he sashayed over to Elmina and wrapped his arms around her. To my astonishment, he whirled her about, dipped her almost to the ground, and planted a greatly exaggerated kiss on her lips.

We all cheered and feigned embarrassment as Isaac gave her a gentle squeeze and, with a wink, whispered, "I do still love this beautiful woman."

I couldn't help smiling at them. Even in their sixties, they made a handsome pair. Elmina's once-dark hair was streaked with gray, but her petite form was still lithe and graceful. Isaac's hair and beard were full and wavy, with just enough gold left in them to be reminiscent of their former copper color. He wore a homespun shirt and leather breeches that sagged in the seat and the knees from much wear, but he was still broad and strong. The wrinkles around his eyes and mouth suggested years of smiles and laughter.

"Elmina tells me that you've been enquiring about how she joined the church," he stated.

"I am curious to know," I answered. "She was about to tell us when all the excitement broke out."

"I'm pleased that you asked," Papa Behunin replied. "That's a story I want all our grandchildren and great-grandchildren to know." He motioned for us to leave our tasks and take a chair. I was more than happy to leave the work for a minute or two and listen.

"Sometimes, we think the Prophet Joseph was the only one to see angels and the like when the Lord set His hand to organize His church here in the latter days, but that's not so," Papa Behunin said with a nod. "He prepared those pure in heart to receive the gospel in much the same way He prepared the Prophet himself."

I found a seat on a high-backed kitchen chair and leaned in as Elmina settled herself and began to tell us the story of her family's conversion to the Mormon Church when she was a young girl living in Erie County, Pennsylvania.

Chapter notes:

1. In her journal, Mary Ann Rock Williams Pugh describes being driven out of her home in Nauvoo. She tells of the mobbers shooting cannonballs from the temple into the river and splashing muddy water all over them as they attempted to cross in heavily laden flat boats.

2. The episode about Willey and the turkey is fictitious. Utah settlers celebrated their first Thanksgiving in 1853. However, it was not codified as an annual, federal holiday in November until 1863.

Chapter Eight

Elmina's Story

Springfield, Pennsylvania
June 1823

The door slammed so hard I dropped the peas I had been shelling back into the pan—pod and all. I was only ten years old, and that afternoon I felt wonderfully grown-up. My mama, who had to spread herself between a husband and eleven children, had spent a whole hour that afternoon alone with me. We had been shelling peas for dinner at the kitchen table—talking and laughing as we worked—so the sound of angry footsteps stomping into the house was the last thing I wanted to hear.

It was Papa, and something was wrong. His thick, dark eyebrows were drawn tightly together, and his usually smiling mouth was stretched thin.

"Elizabeth, what are we going to do about Dad?" Papa shot a dark look in our direction punctuating his words by dropping the ten-pound bag of sugar he was carrying onto the table. I grabbed for the pan, but it was too late. Dozens of peas sprung out of the pan, rained down onto the table, and bounced to the floor.

I hit the floor almost before they touched the ground and began crawling around on my hands and knees, trying to retrieve the efforts of our afternoon's labor. Papa, however, paid them no mind. Like a drill sergeant, he marched about the kitchen, squashing peas beneath his heavy boots as he unleashed a string of angry words.

"It's not enough that he's alienated half the county—people duck when they see him coming. They don't want him to corner them. Don't want to hear him asking why none of the ministers preach the gospel the way it's told in the Bible. Don't want to argue about how we outta have all those same prophets and miracles today. No—that's not enough for him! Now he's gone and insulted the churchgoers personally!"

46

"Oh no, what's he been saying now, Andrew?" Much to my surprise, Mama didn't pay any attention to the peas either. She just stared back at him with a look of dread spreading across her face.

I kept peeking out from under the table hoping Mama would see what was going on. If we didn't get these peas cleaned up quickly, we wouldn't have any left for dinner. But she wasn't paying any attention at all, so I just kept crawling around under the table, picking up peas and stowing them in my apron.

To my relief, Papa heaved a sigh and slumped down onto a straight-backed chair, shaking his head and laughing a little, even though I was sure he didn't think it was at all funny.

"I noticed at least a dozen people in the general store today. They were talking pretty loud before I went in, but as soon as I opened the door, it got real quiet. Seemed more than a little strange that none of them said 'Howdy do'. But when they turned their backs on me and went about their business like I wasn't even there, I got suspicious. Funny how the store cleared out real quick. I looked down at a bucket of nails, and when I looked up again, it was just me and old Lester behind the counter. So I up and asked him what was going on—and he told me."

I crouched under the table and stayed as still as I could. I didn't want to remind my parents I was still there. They'd have sent me outside for sure.

"And what did he say?"

"Well, it seems that Dad made his weekly visit to Lester's mercantile this morning and spent some time jawing with the other old codgers. As usual, the conversation got around to religion."

"I wonder how that might have happened," Mama said, rolling her eyes.

"Dad got on his usual high horse about ministers not knowing what they're preaching about. Then somebody got mad and called him a heathen, so Dad started spouting scripture about spiritual gifts and signs that follow the true believer. He told them there wasn't a single true believer among them—or anywhere else on the earth for that matter."

"Oh, Andrew, he didn't!'

47

"Yes, he did—and you can pretty much guess what happened next. They were mad as a hornet's nest, that's for sure!"

Papa jumped back onto his feet and stomped around again, squashing more peas as he paced. "Dad didn't back down one bit, not even when they called him an old fool for thinking he knew more than the ministers. He told them that he was so sick and tired of all the squabbling over scriptures that he'd decided to ask God about it himself. And he said that's just what he had done."

"I can well imagine what they had to say about that," Mama muttered.

I was getting pretty uncomfortable under that table by then, but I still didn't dare move.

"I guess it was getting pretty bad—half of them laughing at him and the other half yelling at him. They said, maybe he should be a prophet himself, since he was so high and mighty and on speaking terms with God and all that."

"Oh, Andrew!"

"Just wait—it gets better! He told them he wasn't a prophet—but there was one coming soon. A true prophet who would bring the gospel back—the way God intended it."

"Oh my, he's done it this time for sure!" Mama said quietly, and I could see her hands fidget in her lap. "How are we going to show our faces in church on Sunday?"

Papa leaned heavily on the table, staring out the window at nothing in particular as he continued, "All this is going to cause real trouble for the family, that's for sure." He turned slowly to face Mama. Even from where I sat under the table, I could see worry lines between his eyes and his jaw tensing as he spoke. "It's not that I don't pretty much agree with him, you know. Things aren't as they should be, and there's no talking to the ministers about it—all they do is get mad and uppity—but you can't go marching around saying things like that to folks—not if you want to live in the same county with them."

Mama left her seat and moved softly to his side, paying only minor attention to the occasional pea being squashed beneath her feet. "I think you're getting too worked up about this, Andrew. Your father's an old man. No one will take him seriously."

Papa laid his hands on her shoulders, shaking his head and looking down on her with sad, tired eyes. "Yes, they *will. They know him well enough. They know he's sharp as a tack and he never says a word he doesn't mean. The whole county is all worked up about religion right now anyway."*

"They are at that," Mama replied. "It seems like every time a half-dozen people get together, they end up arguing about religion. We'll just have to try to stay out of it."

By this time, my legs were so cramped and tired that I bumped my head on the underside of the table. Mama turned around, surprised to see me there.

"Elmina, what are you doing under the table?"

"Just picking up the peas, Mama," I answered, showing her the contents of my apron.

"It looks like you've got the better part of them, sweetie. I'll sweep up the rest," Mama smiled back. "You can go on out, now. I'll call when it's time to set the table for dinner."

I climbed out from under the table, deposited the peas from my apron back into the pan, and scurried outside. I couldn't imagine anyone being mad at my grandpa. Especially over something as silly as disagreeing about religion. He was the best person I knew.

***

Papa was right.

Grandpa's outburst did cause trouble for the family. Daniel came home from school with black eyes and a bloody nose quite regularly after that. He was only eight years old, but he wasn't about to take family insults lying down, especially those about Grandpa.

Our family carpentry business fell off sharply, and I knew that Mama was struggling to make ends meet. Worst of all, though, was church. Grandpa didn't attend anymore, but Mama insisted that the rest of us go—no matter what.

I hated it more than anything. Every week, all thirteen of us made our way down the center aisle of the chapel to our pew. My cheeks always flamed red—knowing the sudden rustle of ladies' skirts meant the whole congregation was turning to look at us with disapproving stares. Mama pretended she couldn't hear the whispers that followed us all the way up the aisle; but I knew they hurt her even more than they hurt me. The thing that made me burn inside, though, was the way the minister made pointed comments throughout his sermon, then glowered at our family over the top of his spectacles.

The very worst was the week Reverend Paine stopped us on our way out of the chapel to call us to repentance. Papa had done his best to ignore the whole situation. But when the Reverend Paine called Grandpa an apostate and a follower of Satan, my father lost his temper.

"Has God stopped loving his children then?" Papa stormed at the reverend, "or did He just decide that we're no longer worth wasting a prophet's breath on?"

Reverend Paine responded by shaking his leather-bound Bible above his head and declaring, "This, my brother, is the word of God unto man—all of it! Why should He give us more when we have yet to live what He has already given us?"

"Maybe because it's been almost two thousand years since that last page was written. The God I know and read about in that Bible of yours loves His children and cares about their lives. I think it's our hearts and minds that are closed— not the heavens or the Bible."

Papa began to gather us, preparing to make a timely exit, but he called out over his shoulder, "Seems to me, Reverend, there's something wrong when a sincere believer like my father, who wants nothing more than to know the will of God, is ostracized by the people who ought to be his friends."

Then he turned, and we followed him quietly down the walk. No one said a word, but Mama slipped her hand into Papa's and smiled up at him. I think she was kind of proud of him. And I couldn't help smiling too.

***

I hated cooked mush—the gooey feel of it in my mouth and the slippery way it slid down my throat. My brothers and sisters had long since finished theirs and were busy with their morning chores. I stirred the mess around with my spoon, scooping up a lump and then plopping it back into my bowl.

Mama poked her head into the kitchen just long enough to warn me, "Elmina, if that mush isn't gone in five minutes, you can plan on eating it cold for dinner. It's time *you get your chores done." I sighed and jabbed at it with my spoon. It was already cold.*

That's when Grandpa came huffing through the kitchen door and collapsed onto the high-backed chair beside me. "Elmina, darlin', get your mom and dad."

Grandpa didn't look good, but that was no surprise. He lived a good half mile down the lane. And with his bad leg, that was a mighty long walk. I was dumbfounded to see him in our kitchen, especially so early in the morning. I got Mama and Papa in a hurry.

"Good glory, Dad, what are you doing—walking all the way down here with that bum leg of yours? Is something wrong?" Papa looked at him, dumbstruck, and Mama, came up behind him, chewing on her bottom lip.

Grandpa just looked back at them for a long moment—a sad expression on his face and a tear forming at the corner of his eye. The white beard that framed his wrinkled face quivered at bit as he tried to explain. "I just wanted to say goodbye to you all. That's why I came."

"You came to say goodbye?" Mama repeated. "But you're not going anywhere."

"That I am, my dear—and soon too." I couldn't figure out what he was talking about, and judging from the look on their faces, neither could my parents. "I had a visitor last night—came to give me a message."

"Who was it, Dad?" my papa asked. He was looking more concerned by the minute and exchanging glances with Mama that I was sure Grandpa couldn't miss.

"Well, as you know, I read the Bible every night before I go to bed, sitting in my rocker beside the fire. Last night was no exception, but while I read, I noticed the room getting mighty light. I looked up to see where the light was coming from, and there he stood, just a few feet from me, looking right at me. The light shone all around him."

"Was he an angel, Grandpa? Did he have wings?" I popped out of my chair, almost spilling my mush in my excitement.

"I reckon he was an angel all right, but no, he didn't have wings," Grandpa nodded in my direction.

"You fell asleep reading, Dad. You were probably just dreaming." I could hear the relief in Papa's voice and noticed Mama nodding her head beside him.

51

"Are you telling me I don't know the difference between being awake and asleep? I'm not that old, you know!" Grandpa leaned forward, his eyes snapping.

"It happens all the time," Mama said. "Sometimes it's hard to tell."

"Not to me, it doesn't," Grandpa shot back. "Now, do you want to hear what he had to say, or not?"

My parents exchanged worried glances, "I think you're going to tell us whether we want to hear it or not," Papa muttered.

"He told me I was going to die soon," Grandpa paused as we all did a quick intake. "That made me upset, because I've been waiting for that prophet the Lord promised me was coming, and I didn't want to go before he got here."

He looked back and forth between us to make sure we were all listening—we were. "I didn't dare say it—him being an angel and all—still, I guess he knew what I was thinking, because he told me I would die before the prophet came, but that my family would join the true church when it got organized, and they would help the prophet to get the work started."

"Elmina, you have chores to do." I knew what that meant. Papa didn't want me to hear what Grandpa was saying, and I was to leave real fast. So I did; but Mama caught me on my way out and whispered in my ear that I was not to breathe a word of what I had heard to anyone. Grandpa was old, and I was not to pay him any mind.

***

A chill ran through me and I shuddered. Cold seeped into my body from the damp earth below me, but the nip in my heart was the real reason for my icy feelings. I wrapped my arms tightly around my folded legs, resting my chin on my gingham-covered knees, and tried to ignore the group of schoolgirls huddled a few yards away. I knew they were talking about me. My cheeks flamed red as they whispered to each other, then glanced in my direction with up-turned noses

I hugged my arms more tightly about myself and shivered, not so much from the cool of the afternoon but from the chilly attitudes that surrounded our family. No, I wouldn't tell anyone about Grandpa's angel—not my so-called friends at school—not even my brothers and sisters. Still, I couldn't help wondering about it.

"He was an angel, all right," Grandpa had said when he told us about his visitor—the one with glowing light around him who had brought such a strange message.

Was Grandpa just dreaming like Mama said; or was he so old he was mixed up in his head?

I thought about some of the dreams that had visited my sleep at night. Sometimes they did seem real—but when I woke up, I knew I had been dreaming. I felt sure that it was the same for Grandpa.

Well then, was Grandpa getting so old his mind was playing tricks on him?

I knew my grandpa pretty well, and I had never seen anything to make me think that.

I tried to look at the situation from every angle, but no matter how I looked at it, I came up with the same answer. Grandpa had, indeed, seen an angel—an angel with a special message, not just for Grandpa but for our whole family. Something inside of me said that was the truth and that Mama and Papa knew it was true too. Even if they would never admit it.

**

It was Saturday the following week, which meant no school, but plenty of chores, so I smiled with relief when Mama assigned me to take some cornbread to Grandpa after breakfast. He was pretty good at fixing his own meals, but I think sending one of us children down the lane with something for his dinner was Mama's way of checking up on him. Today it was my turn, and I was glad. I'd rather spend time with Grandpa than gather eggs or slop the pigs—that was for sure.

The sun shone high in the sky as I skipped down the lane that lead to Grandpa's place with a smile on my face. Before I had gone far though, I began to think about Grandpa's visit. "I came to tell you all goodbye." That's what he had said. And that an angel had told him he would die soon. A chill ran through my body, and I stopped in my tracks.

How soon? I wondered. The terrible thought made me fly down the lane toward Grandpa's house, trying to get there as fast as I could but dreading it just the same.

The first thing I noticed as I rounded the corner and started down the graveled path was Rosie. She wasn't in the pasture.

Grandpa should have milked her and turned her out by now. I thought I could hear her gentle lowing from the barn. But maybe he was just running late, I reasoned. Maybe he was in the barn milking her right now. I pulled the heavy barn door open and peered inside. Rosie lowed impatiently at me, her full and dripping udder a sure sign that she had not been milked.

I threw her an armful of hay before I forced my steps toward the house. With trembling hands, I opened the door and called, "Grandpa?", hoping to hear his booming reply.

Jack, Grandpa's old brown dog and constant companion, wandered out from the back room and came to sit beside me, his tail thumping. But I could see no sign of Grandpa. Then I knew for sure. It took all my strength to resist the impulse to turn and run home.

At last, my racing heart slowed a bit and I reached out for Jack's brown head. "All right, Jack, show me where he is." Jack turned and led the way. I followed stiffly behind him.

I stopped in the doorway, but Jack went on into the room and sat beside the bed, resting his head on Grandpa's still form. He was lying on his back, his white hair fanned out across the pillow. The slight smile across his lips made me think, for an instant, that all was well. His eyes were open, and he seemed to be looking at something. But there was nothing there. "Grandpa?" I whispered, but he didn't turn toward me. I saw no movement, not even the rise and fall of his breath.

My heart froze within me. I turned and ran, my arms slamming the door behind me and my legs pounding the dirt lane that led toward home. My breath came in huge sobs, and tears streamed down my cheeks. I couldn't face this alone.

"Mama! Mama!"

She must have seen me coming, because she met me at the drive. I ran straight into her arms, not even slowing down, and buried my sobbing face in her soft, warm body. Wrapping my arms about her waist, I held on tight and cried until I could cry no more. She led me gently to the house—not even asking what was wrong. I'm sure she knew.

Chapter Nine

Elmina's Story

Springfield, Pennsylvania
December 1832

Eight years went by before Grandpa's prophecies began to come true. I was working as a live-in maid for the Hansen family by then. They had recently joined that new Mormon Church, and I had been attending meetings with them. It was true, and I knew it, but telling Papa about my decision to be baptized had me about as nervous as a kite on a string.

"Be courageous, Elmina," Mr. Hansen reminded me. "Tell your father how you feel, and don't back down. Be strong and resolute; the Lord will do the rest." His nose was red from the cold. Ice crystals hung in his beard and mustache, but his eyes were warm and his smile encouraging. I knew he thought of me more as a daughter than as household help.

I gave him a quick peck on the cheek. "Pray for me?" I asked. He smiled, nodded, and jumped quickly from the wagon, hurrying around to help me down.

The front door flew open, and my family spilled out. I hadn't been home for several months, so my visit was an event. Mama showered me with hugs and kisses and led me toward the house. Papa paused to thank Mr. Hansen with a hearty handshake before the kindly old man cracked the reins and started his team down the snow-covered road. My brothers grabbed my things and carried them in.

Once inside, we all stamped the snow off our feet on the doormat and Papa threw his arms around me in a huge hug. "Elmina, it's so good to have you home! We surely do appreciate Henry bringing you all this way in his wagon."

"Yes, and he turned right around and went back, despite the weather," Mama said, as she guided me toward the fire and wrapped a comforter about my shoulders. "I wish

he could have come in and warmed up a bit before he headed out."

"I invited him to come in, but he said he had some errands to do in town and couldn't take the time," Papa said as he removed his hat and coat and hung them on a peg by the door. "Henry's a good man. I've always liked him, but I've heard some disturbing things about him lately. Elmina, we'll need to talk about whether you should go back and work for the Hansens after the holidays."

Here it is already, I thought. My heart skipped a beat, and I opened my mouth to reply, but Mama jumped in quickly.

"Andrew, she's just stepped in the door, and we haven't seen her in months. Can't this wait?" I smiled gratefully at my mother as she settled me into a chair by the fire and headed for the kitchen, promising to be right back with something warm to drink.

I was happy to be home, and it felt good to see my family again, but a sense of dread had hung over me all day. I knew it was just a matter of time until everything came out, and I didn't know what would happen when it did. This situation was about as prickly as a cornered porcupine.

That evening, when dinner was over and the dishes were done, the family gathered around the fire to relax a while before bedtime. I, however, didn't feel at all relaxed.

Mama placed a basket of mending by her side and picked up a sock to darn. Papa smiled at her and continued to rub grease into the harness he was mending. My brothers sprawled on the floor in front of the fire, and I leaned over to pick up a darner and a sock from Mama's basket. That's when it all started.

"Elmina, is it true that Henry and his wife have joined those Mormons?" Papa's dark eyes bore into mine.

"Yes, Papa, it is." I took a breath and tried to stay calm, but my heart almost leapt right out of my chest.

"And is it also true that you have been attending meetings with them?" Papa's voice picked up in volume, and Mama's eyes darted nervously between us.

"Yes, it is, Papa, and I—"

"Elmina, haven't you heard the terrible things that are being said about those people?"

"Of course I have, Papa, but none those awful stories are true. If you would go to one of their meetings, you'd see they have answers to the questions our family has been asking

all these years. Joseph Smith is the prophet Grandpa told us about. I'm sure of it."

"Don't you dare bring your grandfather into this! He was a foolish old man who didn't know when to keep quiet. And our family paid the price for it. It took us years to get beyond the consequences of his thoughtless actions. Years! Never again will I allow a member of this family to put the rest of us through that kind of humiliation. Do you understand me, Elmina? When the holidays are over, you will not be returning to the Hansens'. And you will never again attend a meeting with those Mormon devils or speak about them in this house!"

I stood up and returned the darning to my mother's basket as calmly as I could. Facing my father with all the determination I could muster, I said quietly, "Papa, I am not a child. I'm old enough to make my own decisions, and I intend to be baptized a Mormon."

Papa sprang to his feet with a suddenness that brought the whole family to attention. He boomed out at me, "Elmina, you're still my daughter, and this is still my home. If you have any intention of remaining a part of this family, you will follow my direction as head of this house. I say again, you are to have nothing more to do with the Mormons!"

Tears stung my eyes, but I stood my ground. "Papa, if you'll just listen to them, you'll know. You've studied the scriptures for years. I know you've seen the inconsistencies between the Bible and what all the other ministers preach. Talk to the missionaries, Papa," I pleaded. "They have answers."

To my surprise, Papa thundered back at me, "I have talked to them, Elmina, and I have been to their meetings!"

"You have?" I stared at him in disbelief.

From behind me, I heard my mother's voice, "Yes, we have, dear, several months ago." I spun around to face her, my eyes wide with shock. "Joseph Smith's brother, Samuel, and a man named Orson Hyde held several meetings in town. We heard about them and were curious, so we went."

"And?" I demanded.

"I have no quarrel with their teachings," Papa's voice was quieter now. "The things they said made sense; we even thought of joining, but . . ."

"We started hearing things, Elmina—terrible things!" Mama's voice trembled, and I could see fear etched

into her features. "We knew something was wrong. Since then, we've stayed very far away from them. And so should you."

That's when William jumped up and elbowed his way into the conversation. At eighteen, my brother was headstrong and impulsive. I felt quite sure he didn't care one way or the other about religion, but he wasn't going to let an opportunity to flex his muscles pass him by. "Joe Smith is crazy and dangerous! I've heard all about him walking on water and catching angels." He looked quickly around to make sure everyone was listening. "And that book he's got is bewitched! Any Mormon who tries to baptize my sister or anybody else in this family will have me to deal with. I'll shoot him dead!"

Mama and Papa turned their attention away from my baptism to William in an effort to temper his unruly and aggressive attitude. I stood watching and listening as if from a distance. I would be baptized. As much as I loved them, not even my parent's fury would stop me. I doubted my father would actually disown me, and I didn't think William would try to kill the missionaries. Still, I knew that if I joined the Mormons, I would cause a huge rift between my family and myself. The very idea left me weak.

***

With the holidays over, the time had come for me to return to my employment at the Hansen residence. Although we had avoided the subject of "the Mormons" and my desire to be baptized, it had hung over our family like a thundercloud about to break. I knew I couldn't avoid the subject any longer. When Papa came back from town, I would get it over with; I would tell him I had decided to be baptized a Mormon and return to the Hansens' home.

I sat in the parlor, waiting for him. When I heard the wagon rattle onto our drive, I bowed my head and pleaded with the Lord, one last time, to soften my father's heart and allow my baptism to take place without tearing my family apart. But I was not prepared for what happened when Papa stepped through the door.

With him were two men. One of them was Hyrum Smith, brother of the Prophet Joseph, and the other was a man named Orson Hyde. Papa invited them to come in and visit with us in the parlor.

"I believe you have met my daughter, Elmina," Papa began. "She is determined to be baptized a Mormon, but I am telling you now, I will never allow it."

"Papa," I began, but Hyrum threw me a warning glance and shook his head slightly in my direction as he began to speak.

"Mr. Tyler, we will not baptize you daughter against your will. I would advise you to consider carefully, however, because if our doctrine is true—and I testify to you that it is—and you prevent her from embracing it, the sin will be on your head—not ours or your daughter's."

The tension in the room was tangible. Papa stared down at his boots for a long while before he looked me sternly in the eye and said, "Elmina, if these men are telling the truth, this new religion is a wonderful thing; but if they're wrong, it's the most terrible lie the world has ever seen. I just don't know. I've decided to let you to make your own decision about this. But I'm your father, and I'm begging you not to make a commitment you might regret the rest of your life."

Tears welled up in my eyes; then I flew across the room and wrapped my arms around his shoulders. "Papa," I whispered as I studied his eyes with mine, "Every word these elders have told us is true. I know it deep in my heart, and you're right—this new religion is the very best thing that could happen to the world. Someday I hope you'll know that it's true too."

The next day my father drove me in an ox-sled to Lake Erie to be baptized. The two-mile ride was cold, but the sun shone overhead, and my heart felt light. Papa said very little. I sensed that he was deep in thought and torn by conflicting emotions.

At Lake Erie, Papa helped the elders cut a hole through the three-feet deep ice. Hyrum Smith baptized me there, in the frigid winter waters of Lake Erie, and then confirmed me a member of the Church of Jesus Christ of Latter-day Saints. Mama worried I would catch my death, but of course, I didn't. My baptism day was the warmest day of my life.

***

I returned to the Hansens' happy and contented. Oh, yes, I did have to endure the pointed fingers and whispered words of persecution, but I ignored them.

I thought my life couldn't get any better, but to my surprise, it did.

"Elmina, come quickly," Sister Hansen called to me. "You have a visitor."

I scurried down the stairs and peeked into the parlor. There in the doorway, holding his hat and beaming as if someone had lit a candle inside of him, stood my father.

"Papa, is everything all right?" I asked when I reached him, confused not only by his presence, but by the light that sparkled in his eyes.

He threw back his head and laughed at my confusion, kissed the top of my head, and said, "Elmina, I've come to get you, because your mother and I are getting baptized today into that church of yours, and I thought you would like to be there."

I saw his mouth move; I heard the words he spoke, but I truly could not believe I was hearing them. I had to be dreaming.

"Close your mouth, Elmina," Papa said, his eyes dancing with amusement. "You look like a codfish washed up on the beach. You'd better breathe sometime soon, or you're going to pass out."

I shrieked for joy and jumped into his arms. He swung me around like he used to do when I was a little girl. And we laughed together like children in the park.

***

During the wagon ride to their baptism, I learned of the amazing events that brought my parents to this unexpected decision. "Your grandfather came to me in a dream," Papa said. "He told me that Joseph Smith is the prophet the angel said would be coming—the one who would bring the true religion of Christ. He said our family should join the Church and be true and faithful, because the Lord has work for us to do."

"Now, you know that I don't take much stock in dreams, Elmina, but this dream was different. I saw your grandfather, as clearly as I'm seeing you, and the message he brought to me was from God. I knew it in my heart when I

woke up, and your mother knew it as soon as I told her about it. Our lives would be a lot simpler if we didn't join this church, I'm pretty sure of that, but you're right; we have looked for the truth all our lives, and now that the Lord has brought it to us, what else can we do?"

***

"My family all joined the church," Elmina said, smiling wistfully at the cluster of family members gathered in her kitchen, listening to her story. "First I joined, then my parents. It wasn't long until my brothers joined too."

She closed her eyes and drew a deep breath, smile wrinkles creasing her cheeks where, perhaps, youthful dimples had once been. And then she opened them again.

"Papa was right. Life would have been easier if we hadn't joined. We were driven out of homes in Kirtland, Missouri, and Nauvoo. We came all the way across the plains in covered wagons and settled here in an untamed land—all for the sake of the gospel." The little woman leaned forward in her chair and extended her hands toward us—hands callused and worn from toil, struggle, and care. "But I'd do it all again in a minute," she whispered, her eyes glowing as if lit by a flame deep within her soul. "Because the gospel is true—and it has brought me joy."

You could have heard an angel sigh when she finished her story. No one wanted to be the one to break the spell her tale had spun around us, glowing inside our hearts like a candle lit by some unseen hand.

Tears ran down my cheeks, only to be replaced by fresh ones each time I brushed them away. And I wasn't the only one. Jane, Percilla, and Mary all wiped tears from their eyes before they moved silently back to their tasks. Isaac stood and wrapped a strong arm around his wife's shoulders, mingling his tears with hers as he dropped a kiss on her upturned forehead. I sat still as a statue, not knowing what to say.

At last I stood, moved to her side, and reached out to touch her hand with mine. "Thank you, Mama Behunin, for sharing that part of yourself with us. I will remember it and cherish it—and I'll tell the story it to my children. Every one of them will know that Joseph Smith was a prophet and the gospel is true."

She patted my hand and smiled at me in a way that made her cheeks bunch up and her eyes sparkle. "Thank you, honey, it will mean more to me than you can ever know if you will do that very thing. I won't always be here to tell the story myself, you know. And I want all my family to hear it."

———————————

Chapter notes:

1. Although Elmina was certainly aware of and affected by her grandfather prophecy and angelic visit, the story of her direct involvement was created by the author. I have changed the timeline somewhat and made Elmina several years younger than she actually was at this time.

2. This account of the conversion of Elmina Tyler and her parents, Andrew and Elizabeth Tyler, is based on the family record written by Elmina's younger brother, Daniel Tyler, in "Incidents of Experience." The following are excerpts from "Incidents of Experience" dealing with the conversion of the Tyler family:

"In 1823, my father (Andrew Tyler) with his family moved to Springfield, Erie County, Pennsylvania, where his father and some other relatives had previously gone. About this time my father and grandfather became unusually interested in reading the scriptures and talking about them to their neighbors. One day my father happened to open to Mark, 16th chapter, 16th and 17th verses. After reading them several times carefully, he said, 'There is not a true believer in the world,' as the promise was that the signs spoken of should follow those who believed. He showed the passage to several ministers, mostly Methodists, and argued with them. The more he argued, the more convinced he was that the gospel was not on the earth, and he was able to confound the most learned divines, although he was quite illiterate. My grandfather also had the same views and he prophesied that he would die, but my father would live to see the true church organized with all the apostolic gifts and blessing...

"After my grandfather was taken with his last illness, he told my parents that an angel appeared to him clothed in white, and told him that he would not recover, for his sickness was unto death. Ten days later he died... the true church was not then on the earth (February 1829) nor had such an occurrence been heard of by us at the time. Although the Father and Son had appeared to Joseph Smith (Jr.), we had not heard of the vision. The vision of my grandfather seemed so strange that my parents hardly knew whether to attribute it to imagination or a reality, as they could not question his sincerity, he having always been strictly reliable. I have never doubted, however, his having the vision.

"He walked a half mile to bid my parents good-bye, although in poor health. On parting, he wept like a child, and said, "This is the last time I shall ever visit you while I live...."

"In the spring of 1832, Elders Samuel H. Smith and Orsen Hyde, of the Church of Jesus Christ of Latter-day Saints, came to our neighborhood and held a few meetings...My father soon became a bitter enemy. I believed every word ...but dared not make it known because of my youth and the bitterness of my father... I soon learned that she (Elmina) like myself, had believed the work from the beginning and was resolved to be baptized at the first opportunity.

"She was in the service of one of our neighbors. When she came home on a visit, father asked her if what he had heard, that she intended to join the "Mormons", was true. She answered that she believed they were right and felt it her duty to join them. He said, "If you do join them you must never darken my door afterwards"... My older brothers told her that they would shoot any "Mormon" elder who dared to baptize her...

"About Dec. 1832, Elder Hyrum Smith, brother to the prophet, came to our neighborhood. My father told him that his daughter, who was present, was bent on being baptized into his church, stating at the same time, that the elder who baptized her would do so at his peril. The Elder mildly remarked in substance as follows: "Mister Tyler we shall not baptize your daughter against your wishes. If our doctrine be true, which we testify it is, if you prevent your daughter from embracing it, the sin will be on your head, not on ours or your daughter."

"This remark pricked him to the heart.... He took her on an ox-sled to Lake Erie, a distance of two miles, where, after a hole was cut through three feet of ice, she was baptized and confirmed into the Church by Elder Hyrum Smith......

"Soon after, my grandfather appeared to my father in a dream, and told him that this was the people he had prophesied of while living, and my parents were baptized.

Chapter Ten

Rockville, Utah Territory
Thanksgiving Day, 1869

"Father, on this Thanksgiving Day, we feel to thank thee for the bounty spread before us and for the joy of family which brings us together." Isaac's clear voice boomed across the room where twenty-eight members of the Behunin family, plus myself, were seated at two long tables.

Mosiah's parents, Isaac and Elmina, and his single brothers, Alma and Hyrum, sat across the table from us. Cutler and Jane with their baby, "Little Ligie", bowed their heads at our left, and six-year-old Willy squirmed through the prayer between Mosiah and myself. Percilla and Amos with their baby, along with Andrew's widow, Mary, and her remaining five children, occupied the other large table in the room. We were missing Mosiah's two older brothers, his sister, and their families, but wondered where we would have put them if they had been able to come.

Conviction resonated in Isaac's every word as he continued with the prayer: "We are grateful for each precious member of our family gathered here and for those who, although unable to join us, hold a place in our hearts. We are thankful also, Father, for our dear sons, William and Andrew, whose empty places at our table are so keenly felt, and for the gospel, which brings peace to our souls and the knowledge that our family will one day be reunited before Thee. For these and all other blessings, we humbly thank Thee. In the name of our Lord and Savior, Jesus Christ, amen."

I joined in a hearty communal amen, which was followed quickly by the clank of silverware and the rustle of napkins. Across the table, I caught a glimpse of Mosiah's mother as she wiped a tear from the corner of her eye. She smiled at Isaac before starting a steaming bowl of mashed potatoes around the table. The room echoed with laughter and happy voices as heaped-up dishes of food made their way from person to person.

"Mighty fine turkey," Mosiah grinned at Willy as he handed him a platter of meat almost as big as the boy himself. I came quickly to his rescue, smiling at the feathers that stuck out from a cloth band tied around his tussled blonde hair.

Across the table, I couldn't help noticing Isaac cover his wife's small hand with his large one and smile knowingly into her eyes as they exchanged a private moment.

Isaac and Elmina's marriage had been one of convenience, Mosiah had told me—a lot like that of my own parents. Meriba, Isaac's first wife, died shortly after the couple moved to Kirtland, leaving him with three little boys aged six, three, and one.

I'm sure Elmina held no illusions of romance when Isaac knocked on her door and asked for her hand. He needed a mother for his children and she, at twenty-three, was still unmarried. Isaac Behunin was a good man and a faithful Latter-day Saint; so she married him and raised his children as her own. Somewhere between the bowls of cooked mush and the tubs of laundry, Elmina carved out a place for herself in Isaac's heart, and today, he couldn't take a breath without her by his side.

How like my parents—and yet how different! I could see Ma in my mind's eye, rocking fiercely in our St. George parlor, head held high and her jaw tight. Unable to return her husband's love, she had lost it.

Things couldn't have been easy for Elmina either—I was sure of that—but she had never asked Isaac to give up the memory of his first love. And she had even named her own first daughter, Nancy Meriba—the one with the red curls that hung down to her waist—after Isaac's first wife. To me, this was evidence of love so pure I could hardly imagine it.

I stole a sideways glance at my husband-to-be. No doubt, many a pretty girl had caught his eye before I came along. I held no worries that any woman, past or future, could ever challenge me for his heart; but there are other sirens that call with golden voices, luring away men's hearts from hearth and home. I already felt nudges of jealousy when Mosiah talked about the solitude he found in the mountains and of his love for the people who inhabit them.

I knew it was ridiculous to allow my mother's shallow words to affect me like they did. But planted like tiny seeds of doubt, they kept popping their nasty little heads into my mind.

"Caroline, could you pass us down some gravy?" Jane asked at my elbow, bringing me back to the present. I nodded, passed the gravy, and turned my attention to Willy.

"Well, Chief," I said with a smile, "you are indeed a mighty hunter. This turkey is the best I've ever eaten, and just think—he almost got away!"

Willy pulled himself up to his full height, puffed out his chest, and said, "Me and Uncle Mosiah did a real good job, didn't we?"

"You bet we did, tadpole," Mosiah laughed as he reached for another hot biscuit. "And just look at him now—a bit of a stuffed shirt, wouldn't you say? Yes, indeed, Willy, I'd say you are fast on your way to becoming a mighty warrior." Everyone laughed and Willy grinned with obvious pride.

Across the table, Elmina pushed a bit of her food around on her plate with her fork, then without looking up, she began, "Speaking of Indians, I have a feeling that you boys have some explaining to do—something about a raid and sneaking out at night?" She looked up and threw a sharp glance in Mosiah's direction.

Around the table, half a dozen forks stopped in midair, and it became very quiet. The boys all looked questioningly at each other and shrugged. Cutler turned to look at Jane; who muttered a quiet "oops" under her breath and turned beet red.

About that time, Mosiah's mouth seemed to explode, half-chewed food spraying across the table. "Well, I thought we'd actually gotten away with something for once, Mama, but I guess I should have known better. Here I am a grown man—going to be married in less than a week—and about to get the whipping of my life!"

"All right, out with it, Mosiah," Isaac replied. Papa Behunin tried to look stern, but the corner of his mouth kept twitching.

"Why is everybody looking at me?" Mosiah threw his hands into the air, an innocent expression on his face. "You were the oldest, Alma."

"I might have been the oldest," Alma answered back, "but the whole thing was your idea, and you were bound and determined to go alone if I didn't go with you." He nodded toward his mother. "You wouldn't have liked that, I'm sure."

"Well, everything would have been all right if Hyrum and Cutler hadn't followed us," Mosiah said, turning to look at his younger brothers. "We didn't even know you were there until we'd almost made it to the camp. How in the world did you know we were going anyway?"

"Oh my goodness!" Elmina's hands flew to her cheeks, and her eyes popped open with horror. "Hyrum and Cutler couldn't have been any more than five and six!"

"We heard you two talking," Cutler stated matter-of-factly. "And we weren't about to be left out. We knew the grown-ups were all stewed up, and the drums had been beating for days. We were curious."

"I hated having the Indians camped right around us like that," Elmina whispered. "All the whooping and laughing—and the pounding of the drums. I thought I would lose my mind!"

"You know why they camped so close to us." Isaac said, "They wanted to show off their captives from the Shoshone raid."

"Their captives and the scalps they'd taken," Alma said. "They were awful proud of those scalps; kept parading them all around on poles—all covered with blood."

"It was something to see all right," Mosiah said, "but I felt real bad for those women and children. The Utes made them dance around the campfire in front of the scalps of their dead husbands and fathers. The way they treated them made me sick."

"I wish I hadn't gone," Hyrum said. "It scared us real bad. We hid in the bushes and watched; then we crept home and snuck back into bed. But it stayed in my head for days. Every time I closed my eyes I could see Shoshone women and children crying. I can still see them."

"Some of the men rode out and got Captain Nelson from the Mormon Militia to come and put an end to it," Isaac said. "We were all mighty relieved when the Indians finally broke camp and left. I'm sorry that you boys had to see it. It was nothing for a child to see."

"The worst part for me," Mosiah said, his eyes still on his plate, "was seeing my friend Two Owls and his family be a part of it all. Couldn't believe my eyes. When I asked him about it the next day, he just laughed and said it was nothing." He stabbed a piece of turkey with his fork and looked up. "Talked about the Shoshones like they weren't even human."

68

"That's how he'd been raised to feel. Couldn't hardly have expected any different," Cutler said, shaking his head.

"But Two Owls was my best friend; he'd have given his life to save me if I was in trouble. He and his family were the kindest people I knew. It just didn't make any sense to me at all."

"What did he say when you told him how you felt?" Cutler asked.

"Oh, he got so mad he shoved me off the log we were sitting on. Then he jumped onto his pony and took off with a war whoop. Left me sitting there in the dirt trying to figure it all out."

"Were you still friends after that?" I asked.

"Sure, he'd forgotten all about it by the next day. But I never forgot it. I've heard white people talking about Indians the same way he was talking about the Shoshones. Like they aren't even human."

"Feelings like that run deep," Isaac said. "When the Indians massacred our William at Eagle Mountain, I struggled with some of those feelings myself. If it hadn't been for the gospel, I think they might have gotten the better of me."

"Did you ever kill an Indian, Uncle Mosiah, when you were in the militia?" Willy asked.

Mosiah turned to look at his nephew's small face but didn't answer.

"We all do what we have to do when we're in the military, son," Isaac answered. "It's our duty to protect our homes and families. But there's no glory in it." Then wiping a napkin across his bewhiskered mouth he added, "Enough of this disagreeable discussion. Let's get back to enjoying our splendid feast."

Everyone, including me, agreed very quickly to that suggestion, but somehow I had lost my appetite.

Chapter notes:

1. Events following the San Pitch Ute Indian raid on Shoshone Indians in 1854 are depicted in Ruby Noyes Tippets's history of the Cutler Behunin family, *A Song in Her Heart*, (pp. 46).

Chapter Eleven

Rockville, Utah Territory
December 1, 1869

I peered into the looking glass that hung in Mama Behunin's bedroom. The mirror was small and cracked, but the eyes that stared back at me danced with happiness.

Two sets of hands worked behind me, untying the rag curlers from my hair and gently coaxing my locks into ringlets that cascaded down my back. Jane and Percilla giggled softly as they worked, and Mama Behunin hummed while deftly fastening buttons up the back of my dress. I tried to tie a yellow bow around my unruly curls, but my shaking fingers wouldn't allow it.

"Here, honey, let me do that," Percilla whispered and quickly took over, fluffing my hair into a chestnut frame and pulling a shower of tiny ringlets about my face.

The soft yellow ribbon matched the beautiful dress from Pa, pulled from its place in the old chest for this—my wedding day. I wished that he could have been a part of the crowd waiting outside of Mama Behunin's bedroom door. But wearing this dress, chosen just for me, reassured me of his love. Even if he couldn't be here on my special day.

I touched the pearl-encircled cameo brooch pinned at my throat and thought of Ma. "Be happy, Caroline," she had said to me as she pressed her most-valued possession into my hand on that well-remembered day. The uncharacteristic softness in her voice and her briskly offered hug had reassured me that, despite her crusty exterior, she too loved and cared about me.

A knock sounded at the door, and Papa Behunin's voice called, "Bishop's here; everybody's waiting."

My breath caught in my chest.

Peeking anxiously around the bedroom door, I scanned the parlor, which was filled to overflowing with guests. Through the open front door, I could see more guests waiting for us in the yard. A wedding was a great occasion in Rockville.

The bishop married us for time only. That's all he could do. We would be sealed for eternity as soon as we were able to make the trip to Salt Lake.

I could have sworn I heard angels singing when the bishop pronounced us man and wife. The strength of the hug and kiss that followed took my breath away.

Minutes later, as we stepped out the front door, a cheer went up that must have echoed all the way to the mountains and back again. A fiddler struck up a tune, and everybody started to dance. It was the first day of December, and there was a definite nip in the air. But the sun smiled above us, and I was too excited to feel cold. A bonfire blazed to warm the guests, but once everyone started dancing, we didn't really need it. The neighbor ladies helped Mama Behunin bring out the food and set it on boards while the guests laughed, talked, and danced up a storm.

Mosiah and I danced 'til my feet almost fell off. I think he could have kept going 'til the cows came home. I always did feel proud to be the one he chose at those dances down in St. George. The other girls batted their eyes at him real good, hoping he'd choose them. But it was me he chose— and now he was mine for good.

I was out of breath, so we stopped dancing for a minute to visit with Jane and Cutler. That's when the men rode up. We could see them coming from a ways off—a cloud of dust announcing their approach. They rode in fast, jumped off their ponies, and plowed into the crowd, heading straight for us. As people moved back to let them through, I could hear the crowd murmuring, "Indian trouble". Isaac and Elmina moved quickly to our sides, their faces grim.

Before the men could get a word out, Isaac took the lead. "What's wrong, boys? As you can see, we're having a wedding here."

"Yes, and I'm mighty darn sorry about this," the short man with a barrel chest replied. "But we need Mosiah's help, and we need it now."

"Whatever it is, it's going to have to wait; this is my wedding day," Mosiah answered at my side, wrapping his arms tightly around my waist.

"Now, Behunin, you know we wouldn't be here if there was any other way. But those confounded Indians are all

71

riled up and fixing to come down on the homesteads here abouts," said a lanky man with a bushy mustache. Taking a slow step forward, he pulled his hat from his head, fidgeting with it as he talked.

"They were just fine a few days ago; what's got them all riled up now?" Mosiah asked, his jaw tight and his face dark with suspicion.

The fellow with the mustache and a powerfully built man with a bald head and one front tooth missing glowered down at the short one. The little man in the middle began, "Well, some of my stock wandered away from the herd, so Jim and Mac, here, were helping me hunt them down. Seemed like the cattle were heading in the direction of the Indian camp, so we rode up to the top of the bluff to take a look, and we saw them. Those thieving Indians shot my cattle and dragged them into their camp!"

Mosiah's face turned red. "You'd better have left things alone. I've told you before to keep your stock away from their camp. The Indians are used to living off the land, so if some cow wanders close to their camp, they think the Great Spirit has brought it to them. They feel they have a right to it."

"They were my cattle, and this is open range! They'd best learn to keep their thieving hands off of my property, or there will be heck to pay!"

Mosiah stared hard into the little man's face, his fists balled at his sides, and his jaw clinched.

"He fired into their camp," the tall man said.

Mosiah stamped his boot into the ground, barely missing my toes and let out a string of expletives I had no idea he knew.

"I didn't kill none of them. Just shot their durn dog!" the little man muttered with a sneer.

"The whole camp turned into a hornet's nest, and we lit out fast," the thick, muscular man at his side replied, kicking a clod of dirt with his heavy boot. "We headed straight for your place. I know Harlin, here, done a dumb thing, but it's done now, and there's lives at stake. We need you to come settle them down."

Mosiah's eyes narrowed as they bore alternately into each rancher's face, fixing at last on the short one's defiant gaze. "Well, Harlin, it sounds like you made this mess, so you'd best get yourself back up on that horse of yours and go fix it." Then I felt his strong arm begin to turn me as he

72

concluded, "My wife and I are just about to disappear into that cabin yonder, and nobody is going to see hide nor hair of us for several days, so if you fine gentlemen will excuse us . . ."

Mosiah whipped me about and began to move me firmly through the crowd, but a hand from behind us grabbed my husband's arm, pulling us back. The tall rancher dug his bony fingers into Mosiah's forearm, his Adam's apple bobbing up and down as he demanded, "Behunin, you know very well that he can't do that. Those Indians would have his scalp before he got anywhere near their camp. Besides, that he don't speak their language."

Mosiah jerked his arm away and spun around, glowering back at the man, "And what makes you think I care about his scalp? Right now, I'd like to see it dangling from a pole myself!" Taking two steps forward and pulling me with him, he pushed into the ranchers' faces, his body hard and tense at my side, his arm almost crushing me with his strength.

Two of the men danced backwards and dropped their eyes, but the broad, strong one held his ground and returned Mosiah's determined gaze. "I know this is a bad time and all. We're real sorry—but it ain't just Harlin that's in danger here, and you know it. When them Indians get riled, they don't much care which white man has done 'em wrong. We're all in danger now, and you're the only one who can talk any sense into them—we need you."

Mosiah's body went slack. He took a deep breath and shook his head. Then he turned to look into my eyes with an expression of regret so intense it sent knives of fear down my spine. "So, you want me to ride into their camp and try to talk to them? I'm white too, you know."

"But you can talk their language, and they respect you. You're the only one they'll let anywhere near their camp. The settlers' lives are depending on it, Mosiah; you've gotta go."

I felt his body tense again. "There's lives depending on it, all right, and they aren't all white!" Mosiah's arm snaked forward, his fist grabbing a wad of Harlin's shirt just below his chin and pulling the little man's face close to his own. "If I ever hear of you endangering the settlement with a stupid stunt like this again, I'll turn you over to the Indians myself!" Then he let go of Harlin's shirt with a shove that sent the small man flying backwards into the dust. As quickly as

Harlin could scramble to his feet, the three men hurried back to their ponies, mounted up, and were gone.

Mosiah turned to me, gathering me gently into his arms. I clutched at him, my fingers digging into the flesh of his back, as a voice in my ears screamed, "No! No! No!" I was only vaguely aware that the voice was mine.

Mosiah released me and turned away as other arms gently restrained me from running after him. I struggled to free myself, but Mosiah moved through the crowd toward the barn where Cutler waited with two saddled horses and two rifles.

"Cutler always goes with him," Jane whispered.

"Always?" I blurted out. "Always?"

"Trouble with the Indians happens now and again, honey," Mama Behunin's soft voice spoke into my ear. "Mosiah's the only one who can calm them down at a time like this."

"But what if he can't?" I screamed back at her, hysteria mounting and swirling about me. "What if they kill him?"

"They won't," Isaac said from behind me. "He's got a way with them. He'll be back by sun up."

I pulled away from the hands that held me and ran, stumbling through the crowd that parted like the Red Sea to let me through.

Mosiah mounted resolutely and turned with sad eyes as he sensed my frantic approach. Leaning low from his mounted perch, he swept a strong arm about me and whispered, "It's all right, darlin'. Don't cry. I'll be just fine and home before you know it. You just keep that bed warm for me." Without another word, he nudged his horse, nodded to Cutler, and they were gone.

***

I slammed the cabin door with all the strength I had in me. Then I turned and hammered it with my fist. I had run all the way there, leaving the wedding guests and festivities behind me. I had an idea the party was over anyway. No one tried to stop me or follow me. I guess they knew I needed to be left alone. I had made a scene, but I didn't care.

When at last my sobbing stilled and the pounding in my head quieted, I turned to look with vacant eyes at the rough-hewn bed that dominated the room. Mosiah had crafted the bed himself, and I had covered it with the lovely quilt from the quilting bee. On a chair beside it, folded with care, laid a snowy-white flannel nightgown and the beautiful moccasins made by the little old Indian woman.

Indian! As the word crashed into my consciousness, I darted across the room, snatched up a moccasin, and flung it at the cabin wall. It was followed quickly by the second moccasin and lastly by my white nightgown. One by one they slid down the cabin wall and landed in a heap on the dirt floor.

I stood staring at them for a moment before I ran quickly and picked them up, dusting off the flecks of dirt and pressing them desperately to my breast. In my mind's eye, I could see my new husband riding across the red hills of the untamed desert as the December sun dipped low in the sky.

Is he riding to his death? The ranchers had described the Indian camp as a hornet's nest ready to kill any white man on sight.

Can Mosiah and Cutler get close enough to let the Indians know who they are without getting shot? Visions of raids and scalps hanging from poles ripped at my heart. Crippling fear, too intense for tears, closed around me.

I crept to the bed, sat on its edge, and undressed, slipping into the soft white nightgown and buttoning it up to my chin before I climbed alone between the sheets. Sometime in the night, after crying myself into utter exhaustion, I fell asleep.

***

The first rays of the early-morning sun were just creeping in through the window when the rustle of bed sheets and the sensation of two strong arms closing around me roused me from my slumber. My eyes flew open as Mosiah pulled me to his chest. Relief washed over me like a summer rain, and I threw my arms about him, buried my head in his chest and sobbed.

Mosiah's large hand caressed my sleep-worn locks and whispered, "It's all right, darlin'. Everything's fine, and I'm here now. Still in one piece."

As my feelings of fear and relief began to subside and my sobbing stilled, anger surged up within me, and I found myself pounding his chest and screaming, "Don't you ever do anything like that again, Stephen Mosiah Behunin! How could you do that to me on our wedding night?"

"Now, darlin', I had no choice. It had to be done, and you know it," he whispered into my hair. "But it's done now, so if I promise to stay right here beside you, will you forgive me and give me that kiss I've been dreaming about all night?"

That's how my life as Mrs. Stephen Mosiah Behunin began, and it never did get any easier. But I wouldn't have traded it for the world.

Chapter Twelve

Rockville, Utah Territory
May 1870

The world around me swirled uncontrollably and bile rose in
my throat each time I opened my eyes or raised my head; I
tried to do neither. The cow should have been milked an hour
ago, but I didn't care. It was hard to care about much of
anything these days.

Mosiah was gone again and I did care about that. I'm
ashamed to say it, but sometimes I felt so angry with him for
leaving me sick and helpless that I screamed and kicked at
anything in my way. I guess I wasn't all that helpless, but I
sure was sick. I knew I shouldn't be angry with my husband.
After all, it wasn't his fault that I was sick. Well, maybe it
was—but it's all a part of the natural way of things.

We'd planned to go to Richfield together when
spring came and get started on our farm there. I guess we
shouldn't have been surprised when I found myself in the
family way after being married for only a couple of months.
But we were. After all, I was barely fifteen.

My heart told me that having a baby should be
exciting, and down deep I did feel happy, but by the time I
realized what was making me so sick, I was too ill to care.

Mosiah decided to leave me in the relative comfort of
the cabin while he got the land cleared and crops planted in
Richfield. His solution sounded logical, but I was lonely and
scared—and sicker than I had ever been in my life.

I gripped the side of the bed with one clammy hand
and rolled out. As my knees hit the dirt floor, the walls began
to roll. Two seconds later my head was in the pot.

At last the stomach spasms subsided, and my
spinning world righted itself. I wiped my mouth on my sleeve
and pulled myself up to sit on the edge of the bed, staring
down at my pillow. I wanted to lie back down and forget all
about the lowing cow and the hungry animals. But Mosiah had

his work to do in Richfield, and I had mine to do here. I reminded myself that women had been doing this for centuries, some of them a dozen times or more. I could do this.

I forced my unwilling body into a standing position and started across the room for the milk bucket. My legs were rubber beneath me. I reached out a shaking hand to steady myself, and the cabin door flew open, startling me so badly that I almost fell on my nose.

Jane barged into the room with Cutler at her heels. She threw her arms around me and began to hustle me out the door without so much as a howdy-do.

"There's trouble with the Indians, Caroline," Cutler explained. "Nobody seems to know what set them off, but they're burning homesteads and stealing stock. They say a whole family got burned to death in their own cabin. The settlers around these parts are heading for the fort as quick as they can. You can ride with us."

"Stop! What about Mosiah?" I cried as I planted my feet and pushed their arms away. "I can't go without my husband—and what about the animals?"

"Caroline," Cutler's voice cut through my unreasoning anxiety, "Mosiah's in Richfield—he's miles away. You've got to come with us now." I felt the blood rush from my face, and the world began to spin as everything went dark.

***

When I came to, Jane's head hovered above me. I jerked up, but she pushed me gently back down again. We were in the bed of the wagon, my head in her lap. "You fainted, Caroline. Just breathe slowly. Try to calm down and listen to me. You don't need to worry about Mosiah—he'll be fine. When he hears what's going on, he'll head to the fort and meet us there. Word travels like wildfire at times like this."

"What about the animals?" I asked, pulling myself slowly into a sitting position and propping my back against the wagon side.

"Cutler's gone to get your horse and your cow," she answered. "We'll tie them to the back of the wagon and bring them along. The other animals will have to fend for themselves for a few days."

"Molly hasn't been milked," I said, guilt adding to my discomfort. "I should have milked her earlier, but I just couldn't make myself get up."

Jane bit her lip. "We can't worry about that right now. We've got to hurry and meet the others. She'll be all right."

Cutler came, leading Molly and Lucy, and tied them to the back of the wagon. "Alma's gone into the canyon to get the folks and Hyrum," he said. "They'll catch up with us on the way." He jumped onto the wagon seat and picked up the reins. Jane joined him on the seat, but I stayed in the wagon bed, resting my head on a pile of quilts as we jolted into motion.

Molly lowed her discomfort, her heavy bag swinging to and fro and leaking milk as we traveled. Cutler finally pulled the wagon to a stop, got down, and milked her enough to make her comfortable before we started out again. I wished there was something I could do to ease my own discomfort. My stomach didn't have much in it, and I lost what little there was over the edge of the wagon soon after we started. Dizziness and dry heaves made my ride miserable. Jane coaxed me into eating a little bread and drinking some of Molly's warm milk, but I lost that over the side too.

We met up with the other settlers and continued on our way. I slept off and on despite the bouncing of the wagon and the noise of the group. Mama and Papa Behunin joined us about mid-afternoon. It was almost dark by the time we made it to the fort. Mosiah hadn't arrived yet, so I was pretty worried; but when I woke up in the morning, he was sleeping beside me. I curled close to him and sighed. All was right with the world as long as I had my Mosiah

***

The fort on the Santa Clara River was twelve feet high, and the walls were two feet thick. With only fourteen cabins inside, several families had to share each cabin and others lived out of their wagon beds. We were cramped in together like eggs in a basket. Privacy was next to nonexistent, but we managed. Living in such close quarters, people tended to get on each other's nerves, so every now and then, tempers flared and an argument would break the monotony. We almost looked forward to it.

Most of the settlers were pretty used to the fort routine. They'd all spent a lot of time at the forts during the Walker and Black Hawk Wars. Mama Behunin said she quite liked it—gave her a chance to spend time with the other settlers' wives—and she always felt safer inside the strong walls of a fort. The women did most of their chores together. Washing the dirty clothes actually became a social event. In the afternoon, we'd all find a comfortable place to sit and chat while we darned socks, mended clothes, and watched the children play.

The weather was pleasant most days, so I usually dozed off during those afternoon get-togethers. The older women fussed over me like mother hens, always bringing me a blanket or pillow. They'd laugh and say they couldn't have me falling off a barrel and hurting the baby. It really helped to have other women assure me that everything I was going through was normal. It was all brand new to me.

Mama Behunin was especially good to me, and I felt proud to be with her. It seemed that everybody liked her. They respected her too. She'd endured about everything there was to go through and had come out of it a kinder and wiser woman.

"Elmina, you were friends with Emma Smith back in Nauvoo, weren't you, honey?" a big-boned woman with a wide smile asked, looking up from her knitting.

"Yes, Nancy, I was," she answered. "Emma was friendly with everyone, of course, but we lived near the Smiths in Nauvoo, and Emma and I had a special bond because of the children."

"Oh, my, but the Prophet and Emma did have a time of it with their little ones," said a tiny round woman with a cluck of her tongue. "Lost four of them, didn't they?"

"Yes, three of their own and one of the twins they adopted," Elmina answered. "It was hard on Emma, as you can imagine."

"Had you lost children of your own, dear?" she asked peeking at Elmina over her spectacles. "Is that what brought the two of you together?"

"Well, no. In fact, Isaac and I had only been married for a few months, but he had three little boys from his first marriage, so I became an instant mother. I was quite overwhelmed." Elmina looked about her at the other women, who nodded with understanding. "Emma took me under her wing. She helped me understand what a gift motherhood is and taught me how to mother a child who isn't your own by birth. I learned more from her than I can ever tell."

"She was weak." A tall woman with narrow, angular features declared as she put down her mending and crossed her arms knowingly. "Too bad she forfeited her eternal crown because she didn't have the strength to stay faithful."

Elmina's eyes snapped. She drew herself up with a quick breath and leaned forward to study the other woman's face. "Emma Smith was the most Christ-like person I've ever known. She gave of herself every waking minute of her life. Not only to her children and her husband, but to her mother-in-law, every sick or needy Saint, and every stranger at her door. I simply cannot imagine anyone thinking or saying such a thing about Emma."

Raising her eyebrows and repositioning her spectacles over her hawk-like nose, the woman drew back slightly and looked about for support as she demanded, "Where is she now, then, Elmina? She sure ain't here, sitting around on barrels in a fort, hoping she won't get her hair lifted by Indians. And where was she when we all struggled across the plains, near starving and freezing to death? In the comfort of the Nauvoo House—that's where."

"Yes, Myra, in the Nauvoo House—in the very house where her husband's body was secretly buried. Were you there when we buried caskets filled with sand, pretending they were Joseph and Hyrum, to keep the murdering mob from digging up their bodies and desecrating them?"

"She fell apart, poor thing," a sister with grey curls peeking out from under a faded sunbonnet whispered. "She was completely beside herself with grief."

"Yes, she fell apart," Elmina answered. "And she had every right to fall apart. She'd been driven from home after home. Her husband had been tarred and feathered, beaten and jailed. She'd buried four of her precious children. And then she had to see Joseph's lifeless body brought home to her in a wagon bed."

"It was her own letter that brought him back to stand trial and be murdered," Myra said. Her voice had softened a bit but still carried an accusing tone.

"Don't you think she knew that?" Elmina answered, her voice quivering. "I held her hand while she cried until I thought there would be nothing left of her. She couldn't leave him. Not in life or in death. Joseph was her crown." Mama Behunin sighed, wiped a tear, and settled back. "Yes, Emma was my friend."

The women suddenly became very busy with their darning and mending. Elmina didn't give any lectures about not judging other people, but I think they got the message nonetheless.

***

The crescent moon hung high in the sky, and a million stars spilled across the heavens. They seemed so close I felt like I could reach up and catch one. The air nipped at my cheeks, so I snuggled against Mosiah's side, enjoying his closeness as we walked about the common area in the center of the fort. A bonfire blazed high, its light reflected in the faces of the settlers who had taken refuge within the fort's walls.

An Indian attack is a strange reason to have a social; but when you live miles from your nearest neighbor, every get-together turns into a party. Luckily for us, there was a fiddler among the group, and someone called out a square dance while everyone sang along.

"Like to join in the dance?" Mosiah asked hopefully; but I smiled and shook my head.

"Let's just walk together," I murmured. "It's a right nice evening, and it feels good just having you hold my hand. I think it's almost worth an Indian scare to have you with me for a few days."

Mosiah chuckled, and we stopped to share a long, sweet kiss in the shadows before we wandered on. "Guess what? I felt the baby move today," I beamed up into my husband's face, basking in his radiant smile. "It felt like a tiny bubble moving across the inside of my tummy. At first, I wasn't sure what it was. But when I felt it again, I knew."

Mosiah covered the small bulge in my rounding belly with his large hand and waited expectantly.

"No, silly, you can't feel it yet; but pretty soon you will. I hope he looks just like you, curly red hair and all!"

"Like me? I hope *she* looks just like you; we'll call her Caroline."

"It's a boy," I answered, "and I think we should call him Isaac, after your father."

"He'd be right proud." Mosiah smiled down at me and gathered me in for another kiss. But he stopped mid-embrace and peered at something over my head. "Oh, no, here comes trouble. How is it that whenever I get a little time with my wife, those cockeyed ranchers show up?"

I remembered Harlin and his cohorts all too well. Their audacity took Mosiah away from me on my wedding night and left me huddled in my bed, all alone. Just the sight of those skunks made my blood boil.

"Behunin," Harlin called out and marched towards us on short, thick legs. The way the little man's head sat on top of his shoulders with almost no neck in between reminded me of a turtle, but he certainly wasn't slow. "We got to talk to you about this here Indian trouble." He gave me a pointed look, making it obvious that he wanted to speak to my husband alone. But I threaded my arm through Mosiah's and stared back at him, letting the little man know that I wasn't going anywhere.

"What have you got on your mind, boys?" My husband gave me a wink and pulled me close to him, validating my intentions to stay.

"Half the men here have been out searching for the Indians what's responsible for this here mess. And they've seen Indians, all right, but none of them war parties—just little bands with women, children, and old men in them. 'Course they all say they don't know nothin'."

"Well now, that's the way most of the Indians in these parts live—in small bands. They only get together for war." Mosiah folded his arms across his chest, tucked his hands under his armpits, and squinted down at the rancher, waiting to hear what foul plan he might have up his sleeve.

"So, where's all the young bucks?" the ranchers asked together.

Jim—the one with the bushy mustache and the bobbing Adam's apple—spat on the ground and narrowed his eyes as he looked back at Mosiah. "They're lying, Behunin, I know it! They've got themselves a war party, and they're hiding out some place, just waiting to come down on some poor settler. Well, we ain't going to let it happen."

Mac nodded, sucking on the space where his missing tooth should have been and added, "I think it's about time we ride into one of them camps and stir things up a bit—let them know that we ain't going to put up with this business. They'd best be talking if they want to keep their lousy hides!"

"You aren't thinking about *attacking* a camp of women and chidren, are you?" Mosiah drew himself up to his full height, set his jaw, and glared at the ranchers through narrowed eyes.

"They're Indians, ain't they? And they're all in cahoots together!" Harlin glared back at him.

I glanced up at my husband, suspecting that he was about to make mincemeat out of the cocky little man. Without thinking, I jumped between the two of them and began to scream into the rancher's face, "That's murder—and the lowest kind on earth. You ought to be lynched from the highest tree for even thinking such a thing!"

"Atta girl, Caroline!" "You tell him!" "Give him a good left hook on the chin!" I glanced quickly about— shocked to find that we were surrounded by cheering settlers—and shut my mouth real fast. Mosiah was scratching his head and looking down at me with a funny, twisted grin on his face.

The ranchers stepped back a bit in surprise. The tall, skinny one held up his hands in surrender. "Now hold on, little lady, we didn't say nothing about killing any women and children. We just thought we ought to make them a little nervous—so they'd tell us what they're up to. They need to know white folks ain't going to let them get away with killing people or burning cabins or stealing stock."

Mosiah crossed his arms and leaned back a little. "Well, it seems to me you've got a few things mixed up here. In the first place, they haven't killed anybody. That family we all thought was burned to death in their cabin turned up in Cedar City a few days later just fine."

"I don't think I'd call them 'just fine', Behunin," the rancher answered back. "They was scared out of their wits, their cabin was burned to the ground, and all their stock was stolen."

"That's a fact!" voices from the crowd called out. "We ain't going to take this lying down!" "Weren't they all supposed to go live on a reservation after they signed that treaty?" Encouraged, Harlin looked about with a wide-toothed grin and puffed himself up while adjusting his belt.

"There's a thing or two you've got to understand," Mosiah continued. "It was the Utes that signed the treaty. Most of the Indians around here are Paiutes."

"That don't make no never mind. An Indian is an Indian! They were all supposed to go," someone called out from the back.

Mosiah turned to face the man who had spoken. "If you were a Paiute, would you want to go live on a reservation with the Utes after they stole your wife and child and sold them down in Mexico?" he asked.

"I don't think it rightly matters what they want," the man called back. "Their chiefs signed the treaty, and they need to abide by it." The agitated crowd cheered him on.

"They took the cattle and the flour we gave them," another voice called out. "Don't that make them beholden to the treaty?"

"You mean those scrawny, half-dead cattle the government sent and the flour that never arrived?" Mosiah's voice was getting louder and more agitated. "The federal government didn't ever ratify that treaty anyway. So, no— they're not beholden to it. A good many of them don't want to go live on the reservation. And nothing says they have to."

I could feel the tension mounting within my husband and glanced up just in time to see a hand settle on his shoulder.

We both turned quickly to face a man with a gentle smile. He extended a large hand toward Mosiah and began to introduce himself. "Brother Behunin, Sister Behunin?" he said as he nodded in my direction. "My name is Jacob Hamblin."

There was a murmur from the crowd, and I felt my eyes grow wide. Not only was Jacob Hamblin an apostle, but he was also a missionary to the Indians. From what I'd heard, he'd risked his life more times than you could count during his ten years of service.

The ranchers melted into the crowd like snow on a sunny day, and I found my husband tongue-tied for the first time since I'd known him. "I was just returning from a mission to the Hopis when I heard about the Indian trouble around here. They tell me you're a man with some Indian experience yourself."

"Brother Hamblin," Mosiah sputtered as he grasped Jacob's hand with his own and began to pump. "It's mighty fine to make your acquaintance. We've heard a lot of good about you and all you've done with the Indians. I'm pleased to meet you. I surely am." When he recovered a bit, my husband remembered I was standing by his side and introduced me. "This here's my wife, Caroline, as you most likely guessed."

"It's a pleasure to meet you, ma'am," he said as he tipped his hat and flashed me a wide smile. There was something warm and comfortable about this man.

"I surely didn't mean to interrupt your conversation with these fine gentlemen," Jacob continued. "From what I overheard, it seems to me that you about hit the nail on the head. We're in a real sticky situation here with the Indians. And there aren't any easy answers. But it helps a great deal if you understand the problem."

Jacob reached out, laid a hand on Mosiah's shoulder, and studied my husband's eyes with his own. He continued, "I hear, Brother Behunin, that you're one who does. I think you could be a great deal of help to us while we're trying to iron out this problem."

Mosiah looked down at his boots and gave the dirt a little kick before he looked back into Jacob's eyes. "I don't rightly know how much help I'd be, Elder Hamblin, but I certainly am willing to do what I can."

Jacob chuckled and hooked his thumbs into his pants pockets. "From what I hear, you're being a bit modest. I've been told the settlers down Rockville way pretty much depend on you to handle the Indian problems in their neck of the woods."

"I don't know if I'd go that far, but I do try to smooth things out when I can. The Indians around here don't usually cause a lot of trouble. They're pretty quiet as Indians go. But every once in a while, they do get a bit fractious. Usually it's some fool thing somebody did that set them off."

"That's most often the case, now, isn't it?" Jacob replied as he shook his head. "Is it true that you speak Paiute?"

"Actually, it was the Ute language I learned to speak first," my husband replied. "Spent quite a lot of time with the San Pitch Indians when I was growing up. They're Utes, you know, so that's the language I learned first. But the Paiute language is pretty similar. Didn't take much to pick it up when we moved down here."

"It was the other way around with me." Jacob nodded toward the fire, so we turned and wandered slowly in that direction as he talked. "Paiute was the language I learned to speak first. I do well with Hopi, and I can manage Ute. As you say, the language is pretty similar. But I need an interpreter with the Navajos."

We settled down on logs by the fire, and the men got to telling Indian stories. Jacob was older and a lot more experienced than my husband, but they both had a respect for the Indians not many men shared. Some of the stories that Jacob told made me shudder clear down to my toes. I couldn't help thinking how hard it must be to be married to someone like Jacob Hamblin. *What would I do if my husband was away with the Indians half the time?* I couldn't handle wondering if he was going to make it home alive or not. I remembered all too well what that felt like.

After a while, I got sleepy and laid my head on Mosiah's shoulder. I had just dozed off when I heard words that woke me up in a hurry.

"Well, Brother Behunin," Jacob said, "I'll be riding out tomorrow looking for the Indians who've caused our current predicament. I'm not sure what I'll find. We don't know if the Indians responsible for this are Paiutes, Utes, or Navajos. I could surely use someone with me who understands Indian ways and speaks their language. Between the two of us we pretty much have Paiute and Ute covered. How about it?"

I felt as if a ton of lead had hit the bottom of my stomach. *Oh, no! Why does it always have to be my husband?* I tried to protest but bile rose in my throat.

Mosiah looked down at me, his brows knit together with concern. "I'd be more than pleased to accompany you, Brother Jacob. First light then?" With that, my husband wrapped his arm about my shoulders and led me away from the crowd toward the wagons, where I lost my dinner in the dirt.

***

When I woke up the next morning, Mosiah and Jacob were gone and they didn't come back until after supper. I felt sick all day so Jane and Mama Behunin stayed close by me. As the sun began to set, the lookout signaled that he could see riders coming in the distance. Weak kneed with relief, I watched as Mosiah and Brother Hamblin rode in through the gates and everybody gathered round to hear what they'd found out.

Jacob took off his hat and stood tall in the stirrups so that everyone could hear him, "Well now, folks, here's the situation. There's a group of renegades from the Colorado Utes who've been going around to the local tribes trying to pick up recruits."

Waiting a few moments for the buzz to die down, he continued. "They're unhappy about the treatment they've received from the government and they're tired of seeing their families going hungry. They've been doing their best to stir things up, but most of the local Indians want no part of it."

I could see people look at each other with relief. "The Indians we talked to said their families are hungry too, but they don't want to fight a war they can't win. Some of the hotheaded young bucks have joined the renegades, and that's who's responsible for the cabin burning and the cattle stealing we've been hearing about."

"What do we do now, Brother Hamblin?" someone called out.

Jacob reached down to give his horse a pat and answered. "It seems they've headed northeast and are out of the territory for now. They probably won't be coming back for some time, if at all, so the best thing to do is to go home and get on with spring planting."

My husband rode over to me, swung out of the saddle, and wrapped me in his arms. I snuggled in and started to cry. I wasn't quite sure whether my tears were relief that he was back safely, or sorrow that he would be heading back to Richfield tomorrow while I returned to Rockville with Jane and Cutler. Maybe it was both.

Chapter Thirteen

On the road to Rockville, Utah Territory
May 1870

I sat beside Jane on the buckboard seat, feeling gloomier as
each clop of horse hooves took me farther away from Mosiah.
Cutler's dog, Spook, who had been trotting along beside us,
spotted a rabbit and bounded off after it, only to return
minutes later with his tongue hanging out. He was a mangy
critter, but Cutler seemed unusually attached to him.

"Why did you call him Spook?" I asked.

"Now that's a right good question," Cutler answered,
throwing me a wink, "and it's got a right good story attached
to it, too."

Jane rolled her eyes. "Oh, no, here we go again."

"I want to hear it," I answered.

Tired of watching mile after mile of sand roll by, and
even more tired of the dust our wagon wheels continually
churned up, I welcomed anything that would break the
monotony.

"Found him when he was just a pup," Cutler began,
"while I was serving in the militia during the Black Hawk
War."

I turned to face him with interest.

He flicked the reins and smiled in my direction. "Our
regiment was all bedded down for the night. I must have been
the only one still awake when I heard a noise in the bushes, so
I reached for my gun. Before I knew it, an Indian with a knife
in his hand jumped out from the bushes and landed on top of
me. In the tussle, he knocked the gun out of my hand, and I
thought I was a goner."

Cutler swatted at a fly with his hat and went on with
his story, "Somehow I managed to get out from under him,
roll to my gun, and grab it, just as he raised his arm to stab me
with his knife. As soon as I felt that gun in my hand, I shot.
Hardly even had time to aim, but I got him. Bullet went right

through his side. He was in pretty bad shape, but he wasn't dead."

"Oh, my goodness," I murmured.

Cutler gave me a big grin, and Jane rolled her eyes again. It seemed maybe he'd told this story a time or two before.

"As soon as we realized who the Indian was, I knew I was in trouble. I had shot White Horse, or Tamarisk, as the Indians call him—the chief's son. While the other soldiers helped to patch him up, I cussed under my breath. I knew I would spend the rest of my life watching my back, because he was sure to come after me, looking for revenge. Him and the rest of his tribe.

"The next morning he was weak from losing so much blood, but there was no holding him back—he wanted to get to his camp. So, I put him on his horse and rode with him. I didn't want him to fall off and get hurt worse. When we got about a mile from camp, I stopped and watched him ride back to his tribe."

"He should have been grateful—you could have killed him." I said. "Didn't he know that?"

"Oh, he knew I could have killed him, but I hurt his pride more than anything, and that's a mighty serious thing for a Ute warrior," Cutler answered. "I felt mighty nervous for quite a while after that—you can bet."

"So, what did you do?" I asked.

"Well, a few nights later, I heard a noise in the brush and thought it must to be him, so I drew my gun and circled the bush. Kept hearing a kind of whimpering sound coming out of it. Thought for sure it was White Horse trying to trick me. I finally got brave enough to get closer and have a look-see. Then did I have a laugh!"

Cutler looked at me, his eyes twinkling, and gave me a wink. "It weren't no Indian at all, just a little gray pup with a hurt leg. I patched him up and carried him along with me on my horse 'til he could walk. Called him Spook because he sure did scare the tar out of me. He and I have been best friends ever since. Wouldn't trade him for anything."

"White Horse—he's a chief now, isn't he?" I asked.

"Yes, indeed, one of the fiercest around," Cutler answered. "Not a good man to have for an enemy."

"Has he ever come after you?"

"Not yet," he answered, throwing me a wide grin and flicking the reins.

"He probably admires you for fixing him up and taking him back to his tribe when you could have killed him."

"Could be. You never can tell with Indians." Cutler turned his eyes back toward the road and fell into a pensive mood.

Nobody said anything until he turned back to me. "You don't need to worry none, though, about Indians bothering you. The troublemakers are all gone now. Mosiah wouldn't have left you if he had any doubt of that. Besides, you're Shoken's wife. No Indian is going to bother you."

"What?" I said in amazement. "Who's Shoken?"

"Your husband, silly," Jane laughed back at me. "Shoken is his Indian name. Didn't he ever tell you that?"

I shook my head and stared back at her. "What does it mean?"

"Fast Rabbit," Cutler replied, grinning slyly, but never taking his eyes off the trail.

"Fast Rabbit!—Mosiah's Indian name is Fast Rabbit?"

"It's really more complimentary than you might think," he answered, flashing me a big grin. "You see, we used to play with the Indian boys quite a lot, growing up there on Pine Creek. Mosiah spent more time with them than he did with the white boys—much to our mother's displeasure. Sometimes we'd play games—you know, white boys against the Indian boys. It wasn't much of a contest. The Indians always won."

I just looked at him. I couldn't even imagine such a thing.

"Mosiah was real good at those games, though. He was a scrawny little guy, but he was quick. He could dodge around so fast that nobody could catch him. The Indians called him, Shoken—Fast Rabbit—and they always wanted him on their team. Made the white boys real mad. They didn't think it was fair."

I looked at him kind of strangely, I guess, and asked, "Do you have an Indian name?"

"Sure do," Cutler replied, giving me a grin and a wink, "Red Bull."

I looked over at my brother-in-law's red hair that fell to his shoulders and his red beard, shining in the sunlight, and chuckled to myself.

Chapter notes:

1. The incident about Cutler, young White Horse, and Spook is related in *A Song in her Heart* by Ruby Noyes Tippets, (pp. 80-81).

Chapter Fourteen

Rockville, Utah Territory
November 1880

I struggled to cross the shallow irrigation ditch, my hands supporting my huge abdomen. Ordinarily those hands would have lifted my skirts to keep them out of the way of my feet. As it was, I couldn't even see my feet. I think that's why they got all tangled in my skirts. Halfway across the ditch, I lost my balance and felt myself falling.

Frantically, I stretched out my arms to avoid landing on the baby, and a moment later, I found myself on my knees in the mud. My hands, which had taken the full brunt of my fall, were skinned and bleeding. Dirt and gravel were imbedded in the tender flesh.

Through my tears, I could just make out Mosiah's silhouette on the other side of the field. He was bent down digging potatoes. I had to reach him. I could not do this alone.

Gritting my teeth against the throbbing in my hands, I pushed myself to my feet and waddled forward, calling out his name as I stumbled across the field. Maybe he heard me, or maybe he just stopped to wipe his forehead with his handkerchief. Either way, as soon as he saw me coming across the field, he dropped his shovel and took off toward me at a dead run.

"It's coming," I called as soon as he came within hearing distance. "I need your help."

When he reached me, Mosiah stopped just long enough to swoop me up in his arms—not an easy task considering my condition—and head off toward the cabin.

"What in the world are you doing?" I asked in amazement at his strange behavior.

"Getting you to the cabin the quickest way possible," he answered as his long legs ate up the distance between us and the house. "You can't have the baby out here in the field."

"Not me, silly! Lucy!" I told him. "She's having her foal."

Mosiah stopped, set me on my feet, and sat down hard in the dirt, his face white and his hands shaking. "Caroline!" he said as he picked up a clod of dirt and gave it a toss. "That was a terrible thing to do to me!"

"But I think there's something wrong," I said, realizing what an unnecessary fright I had given him. "I really do need your help. She keeps lying down and getting up again. And she's been kicking at her belly and rolling."

"That's what they do, Caroline," he answered, the irritation evident in his voice. "Either you're right and she's having the foal, or she's got a case of colic. Guess I'd better go take a look. I needed a break anyway." Then he grinned at me, wrapped his arm about my ample waist and helped me across the field to the barn where we found Lucy in her stall, calmly munching hay.

My husband looked at the mare, who was ignoring us as she devoured her breakfast, and then back at me with his eyebrows raised. "Um-hmm," he said, a little smile playing about the corners of his mouth. "She's in real trouble, all right. Looks like she's going to drop that foal any minute now."

"Well, she was—" I began, but I didn't need to finish; Lucy's head jerked up from her hay, and a huge gush of liquid escaped from under her tail.

"On second thought...," Mosiah muttered, stroking his chin.

Lucy went down onto her front knees and rolled over onto her side. We watched as she bore down through two powerful contractions. Then, to my amazement, a large white bubble appeared under her tail.

My husband quietly unlatched the stall door and motioned me inside. We crouched together by the mare's hind legs. There was something moving inside the bubble. He reached down and tore the thick membrane with his hands, exposing two little hooves, one slightly in front of the other. Mosiah smiled and nodded at me. "We'll be seeing the nose in a minute, here," he said.

Lucy bore down again with all her strength, but nothing happened. Mosiah's brows knitted into a frown. Each contraction was more powerful than the last. Lucy groaned with pain and effort, but still nothing happened. Suddenly, my husband went into action. "Get the buggy whip," he hollered at me as he grabbed a halter and crammed it on the mare's nose. By the time I got back with the whip, he had attached the lead rope to her halter and was trying to pull her to her feet. Lucy refused to budge.

He took the whip from me and snapped it across her backside, making me flinch. "Pull," he said, handing me the lead rope. "Pull hard!"

I leaned back and pulled with all my strength, but Lucy was dead weight. "I can't do it; she won't get up!" I huffed.

The whip came down harder on Lucy's hindquarters, and I felt my eyes sting with tears.

"Don't!" I cried. "Please don't hit her again."

"Caroline," he yelled back at me, "I have to. Something's wrong, and I can't help her unless she gets up!"

At last, she rolled over and pushed her heavy body onto her feet.

"Keep her moving now," he instructed me firmly. "Whatever you do, don't let her go down."

I pulled her into a reluctant walk, and Mosiah followed behind her. Then, much to my amazement, he thrust his arm, right up to the armpit, inside of her. "The head is turned to the side," he told me as we moved slowly about the stall, "I have to push the foal back down inside so the head can turn the right way."

I pulled Lucy forward, trying not to think about what was going on behind me.

The moment he withdrew his arm, Lucy went down heavily into the straw and rolled over. One more enormous push, and the foal's head emerged. Mosiah sighed with relief. I stood beside him staring at the blue tongue that dangled out of the foal's mouth. A large, seemingly lifeless head lay in the straw beside two front legs, but the rest of the foal was still inside the mare.

"Is he dead?" I whispered.

"No," he answered with a chuckle. "A blue tongue is normal."

Lucy pushed once more, and a large brown foal slid out onto the straw.

Mosiah and I exchanged tired smiles, and I laid a hand on my own protruding belly.

What have I gotten myself into?

Mosiah grabbed some rags and began to rub the foal down. "It's a colt," he said. "Looks like a nice one."

The little guy began to thrash around, even trying to get up on those long legs that stuck out in all four directions. He looked a bit like a large brown spider.

Lucy pulled herself to her feet and began to nuzzle and lick him, nickering softly as she welcomed her new little one into the world. Mosiah and I moved out of the way and let her take over.

The process of learning to walk took almost half an hour. His front legs were stronger and more coordinated than his back, but they all seemed at least three times too long for him. A couple of times, he propped himself up on his front end and gave a big push with his hind legs. But that only made him tumble headfirst into the straw, and then the whole process started over again.

I felt sorry for him and wanted to help him out, but Mosiah said he had to do it for himself. When his back legs finally got strong enough, he managed to remain on all fours and take a few wobbly steps forward. In no time, he was all over the stall and enjoying his first meal.

Mosiah put his arm around me, and we slipped out of the barn, leaving mother and son to get acquainted. I couldn't help smiling.

***

I was scared; but there was no time to be scared. The pain started in the wee hours of the morning, and my water broke an hour later. Mama Behunin sat in a chair beside me, holding my hand while I groaned, and Jane and Pricilla bustled about—boiling water, I think; I can't say that I really cared what they were doing. The women chased Mosiah outside to wait by the woodpile, where I'm sure he could hear my groans and screams. I didn't care much about that either.

"Go ahead and scream, honey," Mama Behunin said, "but don't forget to push. It's the pushing that gets the job done."

I did both. I screamed until my throat was sore, and I pushed until my eyes all but popped out of their sockets. I pushed until every muscle in my body screamed with me.

It took ten hours. They told me that was pretty good for a first baby, but it seemed like forever to me.

When I heard my baby cry, though, I forgot everything else in the world—the pain, the labor, the months of waddling around like a duck—everything but him. And when they laid him in my arms—warm and sweet and all mine—I was the happiest woman who ever lived. They said it would be worth it. And it was.

Mosiah came in after the women got me and the baby cleaned up, looking like he'd been dragged behind a horse for about half a mile but with a huge grin on his face. I couldn't help wondering why he looked so awful—I was the one who had just delivered a baby.

The women melted away to give us time together. Mosiah knelt down beside the bed, wrapped his arms around us and started to cry. My big, strong husband—the man who wasn't afraid of anything—not even Indians—cried.

Pretty soon, I was crying myself. And little Isaac was crying too, so I guess we were quite a sight. But it was all right—we were a family.

Chapter Fifteen

Rockville, Utah Territory
Winter 1871

Life kind of slows down in the wintertime. The days are short and dreary, and the nights are long and cold. I was mighty happy to have Mosiah home with me, and since we couldn't do much outside, we spent lots of time together—joking around while we worked and watching Isaac grow.

My husband was as proud of his son as a rooster in a hen house—and for good reason. Isaac was a fine healthy boy. In the evenings, we sat by the fire and watched the flames leap and crackle and lick up the wood. I'd rock the baby and hum, or sometimes, if he was asleep, I'd sew. Mosiah oiled up the tack and whittled a little. The wind might be roaring outside and whistling around the corners of the cabin, but we didn't care. Those were fine times.

About as quick as a rabbit can wiggle his whiskers, though, spring came knocking at our door. Isaac started to crawl and get into things. Believe me, it's a real chore trying to keep a crawling baby clean when you live in a cabin with a dirt floor. It felt mighty fine to open up the doors and windows and let the sunshine in.

I did a lot of dreaming that spring. Isaac loved to play in the grass at my feet while I churned butter or mended clothes. Sometimes, I'd sit on a stump with a butter churn between my knees, my arms going up and down without needing any thinking on my part, and look out beyond the green fields and the cottonwood trees to where the jagged red mountains met the blue sky.

I liked to watch the wispy white clouds chase each other across that sky and think about the home Mosiah and I would be making for our family in Richfield. It wouldn't look like much at first, of course. Just a little cabin by the creek. But it would be ours—the thought of that made me smile all day.

Maybe I'd make red-checkered curtains for the window when we got a little money to spare. I'd sew a new quilt for our bed and a little one just right for Isaac's cradle. I'd plant flowers down the path and vegetables out back. I'd make the cabin cozy and comfortable. And there were sure to be more babies—lots of them, I hoped. Someday we'd have a real house with lots of rooms and wood floors, a real cook stove, and a white picket fence. I'd have Mosiah build a wide front porch so we could sit out front in summer evenings and watch the sun paint the sky orange and gold. A woman dreams all kinds of things like that when she's young.

***

In May, we left for Richfield. Mosiah said our new cabin was all but finished, so Isaac and I might as well come along. We packed our things into the wagon and headed out. I was giddy as a schoolgirl, but my excitement didn't last long.

Isaac would not sit still. By ten o'clock in the morning, I felt about as fresh as a smelly old shoe. While my baby fussed and wiggled and crawled all over me, we rode mile after mile with the sun beating down on us and the wheels churning up dust 'til we could hardly breathe. I had no shelter but my sunbonnet, and it was almost impossible to keep Isaac out of the sun. I made him a little tent in the wagon bed with a blanket—even tried putting my own bonnet on him—but he just wiggled out of everything. By the time we got to Richfield, he was so burned he got sick. I've never been so tired in my life.

I spent my first days in Richfield frustrated, exhausted, and worried about my sick and blistered baby. I began to wish I had stayed in Rockville where things were settled and Mama Behunin was minutes away. She would have known just what to do with little Isaac. Just a couple of days in a wagon had done all this to me. *How did the pioneers manage this week after week?* I couldn't imagine it.

Maybe that's part of what made my ma so hard.

But Mosiah's mother had been through all that and more—and she was still warm and sweet like a pie just out of the oven. I wondered what it was that made such a difference between them, and I wasn't at all sure that I knew the answer. Maybe it's a choice each person makes deep down inside when things get rough. I knew Elmina leaned hard on the Lord each day. I knew I could make it across a rocky field a whole lot better, even when I was hot and tired, if there was a strong arm around my waist. I'd learned that much.

***

The cabin in Richfield was pretty rustic, but it was ours, and that felt good. I'd planned to work hard, right by Mosiah's side, so we could get things going real good; but Isaac was sick for almost a week, and by the end of July, I was in the family way again. When fall came, we decided to go back to Rockville, spend the winter, and have the baby there.

Joseph was born the end of March, another healthy boy with the Behunin gold in his hair. By the middle of April, I felt fine, so we packed up the rest of our belongings, headed toward Richfield, and never looked back.

***

Richfield felt like home right away. Several young couples settled close around us. The men held barn raisings, and the women got together for quilting bees. We were all poor as church mice, but we didn't mind much. We were working together to make Richfield grow.

Not long after we got our crops in, a call came for townfolk to help build Cove Fort. Trouble with the Indians had us all pretty nervous, so we were glad to help. Mosiah was gone for about a week.

"You'll never guess who I saw there," he said when he got back.

I looked up from rolling biscuits and reached for a tin can to cut them as I retorted, "Well, then, I guess you'd best tell me."

"Jacob Hamblin," he answered, lifting the lid off the kettle to see what was cooking.

"Really? What was Brother Jacob doing at Cove Fort?" I asked as I arranged the soft round biscuits in the bottom of the Dutch oven, covered them with a lid, and nestled the oven into the coals at the back of the fireplace.

"Pounding nails—same as me. It was good to see him though." Mosiah settled onto a chair by the fire and propped his feet up on a stool. "Seems we have an apostle assigned to preside over the Sevier Valley area. Brigham Young's son—Joseph Young."

I rinsed my hands and dried them on my apron. "Was he there too?"

"Yes, indeed. Getting Cove Fort up and running is his first order of business."

"Did you get to meet him?" I asked.

"I did. Elder Hamblin made a special point of introducing me to him. They say Joseph Young looks a great deal like his father—and acts like him too. He's quite a man."

It seemed like a little thing—that meeting between Joseph Young and my husband. Neither of us gave it a second thought. But it changed the whole course of our lives.

***

I pulled the heavy trunk out from under the bed and lifted the lid, tenderly holding a small white gown with delicate embroidery and a matching cap against my heart before I tucked it into the chest. Dressed all in white, Joseph and Isaac reminded me of a pair of angels as our little family surrounded the altar in the newly completed St. George temple and listened to the words that made us all one for eternity.

We had waited for this celestial moment since the day Mosiah and I took our earthly vows. We had to wait for the temple to be finished and then for the crops to be harvested before we could make our journey to St. George. November was upon us before we finally piled into our wagon. Fortunately, providence smiled, sending clear skies and unseasonably warm weather for our trip.

Ma knew we were coming. I wrote her a letter, hoping she could be there for the ceremony, but she declined. A huge lump filled my throat and tears stung my eyes when I thought about how much it would have meant to have her there. She didn't give me a reason. Maybe she was still angry about my marriage, but I doubted that. Likely she didn't feel worthy to enter the house of the Lord.

My mother had never admitted any guilt, holding her head high and glaring back at the raised eyebrows she often encountered as she walked down the streets in Salt Lake, but Ma knew she had done wrong.

I wasn't supposed to know. No one ever really told me; but I did have ears. I heard the whispered stories of Ma's unfaithfulness and saw the way people looked at her.

We had arrived in St. George the day before we were scheduled to be sealed in the temple. Ma welcomed us about as warmly as a chilly December day, but Cynthia's excitement almost made up for it. I couldn't help wondering where the gangly little girl had gone and if this budding young beauty was really my sister. What a difference three years can make!

I laid the boys' white clothing in the trunk, patted and smoothed them into place, and reached for my own white dress. A lump formed in my throat, almost choking me, as tears ran freely down my cheeks, *Oh, Ma! You will never know what this dress means to me!*

I'd planned to wear a borrowed dress, even packed it away in my suitcase. But when I woke up the morning of the temple ceremony, snuggled beside my husband in my old bed in my old room, the first thing that met my eyes was the white dress lying across the chair. I bounced out of bed and started to jump around like a little girl.

The dress was simple in an elegant sort of way. I knew the delicate hand stitches were the work of my ma. It was her quiet way to be a part of my special day.

I ran down the stairs and flew to my ma like an eagle swooping down from the sky, almost knocking her over. "Thank you, thank you, Ma!" I squealed.

"That's a right fine thing you did, Sister Behunin, a right fine thing," I turned to see my husband standing at the foot of the stairs, a warm smile lighting up his face. "And we surely do appreciate it."

"I thought it might be nice if you had a dress of your own to wear today," was all she said. Ma never was one to make a fuss, but I thought I saw a tear on her cheek before she turned away.

***

I couldn't stop crying. I just clutched the dress against my chest and sobbed while huge tears dropped from my cheeks onto the delicate white fabric. I wasn't sure if I was crying for myself or for Ma. I knew that she had never meant to hurt anyone, but she had looked for happiness in the wrong places and ended up giving away all that really mattered.

I gently brushed the tears from the my white dress— the dress whose delicate stitches whispered to me, in words Ma herself could not speak, of a mother's love—folded it tenderly, laid it on top of the yellow dress from Pa, and closed the lid.

Chapter Sixteen

Richfield, Utah Territory
January 1873

They call it cabin fever—the way a body gets to feeling about the end of January after days and days of snow, wind and cold, when no one has seen the sun in weeks. That first winter in Richfield—the winter of '73—I had it awful bad. Maybe it was because I wasn't used to real winters. In St. George, they'd been short and mild—kind of a relief from the summer heat. But that year in Richfield, the snow just kept coming and the wind just kept blowing. The fire at our hearth burned all day long, and we still had to bundle up to keep from freezing in the cabin. I felt as if I would never be warm again.

Isaac, however, never seemed to get cold—maybe because he was too busy getting into trouble. He had turned two in November. And believe me, he kept me hopping every minute.

Joseph had started to crawl too, and I worried about him, because dirt floors are pretty damp in the winter. We didn't have enough rugs and skins to cover the floor like I wanted. And believe me, those two little boys could find a hundred and one ways to turn a dirt floor into mud. Seemed like it was next to impossible to keep them clean. It's a good thing that Richfield dirt is red. It didn't show up on them as bad as brown dirt would have, though it stained their clothes something awful.

Along about the last of January, I looked out from the cabin window just in time to see a carriage, pulled by a pair of fine black horses, stop in front of our place. I had to look twice to believe my eyes. Nobody around these parts drove a rig like that. While I watched from the window, a man in a long black coat and a tall hat climbed out of the carriage, tied his horses, and headed up our walk.

My eyes about popped out of my head, and I went into action. I pulled my soiled apron off and flew about the room, grabbing stray items and stowing them out of sight. By the time he made it up our walk and knocked on our door, my heart was pounding. But I patted my hair, fluffed my skirt, and opened the door with a smile on my face. Like this sort of thing happened every day.

"Sister Behunin?" The gentlemen removed his hat, revealing a balding head as he nodded in my direction. "My name is Joseph Young. I'd like to have a word with your husband if I may."

I caught my breath. "Of course, Brother Young; won't you please come in?" I knew immediately who he was.

This had to be Brigham Young's son, the apostle Mosiah met at Cove Fort; but what was he doing at my door?

"My husband is out in the barn right now," I said as I took his hat and coat. "Make yourself comfortable by the fire for a few minutes while I go out and get him."

"Thank you, Sister Behunin, I'll do that. Your fire does look inviting after my cold ride," he smiled at me as he pulled his chair close to the fire and extended his hands above the crackling flames.

"If you don't mind, I'll leave little Joseph here with you," I said nodding toward the sleeping baby. "I'll only be a minute."

"Naturally, Sister Behunin. He'll be just fine," the stout man smiled back at me. I picked up Isaac, wrapped him in a blanket, and taking him with me, hurried out the door.

What in the world? I thought as I picked my way through the mud toward the barn.

***

"He says his name is Joseph Young, and he wants to talk to you," I said to my husband's back, as he pitched forkfuls of straw into an empty stall.

Mosiah stopped midair and slowly turned to face me, pitchfork still in hand. "Joseph Young is here in our cabin?" he asked incredulously.

"Yes," I nodded back, "and he's asking for you."

"Elder Young is in our house and wants to talk to me?" he asked again as if he couldn't quite understand what I was trying to tell him.

"Yes, and he's waiting," I said as I switched Isaac from one hip to the other. "So you'd better hurry."

Mosiah looked down at his saggy leather britches and his homespun shirt, held out his callused hands, and answered. "I'll be along in a minute, Caroline. You go on back and get something ready to feed him."

I reached out and touched his arm before I turned and headed back through the mud toward our cabin. *What do you feed an apostle when your cupboard is all but empty?* I wondered.

***

I stepped inside the cabin to find Brother Young still seated beside the fire. But now he had little Joseph on his knee. I could hear his booming laughter and Joseph's giggle before I even opened the door.

"I'm so sorry," I apologized as I sat Isaac down and hurried toward them. "I thought he'd sleep."

"It's quite all right, Sister Behunin. This little fellow and I have been having a good time getting acquainted. He's a delightful child. Just look at all those golden curls."

As Joseph learned forward and reached out to tangle his tiny fingers in Brother Young's beard, I couldn't help wondering if his bottom was soggy. Or worse.

Joseph spotted me and held his arms out. I picked him up and took a quick peek into his britches, relieved to find nothing leaking out that would have soiled the apostle's suit.

The door opened, and Mosiah came in, looking as if he had found a bucket of water and made hasty use of it. I smiled at him, knowing he was about as anxious as a youngster on his first day of school.

"Elder Young," Mosiah said as he moved swiftly toward him with an outstretched hand. "I'm surprised and honored to have you here in my home."

Rising to his feet, Brother Young enveloped Mosiah's hand in his own and shook it heartily. "Brother Behunin, it is indeed a pleasure to see you again. Jacob Hamblin speaks very highly of you and your abilities with the Indians."

"Brother Hamblin said that about me?" Mosiah asked.

"He most certainly did," Elder Young answered. "He feels you might be helpful in our efforts to establish a treaty with the Indians and put an end to the war that has caused so much grief and sorrow."

My husband looked into the older man's eyes with astonishment. "Well, I..."

"If you have a few minutes, Brother Behunin, I would like to discuss some things with you." Elder Young's eyes crinkled at the corners, and he motioned toward the chairs by the fire, obviously aware of Mosiah's discomfort.

"Of course, please sit down," my husband said, coming to his senses and giving me a knowing nod.

I scurried to the cupboard. There weren't a lot of choices, but fortunately I had made bread earlier in the day, and it was still slightly warm. I pulled out the jar of blackberry jam I saved for special occasions. *This is an occasion if we've ever had one*, I thought, as I sliced the warm bread and spread it with butter and jam.

"I'm sure I don't need to tell you, Brother Behunin, what a hard time we've had with the Black Hawk War," Brother Young said, his bushy brows pulled together above piercing blue eyes. "It has, indeed, been a terrible tragedy. Not only have lives been lost on both sides, but the hysteria which has prevailed has brought out the worst in many of our own people."

My husband looked into the apostle's eyes and took a big breath before he answered. "I've seen that happen. Seems like when people get scared, they do things they'd never have done otherwise."

"I'm afraid that's true. But how can we possibly expect to teach the Indians the gospel if some of our own people behave in a manner that fosters hate? My father feels it is our responsibility to befriend the Indians and help them. But, as you know, this horrible war has left the natives angry and distrustful."

"I think they're pretty confused," Mosiah answered. "They feel like we extend one hand in friendship and stab them in the back with the other."

Brother Young frowned deeply. "Unfortunately there is reason for them to feel that way. Our colonization has taken land their tribes have traditionally hunted—and the Black Hawk War has been the unfortunate result."

"They're starving, Elder Young. I've seen them," Mosiah said. "Little children so thin a stiff wind would blow them away, eating any awful thing they can get their hands on."

Mosiah shook his head and pursed his lips. "I know everyone's suffered," he continued. "The Indians steal cattle and burn the settlers out. You can't blame folks for being angry when they have to leave their farms and go live in a fort. But the Indians are just trying to find some way to survive. If we're ever going to have any kind of peace, we've got to help them find another way to live."

"They're going to have to farm, Brother Behunin," Elder Young said firmly. "It's the only way for them to survive. We can give them a little flour and beef, but it will be gone in no time. Somehow, we must find a long-range solution. Everyone I've talked to agrees that farming is the only answer for them."

Mosiah leaned back in his chair, folded his arms across his chest, and shook his head with a frown. "Elder Young, I don't think you're ever going to get Indian braves to farm. The women maybe, but not the men. To them it's a humiliation worse than death. They simply will not do it."

I could see the frustration etched across both of their faces as I gently offered them plates of jam-covered bread and cups of milk. They both smiled back at me, thankful for the welcome interruption. But they quickly resumed their discussion.

"They must do it," Brother Young answered, as he clapped his hands onto his knees, his eyes boring into Mosiah's. "They're doomed if they don't. The whole country is filling up with settlers like a basket on apple-picking day. There simply isn't enough open land left anywhere for them to survive by hunting."

"I know that; and you know that," Mosiah said as he extended his hands toward the older man, leaning forward to meet his gaze. "And the Indians know it better than anybody—but it's all happened too fast for them." Mosiah dropped his hands into his lap and shook his head sadly. "Hunting is all they know, and it's not just a way to feed their families. It's the way they prove their value as a warrior—as a man. It's their whole way of life."

"Somehow, Brother Behunin, we must convince them. If they do not learn to farm, their families will starve. Their children will die."

"They already are," Mosiah said softly, closing his eyes as if to block the troubling scenes from before his eyes.

"What can we do, Brother?" Elder Young murmured.

It was silent for a long moment. Each man studied the dirt floor under his boots as if the solution might be written there.

Mosiah finally answered. "You're right—giving them flour and beef won't really solve the problem. But it would help a lot right now. It's going to take time for the Indians to learn another way of life, and in the meantime, we've got to keep them from starving. Is there any way we can get the government to come through with the money and supplies they promised when the treaty was signed back in '65?" Mosiah looked up to find Brother Young frowning.

"Unfortunately that treaty was never ratified by the Senate, and with our current problems, we're not on very good terms with the federal government here in Utah."

"Well, I can't say I'm surprised," Mosiah answered. "The government never keeps the treaties it makes with the Indians—here or anywhere else."

"It's a sad and disgraceful record, I'm afraid," Elder Young agreed. He leaned back, pursed his lips, and shook his head.

"It's more than sad," my husband replied. "It's deadly." Mosiah's eyes flashed, and his jaw tightened.

Elder Young leaned forward, his hands on his knees, and looked deeply into Mosiah's blazing eyes. "I am hopeful the treaty we are here to sign will alleviate this situation, at least to some degree. But unless they learn to farm the land, the Indians simply will not survive."

"If they're going to farm, they have to have good land—not some piece of desert with no water," Mosiah answered resolutely. "And someone's going to have to get them to do it."

"What would you recommend?" Brother Young asked, a hopeful look crossing his face.

Mosiah leaned back and twisted his mouth a bit. "You'll need someone they trust, someone who understands their ways."

"You are right, of course," Brother Young answered, his eyes piercing into Mosiah's. "But there are very few men like that, I'm afraid. Brother Hamblin is one. And you, Brother Behunin—I believe—are another."

I dropped the knife I was using, with a clatter, and turned to stare. What was he suggesting?

Mosiah twisted his jaw but did not respond.

"Enough of that; on to the business at hand," Brother Young laughed, and I felt the intensity of the moment lighten a bit. "I have actually come here to ask for your help in getting the treaty signed."

"What would you like me to do?" my husband replied.

Brother Young folded his arms across his chest and smiled, "The federal Indian agent wrote the treaty, and although the Church has no legal authority to sign treaties, Brother George Bean has been asked to present it to the Indians. Jacob suggested that you might be of help since you're fluent in both Ute and Paiute and familiar with Indian ways."

Brother Young stood and extended his hand to Mosiah who followed his lead and stood as well, "Would you be willing to accompany me and serve as an interpreter?"

"Certainly, Elder Young. I would be glad to." My husband shook the apostle's hand and smiled back at him. I could tell how pleased he was to be asked. It was an honor. But I could feel a hard lump forming in the bottom of my stomach, and I couldn't help wondering what all this would lead to.

"Fine then," he said. "Meet me at my office in Richfield tomorrow morning at nine o'clock." He moved to go, then turned back to me. "Thank you again, Sister Behunin, for the bread and milk. I do believe it was the best I have ever eaten. And, Sister, I hear these things often take several days, so don't be concerned if your husband doesn't make it home for a night or two. Will that be all right?"

"I'll be fine," I nodded.

Elder Young smiled, shook my husband's hand, and walked out the door.

As the door closed behind our unexpected guest, Mosiah turned to me with a wide grin plastered across his face and stammered. "Well, I'll be doggonned! What do you think of that?"

I laughed and reached out my hand for his, "I always knew you'd amount to something someday," I teased.

My husband led me to a chair and pulled me onto his lap. "Can you believe it? The Black Hawk War is finally over, and I'm going to help get the treaty signed."

"It's about time," I replied. "Black Hawk's been dead for more than three years, and the war's just kept on going without him. We all thought it was over when he surrendered. But we thought wrong, didn't we?"

"That war was never really about Black Hawk. It was about the whole, darned Indian situation," Mosiah said as he tucked a stray hair behind my ear. "He was a strong leader all right—militarily brilliant. They couldn't have managed to paralyze the whole territory of Utah if he wasn't. But it's the deeper problems that have kept Chief Tabby and White Horse fighting even after Black Hawk's surrender."

"He came to our sacrament meeting in St. George before he died," I said, remembering the uneasy feelings his presence had brought to our service. "He was so crippled and sick he could hardly walk. I remember he leaned on the pulpit and cried like a baby. Apologized for everything he and his warriors had done—for all the stealing and the killing. You should have heard the people murmuring under their breaths. But we all voted unanimously to forgive him."

"He came to our meetings in Rockville too. I hear he went to meetings all over Utah, apologizing to every community he had raided." Mosiah said. "Did you know he was a baptized member?"

"Black Hawk?"

"Yep. When the saints first settled in Utah Valley, he was friendly. Everybody called him 'The Good Indian.' Whenever the settlers needed a guide, it was Black Hawk they asked."

"What happened?" I asked.

Mosiah's eyes darkened. "Well, for starters, he was nearly killed by a Mormon militia."

"Oh, my goodness!" I gasped, sliding from his lap and picking up the baby, who was tugging at my skirts and begging for attention.

"Guess he was about eighteen when it happened," Mosiah said. "The militia was out searching for stolen stock near Pleasant Grove when four Indians opened fire on them. The braves got killed in the fight that followed, and the women and children, including Black Hawk, were taken captive. Old Chief, the Indian who led the militia to the encampment, told the men they should kill the boy. 'He will grow up to kill Mormons,' Old Chief said. And he was right."

"He really said that?"

"That's Indian logic," Mosiah said as he plopped Isaac on his knee and began to tickle his belly. "They take revenge mighty seriously."

Isaac giggled and tugged on his daddy's beard, which earned him another round of tummy tickling. "The militia didn't do it, of course. They took the women and children and Black Hawk to Salt Lake and farmed them out to Mormon families who took care of them through the winter. The family he stayed with must have been real good to him, because he joined the Church. When the next round of trouble came, he was on the settler's side."

I pulled my rocker close to the fire, settled myself comfortably and began to rock the baby to sleep while I listened with interest to my husband's tale.

"The real trouble started with a settler named Ivie and an Indian they called Bishop because he looked so much like Bishop Newel K. Whitney. The two of them got into a scuffle over a shirt Ivie claimed Bishop had stolen. In the struggle Bishop was killed."

Mosiah glanced at me and nodded. "Now we get into that revenge thing again: Ivie and his friends were afraid that if any Indians found out about the killing, they'd come down on the settlement. For good reason, I might add. If a white person kills an Indian, Indians aren't too worried about which white person they kill in revenge."

I shuddered, trying not to think about what a touchy situation that put us all in. Some people don't think twice before they act.

"Are you sure you want to hear about this?" he asked, raising an eyebrow in my direction.

"Is it that bad?" I asked.

"If you have a queasy stomach, it is."

I looked back at him. "Go on," I said. I wanted to learn everything I could about Black Hawk.

"Well, they sliced Bishop open, took out all his entrails, and filled him up with rocks. Then they dumped him into the river, hoping that he wouldn't be found."

"For mercy sake, no!" I said as I covered my mouth with my hand and stared back at him with wide eyes. "Mosiah, I'm not sure if I want to hear about this after all," I said as I

112

rose from the rocker, carried Joseph to the cradle and laid him gently inside, tucking a blanket snuggly around him.

But Mosiah gave me a you-asked-for-it look and continued. "It didn't work anyway. Some Indians found the body a few days later when they went fishing. They were furious!"

"I can imagine," I whispered, as I moved back to the rocker and sat down. Grisly or not, I had to hear the rest of the tale.

"Not long after that, seventy Indian warriors attacked Fort Utah. They got the worst of it, though, and retreated in the middle of the night. They were in pretty bad shape, left a trail of blood behind them." Mosiah set Isaac on the floor and handed him a wooden toy to distract him. At just over two, Isaac probably wouldn't understand any of this grown-up discussion, but it was still too gruesome for young ears.

"Black Hawk was still helping the settlers at this point. So, he led the militia up Rock Canyon to the attacker's encampment, expecting a fight. But when they got there, it was mostly just *tepees* filled with frozen bodies. Some of the Indians had died from wounds, but a lot of them just froze to death.

"What?" I gasped. "Didn't they build fires?"

"Well, they must have been frantic when they retreated up the mountain. And they were sure the militia was right on their tail. So, when they finally made it to their camp and dropped from sheer exhaustion, the frigid winter night took its toll. A couple able-bodied braves escaped on snowshoes. Most of the survivors in camp were women and children."

"That's horrible!"

"The militia tried to round up the Indians to take them prisoner, but the chief's wife escaped. She ran off and climbed up a rocky cliff—slipped and fell to her death right in front of everybody. They still call that mountain Squaw Peak."

"That's how Squaw Peak got its name? I had no idea."

"And that's not the worst of it, darlin'. There was a Gentile doctor among them who thought it would be a good idea to send the dead Indian's frozen heads to Washington for examination. He hired a couple of settlers and a sleigh to go back up with him and get the heads. When they got there, he tried to use his doctoring tools to take the heads off. But it took him so long that the settlers who were with him got cold. They pulled out their knives and had the heads all whacked off in no time."

I could not believe what I was hearing. *Was it possible that anyone could be so cold and unfeeling?*

"They brought those heads down the mountain on a sleigh and stored them in a crate under the cannon platform. After a while, they started to smell and turn green. Guess they never did make it to Washington."

"Mosiah, that didn't really happen, did it? If you're just pulling my leg, I want you to know."

"Oh, it really happened—I saw them myself. I was about ten. It was pretty awful."

"Oh, my!" I stared at him, my stomach doing flip-flops and bile rising up my throat.

But Mosiah wasn't looking at me anymore. Just staring at the wall with a faraway look in his eyes. "Black Hawk spent the rest of the winter in Fort Utah with those settlers and their Indian prisoners. Nobody thought the heads would bother him—Indians are pretty used to scalps and dismembered bodies. What they didn't consider, though, is that those heads belonged to his friends and family."

Mosiah turned to see how I was taking the gruesome tale, but I was already running for the door, which I flung open just before losing the contents of my stomach.

"I guess, after that, he didn't feel so friendly towards whites," I heard him murmur to himself.

———————————

Chapter notes:

1. Although fictionalized, the episode concerning Black Hawk, the Ute Indians, Squaw Peak, and the militia is true, as described in *Utah's Black Hawk War*, by John Alton Peterson, (pp.49-58).

Chapter Seventeen

Right after breakfast, Mosiah left for Richfield. He was mighty nervous and excited, but it wouldn't take him long to get there. Our place wasn't far out of town.

I spent the day doing the usual things—tending the babies, darning socks, and the like. Along about evening, I started to wonder what I should cook for supper. I didn't know if my husband would make it home or not, but I decided to fix dinner, just in case. Isaac and I needed to eat either way.

I was at the fire stirring stew when I heard the door open. I turned around with a smile, glad that Mosiah had made it home after all, but what I saw took the breath right out of me. A tall Indian brave stood in my doorway—his features proud and unsmiling.

"Young say Behunin squaw give Indians food," he demanded matter-of-factly.

I snatched Isaac who had been playing at my feet, pulled him against my chest and backed up almost into the fire. My heart thundered in my chest, and my mouth flew open to scream, but not a sound came out. Isaac, however, screamed loud enough for both of us.

I clutched the screaming toddler against me and watched wide-eyed as the ferocious looking warrior took several steps toward me. Frozen by terror, I watched helplessly as more braves pushed their way into my cabin until six of them stood staring at me from across from the room.

Still holding Isaac close with my left arm, I reached behind me with my right until my fingers touched the cold metal of the fire poker, "Get out! Get out of my house!" I screamed, waving the fire poker in front of me and taking a few tentative steps forward.

The big Indian didn't budge—just looked at me with an irritated expression as if I was a little child throwing a temper tantrum.

Had I not been so frightened, I would have been impressed by them. They were magnificent. Their clothes

115

were mostly buckskin, but some of them wore white-man–styled shirts. Their moccasins were beaded, as were the necklaces and the chokers which encircled their throats. Their black hair—long and straight—was braided at the sides and feathered. The tall one had a powerful stance, fine-chiseled features, high cheekbones, and an aristocratic nose. His fine looks were lost on me, however. All I could do was tremble and stare.

"Give food, Young say," the leader demanded again, his brows drawing together in anger and his jaw stiffening.

I recovered a bit and managed to choke out, "Where's my husband? I want my husband."

The tall brave pulled himself to his full height as the Indians behind him snickered at my obvious fear. "Behunin great *neab*. He stay with Chief," he answered. "You give Indians food."

The meaning of his words finally trickled into my fear-clouded brain. For some reason, Elder Young had sent these Indians to me, expecting me to feed them. Anger boiled up inside of me, pushing aside my paralyzing fear.

"All right! I'll get you food," I retorted, meeting his glare with a hard one of my own.

He looked at me in surprise, a slow smile spreading across his face. His companions moved into the room and made themselves comfortable around the fire, but the tall, fierce-looking warrior strode toward the hearth and gave Joseph's little cradle a quick push with his moccasined foot. "Squaw, get *papoose* away from fire. Indians get warm."

I crossed the room in a flash, snatched the sleeping infant into my arms, and turned to give the Indian a glower which earned me another round of snickers from the onlookers and an amused grin from the tall one.

Woken from a sound sleep, baby Joseph began to cry.

I crossed the room to the table with a screaming baby in my arms, little Isaac clinging to my skirts, and blood pounding so loudly in my ears I could hardly think.

Somehow I managed to fix the food—hoping all the while that if I fed them, they would leave me in peace.

I sliced bread and set out the stew and cups of milk. Then I backed off and let them have it. They descended on the food like a swarm of locusts, paying no attention at all to me.

Despite my bravado, I was frightened almost out of my wits. I wanted to run as far away from them as I could get, but the frigid January night made escape impossible. Instead, I wrapped my babies in blankets, opened the door and sat in the doorframe. From there, I hoped I could escape quickly if I needed to.

Silent tears ran down my face as I watched them devour the food and lounge about my cabin floor, laughing and talking with words I couldn't understand. Sometimes one of them would point at me and say something to the others, which always brought a fresh round of laughter from the group.

After a while, the tall Indian picked up his food, left the others and wandered over to stand towering above me as he ate. I held my babies close and tried to pretend he wasn't there, but he surprised me by crouching down and gently stroking Joseph's tiny face. Then he touched the tear that slid down my own cheek.

"You scared?" he asked.

My lip trembled as I answered sharply, "I want my husband to come home."

"Pretty soon he come," the Indian answered. "Shoken great *neab*. Talk for Indians. Make treaty good."

I looked up at him, amazed at the tenderness I heard in his voice.

"You no be afraid," he said. "Indians no hurt you. You *heap* white woman. Me like you."

Then he stood and nodded to the other Indians. I caught my breath in wonder and pulled myself up to move away from the door with my babies. As swiftly as they came, the Indians were gone into the night.

***

The next morning the Indians came back for their breakfast. I hurriedly fixed it for them. They ate and were gone. Although I spent the day wondering if they would come back for dinner, I was surprised that I felt very little fear at the prospect.

Along about evening, I heard the hinges of the door screech, braced myself, and turned around, but was surprised to see not an Indian, but my own husband entering the cabin.

A jackrabbit couldn't have made tracks across the room faster than I did. Almost before he was over the

117

threshold, I threw both my arms around his neck and squeezed him so tight it took both of his hands to break my grip.

"Whoa, there, woman," he said with a grin. "Give a feller a chance to come up for air!"

But I didn't give him much of a chance to breathe before I kissed him real hard—and he didn't complain much either.

Before long though, Isaac demanded his share of Daddy's attention and the baby started to cry, so we had to save our kisses for later.

While I got supper on the table, I told my husband about the Indians' visit and how scared I was.

"Oh, I know all about it," he said. "In fact, I've heard little else from those Indians all day. They were pretty impressed with you. Every time I turned around, one of them was pounding me on the back and saying, 'Behunin squaw *heap* white woman!' Then they all laughed, fit to kill."

"They didn't!"

"They sure did! Indians like a spunky woman," Mosiah grinned at me. "By the way, so do I," he said, giving me a little spat on the behind.

I turned around and gave him a hard look. "Fine thing," I muttered, surprised to find anger building up inside of me now that my anxiety and fear had subsided. "You knew that Elder Young sent six Indian warriors to our cabin, and you didn't do anything to stop it?"

"He didn't know you would be afraid, Caroline. He thought since I'm friends with the Indians, you are too. They didn't hurt you, did they?" Mosiah reached out to touch my hand. I could see the sorrow and regret in his eyes, but I pulled away from him, stomped to the fire, and grabbed the kettle that held our dinner, singeing my fingers in my haste.

I'd rather not repeat the words that came out of my mouth before I shook the wooden spoon at him like a weapon and screamed, "Didn't think I'd be afraid of them? Six Indian warriors and me here alone with two babies? I was frightened out of my wits!" I dropped the kettle onto the table with a thud and glared at him.

We ate most of our dinner in silence. Towards the end of the meal, I started to feel bad about the way I treated him, so I said, "The Indians kept calling you a great *neab*. What does it mean?"

"Oh, that's the Indian word for a captain or leader."

"Why did they call you that?" I asked.

My husband looked at me rather hesitantly and said, "Well, to answer that question, I'll need to tell you what went on at the meeting."

Not quite sure I understood the apprehensive glances Mosiah kept sending me across the table, I looked into his eyes for answers, only to find him avoiding my gaze as he talked.

"Well, the Indian agency wrote up the terms of the treaty. George Bean was supposed to interpret it and explain it to the Indians. I guess he's done a lot of that kind of thing. But the more I listened to him, the more uncomfortable I got."

"Who's George Bean?"

"He's done a lot of interpreting for the Church. I think he served on a mission to the Paiutes at one time," he said. "But he doesn't speak Ute too well, and besides that, all the legal gibberish doesn't translate very well into their language. I could tell by their faces they really didn't understand much of what he was saying."

Mosiah stabbed at his dinner with his fork and shook his head. "I'm thinking that's what the government intended all along, because the treaty was so unfair to the Indians. I just sat there getting madder and madder."

"You just listened and didn't say anything?"

"You know me better than that, don't you?" Mosiah snorted. "I couldn't just sit there and listen to how they planned to take the Indian's land—just promising them a little beef and flour in return. Government promises aren't worth the ink it takes to write 'em!" With that Mosiah slammed his fist down on the table, making the utensils jump and the baby cry.

I looked at my husband wide-eyed. It was unusual for him to get so riled up. Isaac's little lip began to tremble, and I reached over to reassure him as I picked up the howling baby.

Mosiah, however, was oblivious to the effects of his outburst. He was just getting warmed up. "So, I leaned over and asked Brother Young if I could say a few words, and he nodded that I could. Then I got up and told that agent what I thought of his cotton-pickin' treaty. Told him if it wasn't changed, they'd end up with another war on their hands. I told 'em it wasn't fair, and the Indians couldn't survive like that."

"Did you really?"

"I did! And Brother Young just sat there smiling and nodding through everything I said." Mosiah settled back, smiling like a kid with an all-day-sucker, and crossed his arms over his chest. "Didn't go over so well with the government agent though," he chuckled.

"The most amazing thing is what happened next. Chief Tabiona jumped up and asked me if I was Isaac Behunin's son, and I said, yes I was. He got real excited and said he remembered wrestling with me when he was young. He said I had come to their camp with my father."

"Really?" I asked. "Did you?"

"Yes! As soon as he said it, I remembered. I was about twelve when my dad and I visited Old Chief Tabby's camp. He had a son about my age named Tabiona, and we had a great time wrestling together. He whipped me good; but we got along great." Mosiah shook his head in amazement. "After hearing all these years about the great Chief Tabiona, I find out now that he's an old friend of mine. It's amazing!"

I just stared at him; this was a bit much for me to take in.

"Well, then all the Indians jumped up, shook my hand, and patted me on the back—laughing and talking. It was really something!"

He paused a moment and glanced in my direction as he slapped his hand on the table. "What do you think of that?"

I tried to appear appropriately impressed.

"The chief asked me if I would speak for the Indians, and Brother Young thought it was a good idea; so, we spent the rest of the time trying to hammer out a treaty that everybody could agree on." Mosiah pushed his chair out from the table and began to strut around the room while he talked.

"It was no easy task—believe me! That old government agent was a stickler, said he wasn't authorized to vary much from the original conditions. But I think we got some workable concessions. The Indians got some good, farmable land and permission to leave the reservation to hunt. That means a lot to them. The government promised to give them farm implements and seed, and Brother Young promised to send missionaries to teach them how to do it."

Then he turned around—with a strange expression I couldn't quite read upon his face—strode to the table, sat back down, and began to eat his dinner real fast.

"Mosiah," I said, my mouth suddenly too dry for another bite of food, "Who's he going to get to do that?"

My husband pushed his dinner around with his fork for a time. Then he lifted his eyes to meet mine. "Caroline, you're going to have a chance to get to know those Indians real good and probably have lots more chances to be frightened, because it's us that's been called."

"No!" I screamed, pushing away from the table and scrambling out of my chair as if someone had just laid a branding iron on my back. "He can't ask you to do that!"

I backed up against the cabin wall and pressed myself against it, my eyes wide and my ribcage aching as if someone had knocked the air out of me.

Mosiah pushed out from the table, his chair digging into the dirt floor, rose to his feet and crossed the room to me. His arms reached out to draw me in, a long, sad look in his deep blue eyes. "Caroline," he breathed into my hair, "he's not asking just me. He wants you to go with me. He wants us to do this together."

"What?" I screamed as I pulled away and speared his eyes with my own. "Take our babies and go live with the savages? You told him *no*, didn't you?" I gave him a shove with the palms of my hands and screamed again, "Didn't you?"

One look into his eyes gave me the answer I could not believe was written there.

With a sharp twist, I squirmed out of his arms and flew across the room. Huge gulping sobs convulsed my body as I ran. I barely remembered my wrap as I threw open the door and plunged out into the night.

***

I slammed the barn door behind me, leaned back against it, and slid to the floor, sobbing and screaming at the same time, my eyes slowly adjusting to the dim light that filtered through the cracks.

"Caroline?"

Hearing my husband's voice on the other side of the door, I jumped to my feet and kicked at door, first with one foot and then the other. "Go away!"

"We need to talk about this, Caroline," I heard Mosiah's muffled voice say through the door. I answered it by hurling the milk bucket against the opposite wall with all the strength of my fury.

"Come in when you're ready. I'll get the boys to bed."

I listened to his retreating footsteps, further enraged by his stoic manner, and launched every item I could find to join the unfortunate milk pail. I wanted to be alone. Just the same, it made me angry that he would leave me. At last I buried myself in the hay and cried myself to sleep.

***

Lightening slashed through the sky, thunder boomed across the hills, and I ran. I ran as far and as fast as I could go, darting between trees, leaping small streams and ignoring the tug of undergrowth on the hem of my shirt. I ran until my chest ached and my breath came in ragged sobs. Above me, the trees swayed to and fro as the wind tore at my hair and called to me with a shadowy voice, "Caroline, Caroline."

Suddenly, light broke through the trees, its golden presence gilding every leaf. The foliage shimmered and danced on the breath of the breeze. I paused to listen to the voice that rustled through the glittering boughs: "Follow me, Caroline."

I turned and saw them—the child and the woman—their brown skin illuminated by the golden light. The little girl was frail and thin, but her dark eyes were huge and deep. I looked into the woman's face and saw an anguish written there that tore at my heart. They reached out their arms to me, beckoning. I took a deep breath and stepped forward.

I woke up with straw in my hair as the early morning sunlight peeked around the door and through the chinks between the logs. I pulled my knees up to my chest, dropped my forehead 'til it touched my skirts, and sobbed.

I knew I would go. It was the hardest thing that could possibly be asked of me. I had no idea how I would do it, or where this mission would take me, but I would go. The call, like my dream, was from God.

Chapter Eighteen

Grass Valley, Utah Territory
May 1873

The day the first robin of spring sang his song outside my window, I swept my cabin floor for the last time, drew the red-and-white-checkered curtains, and closed the door behind me. My babies were already in the wagon along with the few belongings we were able to take.

Mosiah smiled at me and helped me onto the wagon seat. He had been mighty kind these past few weeks. I'm sure he knew I was making a sacrifice and wanted to help ease my way. But he couldn't hide the excitement that danced in his own eyes. To him, this call was an honor and an adventure all rolled into one.

A few weeks earlier, President Brigham Young had come all the way from Salt Lake to set us apart as missionaries. My husband would be the Indian Interpreter for the whole area. Our neighbors had given us a big sendoff too, with a barn dance in our honor.

Mosiah cracked the reins, and the wagon jerked forward. I grasped the seat with tight fingers and held on. After one quick look behind me, I turned my face toward an uncertain future.

***

As we rounded a grassy knoll, an Indian village came into view. *Wikiups* dotted the meadow, horses grazed, and dogs barked. I could just make out the distant forms of women at work and children at play.

We would spend our summer living with this gentle band of Paiutes. Mosiah hoped it would give me a chance to get acquainted with Indian ways before I faced the more hostile Ute bands. Indians from both the Ute and Paiute tribes

123

lived in Grass Valley, where we had been called to serve. We would be working with all of them.

The Paiute village was to serve as a central location. From there, Mosiah could visit the more nomadic Utes. One of these bands, the Weeminuche, led by the war chief Waponey, lived in the Fish Lake area. Another band, the fierce and war-like Shenavagans, led by Chief White Horse, spent most of their time in the area around the Fremont River. Mosiah said the Shenavagans would be our biggest challenge. And he was right.

The Indians who visited me while Mosiah was away making the treaty were Utes. I shivered to think how many white scalps they had each taken.

A stir in the village made it clear the Paiutes had seen us coming. Women and children gathered in the center of the village while the braves walked through the grass to meet us. Chief Etum-tab-boon-zits, which meant Old Fox, led the way. He raised his hand in friendship, and his wrinkled face broke into a welcoming smile. After our initial greetings, the braves escorted our wagon into the village. They had been expecting us.

I had prepared myself for the curious touching of my hair and clothing by the squaws, but I still had to grit my teeth and scrunch my eyes until they were done. Several women patted my belly and exclaimed, "Tow-ats-in!" I wondered how they knew.

When we passed out the gifts we'd brought, the women squealed like children. I soon forgot my fear and laughed along with them. If only white women could be so easily pleased.

On the fringe of the group, I noticed a woman and child who reminded me of the pair in my dream. The little girl was about five, small and frail. She had a twisted little leg and walked with a limp. Her mother was quiet and seemed to hold back, never meeting my eyes with her own. The child's eyes, however, were large and deep. Something about this pair touched a chord in my heart. I made sure that they got their share of the gifts.

With everything distributed and the greetings over, Old Fox lead us to a newly constructed *wikiup*. "Good *wikiup*," he stated with pride. "Good for Shoken's *wyano*."

Mosiah made a big show of gratitude, and I tried to appear appreciative. But, in truth, my heart sank to my toes the moment I laid eyes on the rough A-frame structure covered with brush. *Maybe,* I thought, *we should have gone to the Utes. At least they live in skin-covered tepees.*

I really couldn't imagine how this flimsy affair would even keep the water out in a good rainstorm. "Guess we'll be spending most of the summer outside," I whispered.

Mosiah raised his eyebrows to remind me that spending too much time in my *wikiup* was considered unsociable. One of the many Paiute rules of etiquette he had shared with me as we traveled.

The women helped me unpack the wagon and showed me where to turn out the cow. Then they tugged and pulled me toward the village center where preparations for a feast in our honor were in progress.

The chief's wife, No-ni-shee, a confident woman as beautiful as her name, which meant Dream, was in charge of my orientation. She seemed to command as much respect among the women as her husband did among the men. I watched as she moved about the group, barking out orders like a drill sergeant while the other *wyanos* chatted and worked. I couldn't understand their words, but their warm smiles and welcoming gestures cut through my apprehension and left me feeling surprisingly at home.

I motioned that I would like a job to do and No-ni-shee obliged me by giving me pine nuts she called *tee,* a dished stone she called a *mah-ruch,* and a small cylindrical rock. It seemed she wanted me to grind the nuts into flour.

A round-faced *wyano* named I-oo, which meant Morning Dove, showed me how to rock my body forward and back with the grinding motion. Soon the women were chanting to the rhythm, and I was smiling as I worked.

When I had ground enough *tee,* they showed me how to add water to the flour and fry it into cakes. The flavor was bland, but not unpleasant. I was hungry.

The one thing the Indians have a lot of is time, and it took a great deal of it to prepare that meal. Meat slowly roasted on a spit over the fire. Roots the women had dug from the ground and *panguich,* the Indian word for fish, cooked in the oven, which was really just a pit in the ground, lined with hot rocks and grass and covered with dirt.

They didn't seem to have any metal utensils—not even a pot. They cooked their stew in a basket, if you can believe it. I wandered over to get a good look. They seemed to have sealed the basket with pitch. I found it hard to believe that it could actually hold water—but it did. Right well, in fact. The women dropped in chopped wild carrots and onions along with a lot of other roots I hadn't seen before and a little meat. Then they cooked it all up by dropping sizzling rocks from the fire into it.

I was flabbergasted. The *wyanos* poked each other and giggled, and I tried not to be offended. They seemed to find the silly white woman who didn't even know how to boil a stew in a basket pretty funny.

While we worked, Isaac and Joseph played close around us with the Indian children. They had a great time. It didn't seem to bother them a bit that the other children didn't have any clothes on.

It did bother me a little, but I couldn't help thinking how much it would cut down on laundry if we let our children run around like that. Probably make potty training a whole lot easier too.

The youngest children wore a woven belt around their waists, which was a puzzle to me—it certainly didn't cover up much—'til I noticed one of the *wyanos* grab her child by the belt and pick him up. It did make sense when you thought about it: a naked child can be mighty slippery.

The thing that hit me most, that day, was the way everything the Indians did made sense. *Why can't we be more like that?*

***

In some ways, getting settled was easier than I expected. The Paiute women were kind and accepting. Their way of life was quiet and gentle, and my boys and Mosiah seemed as content as I had ever seen them. In other ways, though, it was unbelievably difficult.

I think the hardest thing was the dirt. It was everywhere: on our clothes, in my hair, and in the food. It turned to dust under our feet, filled the air with every wind, and stirred into mud whenever it rained. No matter how hard I tried, everything in the *wikiup* was covered with dust all the time.

One day I went into the *wikiup* to gather up some laundry. I leaned over my protruding belly to pick up the bundle and was met by beady eyes and a squeak. A mother field mouse scampered out from under the clothes and scurried about the *wikiup*, looking for a new place to hide. I screamed and grabbed my broom. Of course, she darted outside before I could swat her with it, but the mess she left under my pile of laundry left me livid. She had chewed Isaac's sock to shreds for her nest and had left hundreds of detestable brown droppings on our clothes.

I had tried to be patient with the situation. For weeks, I had been doing a pretty good job of it. But at that moment, my patience snapped like a twig in my hands.

"I can't stand to live with this dirt a minute longer!" I screamed. Then, like a crazy woman, I began to scoop up every item in the *wikiup* and chuck it outside.

When at last the *wikiup* was empty, I stepped out the door myself, my hands glued to my hips, my lips pursed, and my brows gathered into a scowl.

At work, not far from my door, every *wyano* in the village turned to stare at me.

"What are you looking at?" I blurted out. "This is my *wikiup* and I am going to clean it. A mouse has done her business all over everything, and it makes me sick!"

Suddenly, I was sick. So sick in fact that I had to run for the bushes before I lost everything in my stomach all over the ground.

When I returned, the *wyanos* kept their eyes to the ground, seemingly very busy with their weaving, but I heard No-ni-shee murmur, "Shoken's squaw, do not fight a battle with *tee-weep* (earth). You will never win."

I sprinkled down the dirt inside my *wikiup* and packed it the best I could before I put my things back in. After that, I watered it down and swept it every day. But No-ni-shee was right. I never did win my battle with *tee-weep*.

To make matters worse, Mosiah was gone much of the time, visiting other bands in the area, which left me alone to deal with a strange way of life and a people whose language I couldn't understand.

I had left my home in Richfield to help my husband teach the Indians, but during those first few months, they did most of the teaching, and I did the learning. I came thinking, like most white women, that the Indians were savages and didn't know much. But it wasn't true—not at all.

They didn't understand white ways—that's for sure. Most of our thinking just didn't make sense to them. But they did know how to survive in an unforgiving land and how to feed their families when it seemed like there was nothing at all to eat. I admired them for that, and the things I learned from them helped me to survive many a hard time.

Most of all though, I learned to love their easy way of living and the way they seem to blend right in with nature. I came to feel a peace that summer I had never known before. And I began to understand what it was about the Indians that Mosiah loved so much.

The Paiute women accepted me without any reservations. It didn't take long before I could understand most of what they said and could speak the language pretty fair myself. Although they were all my friends, I had a special place in my heart for the little girl with the big eyes, Shan-gee Oaeets, Little Lame Bird, and her shy mother, Po-e-chi-co.

Little Bird, as I called her, was very shy at first. She watched me from a distance with her large brown eyes. Whenever I moved toward her, she darted away. Minutes later I would feel her eyes on me again. Closer this time. One day I caught a glimpse of her out of the corner of my eye, creeping toward me with a bunch of wildflowers clutched in her hand. I held my breath and stayed still, tears stinging my eyes, 'til she placed her wilted offering beside me and scurried away. I turned and smiled a thank you. Then I replaced the flowers with a small piece of candy from my apron. Minutes later, when I wasn't looking, she darted in and snatched it.

We played that little game for several days. One sleepy afternoon, as I sat in the shade, she crept up quietly, sat down, and leaned her head against my shoulder. After that she was my constant companion.

As the summer days turned to fall, my family and I became a part of the Indian village. I learned to weave baskets and coat them with pitch for cooking. I even learned to tan hides, scraping off the hair with a sharp rock and rubbing boiled brains into the skins with my hands to make them soft.

I learned to bead and do quill work. I learned which roots and plants were good for food and which ones could be used for medicine. Most important, I learned to laugh and love more easily than I ever thought I could.

By the time the leaves began to show their first color, my body had become so large and cumbersome that I couldn't sit comfortably on the ground with my legs tucked under and to the side, like the Indian women did. It was time to go home.

Mosiah had promised that we could return to Richfield in the fall to have our baby and spend the winter. I was ready to go, but I didn't want to miss the tribal rabbit hunt.

Mosiah had been busy for days, working with the men and older children to build a huge corral. Made from heavily packed brush, it had a small opening with wings that extended out to the left and the right. The perfect trap.

I could hear the men and children in the distance as they whooped and hollered, beating the brush with clubs and sending hundreds of frightened rabbits scurrying before them.

The women positioned themselves toward the back of the corral, their sharpened killing sticks ready in their hands.

As the men and children approached the wings of the corral, they moved in on the rabbits, forcing them through the small opening and into the corral. The older boys quickly closed the gate, and the killing began. The shrill cry of dying rabbits filled the air. It was a hard thing to watch. I was glad that I was very pregnant and not expected to participate.

The rabbit harvest would provide food, clothing and blankets for the coming winter. It was a good thing. But the huge mound of dead rabbits made me sick. And I didn't even want to think about the hundreds of grizzly hours it would take to turn the foul-smelling mountain into food and clothing for the coming year.

The next morning, my family piled into the wagon for our journey back to Richfield. I was surprised to find that I cried as many tears saying goodbye to my friends as I had in coming. Hardest of all was leaving my Little Bird. Just before I climbed into the wagon, she presented me with a beautiful, smooth stone she had found in the creek. I wiped the tears from her little brown cheeks and cried a few of my own.

"We'll be back in the spring," we called to them as our wagon jostled its way out of the village.

"You will have a good *papoose*," the *wyanos* called back to me. "Bring him with you in the spring. We will have a feast."

They followed us as far as they could on foot, then waved and watched us disappear down the dusty road.

Chapter notes:

1. All the Paiute Indians in this chapter are fictional. The author created their Indian names from a Paiute dictionary compiled by Mosiah Behunin and included in his mission notebook.

2. The Paiute methods of cooking and the description of the rabbit hunt can be found in *Utes: The Mountain People* by Jan Pettit.

Chapter Nineteen

Richfield, Utah Territory
September 1873

Brigham Daniel was born just three days after we got back to Richfield. My little cabin felt like heaven on earth after spending and entire summer in a *wikiup*. But Richfield seemed different somehow. I'd been almost beside myself with excitement at the thought of seeing my old friends again, but now, I was losing interest in their shallow conversation.

My friends wanted to hear all about our adventures— but only if I told them what they wanted to hear. And they certainly didn't want to hear anything good about the Indians. When I told them how much I loved my new friends, the *wyanos*, they looked at each other with shocked expressions. Out of the corner of my eye, I could see them whispering to each other. I couldn't hear what they said, and I felt sure I didn't want to. I was ashamed to think that I had been a lot like them not long ago.

I kept mostly to myself that winter. It took all my time to care for my three little ones anyway. Before I knew it, the trees began to bud out and we were packing up to go again.

Mosiah loaded farm implements and seed into the wagon this time. He hoped he had built enough trust with the Indian bands that they would listen to his ideas about farming, and it was time to teach them the gospel too.

The Indians were beginning to ask questions. That was a good sign. They had a natural way of being close to the spirit, so we felt sure a testimony of the Savior would come easily to them. Once they believed, we knew they would be faithful followers.

***

Grass Valley, Utah Territory
Spring 1874

It was as if we'd never left. I settled comfortably back into village life, enjoying sleepy afternoons in the shade and humming along with the *wyanos* as they chanted and worked. I never tired of the stories these ancient chanting songs told. Stories of the Wolf-God, Sin-na'wava; the prankster, Kai-ne-sava; and the evil Wai-no-pits.

Sometimes I would teach them a song about Jesus and tell them stories of his kindness and of his miracles as he walked with men long ago in a faraway land. They listened with great interest as I told them of his visit to their own ancestors after he was crucified and resurrected.

We always worked as we sang, whether we were scraping the hair from deer skins with sharp rocks or weaving reeds into cooking baskets. What I enjoyed the most, though, was the bead work, and these little Paiute women were masters at it.

***

Shpee-rin's old head bent close to mine as we worked together on a cradleboard for Brigham Daniel. It would be white—because he was a boy—made of buckskin and beaded in the intricate Paiute style as a labor of love from this sweet Indian grandmother.

"You must pull the leather very tightly over the frame," she instructed me, her old gnarled fingers working the bone needle and sinew thread through the tough hide.

I had watched the Paiute babies swinging contentedly from tree branches, laced snuggly into their hooded cradleboards, from my first days in the camp. Now, with another baby of my own, a cradleboard was something I had to have. The Indian *papooses* were much quieter than any of my babies, and I was sure it was the cradleboards that made the difference.

It was usually the old women who made the cradleboards, spending hour upon hour creating these beautiful nests for their grandchildren. Old Shpee-rin had agreed to help me with mine, but now all the *wyanos* were helping. I think they were as tired of hearing little Brigham

132

Daniel *yah-gi* (cry) as I was. This cradleboard was being assembled in record time.

"He will be happy in this, I think," my little round-faced friend, I-oo, smiled as she presented me with a soft rabbit pelt to line it with. I smiled back and gave her a quick hug.

It felt good to be back with our Paiute friends. I didn't even mind having to live in a *wikiup* this time—it was only temporary. Mosiah was building a cabin for us across the creek from the Paiute village.

But teaching the Indians to farm was every bit as difficult as Mosiah had feared it would be. It was an effort that required the patience of Job. Occasionally he was able to encourage a few braves out into the field. They would smile and nod as he explained things to them. But then, one of them would see a deer, or mention how good the fishing was this time of year, and they would all be off, leaving the tender plants to scorch in the sun.

The women did a little better, but they preferred to sit in the shade and work the way Indian women have done for centuries. I really couldn't blame them.

***

Our wagon wheels bounced over a rut in the road. We were on our way to the annual Ute bear dance, and I wasn't at all sure that I wanted to go. "Do you think the Indians who came to our cabin the night of the treaty will be there?" I asked.

"Of course," he answered back. "They're Utes, and Wanzitz is one of the strongest warriors in the Ute tribe."

"Oh," I cringed, not feeling at all comforted.

"Now, darlin', there's no need for you to get all worked up. This is purely a social affair. We should feel honored to be invited." Mosiah gave the reins a flick and glanced over at me. "The bear dance is the biggest event of the year for the Ute's. I think it's going to be fun. So, try to relax and enjoy yourself. "

The celebration was already in full swing when we arrived, and the Indians were decked out in their finest. The women were dressed in fringed white buckskin, their hair braided and feathered. I knew very well how many hours of beading and quill work had gone into every dress. The braves wore britches and shirts made of buckskin that had been smoked to a yellow-gray color and fringed down the legs. Their hair was braided and feathered as well, and they wore beaded chokers and necklaces around their necks. It felt strange to be the only pale faces amid a sea of brown ones.

From our vantage point at the fringe of the group, I watched spellbound as two lines of dancers, one male and one female, faced each other and danced forward and back, imitating a bear as he pushes against a tree. At the edge of the group, several old men rubbed sticks against rasp-like instruments, producing a sound much like the growling of a grizzly.

Mosiah smiled down at me, his eyes dancing with excitement as the hypnotic beat of a hundred drums stirred his blood. I lifted my face to his and smiled into his eyes, feeling my own heart begin to race.

Like a gigantic wave, the dancers ebbed and flowed. The music and the rhythm reached deep into the wells of my soul and stirred primitive feelings, touching my very core and causing me to feel at one with nature. A part of Mother Earth herself. Like the bear in the dance, I felt my senses awaken. It was an amazing thing.

I turned as laughter erupted from a group of onlookers and broke the spell. Mosiah pointed to a man dressed ornately in feathers and beads. "The Cat Man," he said, as he nodded in the old Indian's direction. "It's his job to keep everybody in line."

As the crowd laughed on, I watched him tap a dancer on the rear with a long stick. The offender moved quickly back into line with an embarrassed expression.

Mosiah hoisted Isaac onto his shoulders and motioned for me to follow as he headed toward the cluster of spectators. "Come on, let's get acquainted," he called over his shoulder. Isaac giggled and dug both hands into his father's wavy hair as Mosiah broke into a trot.

I swung Brigham Daniel's new cradleboard onto my back and took Joseph's hand, thinking for the hundredth time what a wise idea a cradleboard was when you had your hands full, which, for me, was most of the time.

My husband knew a few of the Ute men and women in the group we joined, but to most of them, we were strangers. They watched our approach with puzzled faces, their black eyes darting from our pale faces to the cradleboard on my back.

Introducing us in his laughing, comfortable way, Mosiah entered the conversation effortlessly.

For me, it was not so easy. However, I found that my newly acquired knowledge of Pauite made understanding these Ute women less difficult. I soon began to laugh and point along with the others as the Cat Man found new victims to chastise.

An ancient-looking grandmother, with so many wrinkles it was hard to see her face, took an instant liking to my red-headed husband. She poked at him with a gnarled finger and grinned up at him with a wide-mouthed, toothless grin until he agreed to join the dance.

"Go ahead," I laughed. "I've never seen a red-headed bear before." But when I realized I was expected to join in the dance as well, the idea didn't seem quite so funny.

"I need to stay with the children," I protested.

It did no good. Many willing hands reached out to take over my responsibilities. I was doomed.

The movements weren't hard. Soon I was dancing right along with the rest of them and quite enjoying myself. Just as I began to get into the spirit of things, I glanced toward the sidelines and saw the fierce-looking Indian who had been my uninvited dinner guest in Richfield staring straight at me.

Something about his powerful stance and his penetrating black eyes unnerved me. I stumbled and skipped a few steps which, to my dismay, brought the Cat Man to chasten me, and laughter erupted from the sidelines. My cheeks flamed red as I stumbled back into step.

At last our turn was over, and I returned to the chattering group of women and my babies. Mosiah left us to visit with a group of several chiefs and warriors.

I had begun to relax and enjoy myself again when the old woman who teased us into joining the dance poked me with her bony finger, nodded in my husband's direction and cackled, "You will have a new husband."

"What?" I said blankly, turning to take in the scene that had drawn her attention.

Standing in front of Mosiah and holding a fine-looking horse by the bridle loomed the Indian who had been watching me dance. My husband was laughing and shaking his head, but the warrior's black eyes were deadly serious.

"See," she whispered. "Wanzitz will buy you for a wife."

As the meaning of her unwelcome words forced themselves upon my consciousness, a sickening sensation crept into my stomach and spread outward, leaving me dizzy with apprehension.

"You will like him," she giggled, "Wanzitz is a strong warrior and very handsome. You will be a happy woman."

"I will not!" I snapped back at her, horrified at the thought. "My husband would never sell me. White men do not sell their wives."

But my angry answer only brought ripples of laughter from the other women who, by now, were all aware of what was going on between Wanzitz and my husband.

"Oh, yes," they proclaimed together. "Wanzitz trades a fine horse for you. He is a strong warrior. He will get what he wants."

But he did not get what he wanted. His angry voice could soon be heard above the din of the dance music and the noise of the crowd. My comprehension of the Ute language was not perfect, but there was no mistaking the death threats Wanzitz hurtled over his shoulder as he stomped off, pulling the offered stallion behind him.

The crowd was suddenly very quiet. Even the dancing had stopped. Beside me, the cluster of women clucked their tongues, shook their heads, and whispered, "Shoken is not very smart. Wanzitz offered a fine stallion for you, and now he will kill your husband when he can."

I gathered my babies and walked to my husband's side. He wrapped a strong arm around my shoulders and pulled me close to him.

The dance went on, but it didn't seem so friendly anymore. Mosiah still smiled and laughed, but his eyes looked worried. Even the huge feast of venison, fry bread, corn on the cob, and melon held no appeal for me. I think we were both very glad when it was time to go home.

Chapter Twenty

Grass Valley, Utah Territory
August 1874

As the lush green of spring turned to the choking heat of summer, Grass Valley's carpet of undergrowth scorched in the sun and turned to straw under our feet. I watched as worry lines around Mosiah's eyes took shape and grew deeper every day.

He'd tried everything he could think of to encourage the valley's Indian bands to work in the fields, hoping they could produce enough food to feed their families through the winter. But nothing he said or did seemed to make much difference.

"Caroline, they're going to be real hungry come winter," he said to me over and over again. "And it's my fault. I just can't get them to listen."

"You've done everything you can do," I told him. "They're free to choose, you know." I reached up to run a finger across his furrowed brow as if I could wipe away the cares written in its creases. "Maybe they'll have to go hungry before they'll listen."

"I don't want to see that, Caroline." He stuffed his hands into his pockets, the sharp edge of frustration cutting through his words. "And neither do you."

***

In August, we moved into our cabin, but we felt little joy in it. One look at the fields, dotted with scrawny plants struggling for sun and water between choking weeds, made it clear that the scanty harvest of Grass Valley's Indian bands would not begin to feed them through the winter.

There was one thing, however, that never failed to bring a smile to my husband's face. He was having wonderful success teaching them the gospel.

"I think it's time to have a baptism," he told me one day, a huge smile splitting his face almost to his ears. "There's near to twenty of them who've accepted the gospel now."

So as soon as Peter Rasmussen could make it down from Salina, we held our first baptism. We chose a spot not far from Fish Lake where the men had dammed a bend in the river to make a pond. The bank opened onto a sunny meadow with tiny, star-shaped flowers peeking through the grass. The air was filled with the scent of pines. The spirit was sweet and strong.

My friends Non-ni-shee, I-oo, and Po-e-chi-co were among those being baptized, and Old Shpee-rin wanted to be baptized with them. We were worried that it would be too much for her, but she insisted that she wanted to make her promises to the Lord before she took the long journey from which she would not return.

I walked with her to the river's edge and helped her into the water. After the prayer, Mosiah gently lowered the frail and wrinkled little woman under the water. I held my breath. But when he lifted her up, her face glowed with a radiance I have never seen in a woman of her age. I wrapped a warm blanket around her shoulders and helped her up the bank into the meadow. Gathering about us, the other women greeted her with tearful smiles of joy.

Our beautiful day was marred, only slightly, by the distant presence of the war chief Waponey, whose seventeen-year-old son was being baptized with his father's extremely reluctant consent. Watching from the trees, surrounded by his warriors, and astride his pony, Waponey left his mark of disapproval on our otherwise perfect day.

***

Our tiny, new cabin had a dirt floor and almost no furniture, but after living in a *wikiup*, it felt like heaven to me. One late August afternoon, while Mosiah was out in the fields harvesting corn, I looked out my window to see Chief Waponey and his warriors ride into my yard. They did not look happy.

Waponey reined his horse to a stop a few feet from my door and dropped an unconscious Indian on the ground. I quickly dried my hands on my apron and headed for the door just as the chief threw it open and angrily surveyed the room.

"Where Shoken?" he growled at me. "You get Shoken now."

"What's wrong with him?" I asked as I fell to my knees beside the young Indian and placed my hand on his forehead. He was burning with a fever so high it seemed to singe my hand.

"He drink water when baptized," Waponey thundered. "He die now, and Waponey kill Shoken. You get Shoken, or maybe Waponey kill squaw too."

With that, he gave me a hard push in the direction of the field where Mosiah was working. I nearly fell over the sick Indian as I stumbled blindly between a dozen warriors, turned, and fled toward the field.

Oh, Lord, be with us now! was all I could think as I lifted my skirts and ran.

Mosiah heard my frantic cries before he saw me struggling through the high corn stalks, and he ran to my side.

"What is it, Caroline?" he demanded, shaking me by the shoulders. "Please, darlin'—stop crying long enough to tell me what's wrong."

Between sobs, I managed to get out, "Waponey's going to kill you! He says the boy drank water when he was baptized. And he thinks he's dying. Now he wants to kill you!"

All the color drained out of Mosiah's face, and he stared at me with a deep fear in his eyes that I had never seen before. "It's that crazy tradition," he whispered. "I've always laughed at it—but here it is. Come to haunt us."

"What tradition, Mosiah?"

"The Utes think if an Indian drinks water when he is being baptized, he will die," he answered. "How sick is he?"

"He looked almost dead to me, and he's blazing with fever." I could feel my heart pounding within me, and I couldn't seem to catch my breath. "What could be wrong with him?"

"I don't know," he answered. "But it really doesn't matter. We'll never convince Waponey that the baptism isn't to blame. Do you know who the Indian is?"

"It's his son," I managed to choke out.

"O-no nint?"

I nodded and swallowed hard as my husband dropped to his knees in the dirt, his head falling into his hands. I went to my knees as well, my head touching his as tears flowed down my cheeks. "What can we do?" I whispered.

"Pray, Caroline," he said raising his intent blue eyes to mine. "Pray harder than you have ever prayed in your life, because only God can save us now."

When we finished our prayer, he helped me to my feet and we walked arm in arm back to the cabin. A strange calm took over my heart. I didn't think much about what was going to happen. I just knew God had everything in His hands. He would handle this in His own way.

As soon as Waponey saw us coming, he began his tirade. Indians are masters of intimidation, and the Ute chief was one of the best.

"This my oldest son. If he die from white man's baptism, warriors kill every pale face in valley."

"Waponey, it wasn't his baptism that caused your son to get sick," Mosiah replied with a calmness that amazed me. "The Lord loves O-no-nint because he has promised to walk in His ways. He will make him well."

With that, Mosiah took a small vile of consecrated oil from a shelf, dropped beside the sick young man, and poured a small drop of oil on his head. As he placed his hands on the boy and gave him a blessing, I silently pleaded with the Lord for his life and ours.

The Indians watched, listened, and waited.

They didn't have to wait long. A few minutes later, the boy stirred and sat up. Within half an hour, he got up and asked for food.

I went into our little cabin and prepared a meal for all the Indians. Before we ate, Mosiah offered a prayer on the food. Tears ran down my cheeks again as he thanked the Lord for the food and for sparing the life of this special young man.

I've never been so happy to feed an Indian in all my life! Brigham Young promised us when he set apart as missionaries that the Lord would be with us and protect us. That day I saw his protecting hand in very deed.

And old Waponey, though he didn't ever join the Church himself, never again discouraged a member of his band from being baptized.

Chapter notes:

1. This story was taken from a similar episode recorded in Caroline Behunin's journal.

Chapter Twenty-One

Grass Valley, Utah Territory
January 1875

I had just pulled Joseph's shirt over his head and was tickling his fat, little belly when a knock at my door made me look up in surprise. We didn't get many visitors in Grass Valley, especially now that it was winter.

I opened the door and saw the gaunt face and hollow eyes of my little Paiute friend, I-oo. Even through her heavy wrap of animal skins, I could tell that her once-round frame was thin and frail.

"I-oo, come in and get warm. What's brought you across the creek on such a cold day?"

"I cannot come in," she answered. "I must go back quickly. Shpee-rin will take the journey soon. She wants to see you before she goes."

"Oh no!" I gasped. "What's wrong with her?"

"Shpee-rin very sick. Too weak to live. I think she die soon—you will come?" she asked hesitantly.

"Of course. I'll come and I'll bring Mosiah," I answered, already reaching for my wrap. "He'll give her a blessing."

I-oo nodded and turned back toward the frozen creek, her small, fur-clad form quickly blending into the snow-covered terrain.

***

"This is going to be hard for you," Mosiah warned as he helped me and the boys across the creek. "It will rip your heart out, believe me."

I hadn't been across the creek to the Indian village in several weeks. It was too hard to go in bad weather with my little boys. Mosiah had been there almost every day, though, taking what food we could spare to ease the hunger there.

But even my husband's warning words were not enough to prepare me for the sight that met me on the other side of the creek. Children stared at me with vacant, lifeless eyes set in pinched, hollow faces. Women too thin to have milk for their babies held infants too weak to cry.

Gone was the playful laughter of the village, replaced by the ugly shadow of cold and hunger.

I saw no men. Mosiah said they were out hunting. But there was very little game. This hunting trip, like the last ones, was unlikely to yield more than a few rabbits. Tears were already running down my face when I entered Shpee-rin's *wikiup*, but she smiled at me with a radiance that warmed my heart. The claw-like fingers that grasped my hand were so thin I could almost see her bones through her skin.

"She has not eaten for many days," her daughter told me. Nodding toward the wide-eyed children huddled at the back of the *wikiup* she added, "She gives all to them."

My heart caught in my throat.

Mosiah produced a small vial of consecrated oil and knelt to give her a blessing, but she smiled and whispered, "It will do no good. It is time to take my journey." She touched his hand, and a tear ran down her winkled face. "My heart is glad that you have come—I will tell you goodbye and say thank you for teaching me about Jesus." Then with a faraway look, she said through trembling lips," It is good that you are here, my friends. Soon I will take my journey."

Mosiah gave her a blessing anyway. But he didn't bless her to live. He simply blessed her to go in peace into the arms of the Savior she had come to love.

I went home, milked my cow, and returned to the village with milk for the *papooses*.

Old Shpee-rin died that night in her *wikiup*.

From that day on, I thought of my friends across the creek every time I put a crumb of bread into my mouth.

***

At last, spring came to Grass Valley. With it, the hard hand of hunger softened her grip on our lives. How good it was to hear the happy sounds of children at play! That year the men went into the fields more eagerly and worked longer and harder. Hunger would visit the Indian villages of Grass Valley again the next winter and the next, but as they learned to farm and grow crops, it would take fewer and fewer precious souls.

***

Grass Valley, Utah Territory
June 1876

John was born in April of '75, and David came one year later—to the day. They were quite a team, those five little boys of ours. They'd scuffle around on the ground like a passel of puppies; then a minute later they'd get their heads together for some mischief. We were in trouble then. And that's a fact!

It was pretty much us and the Indians the first three years of our mission. So when Mosiah came home one day and told me a white family had taken a homestead down the creek from us, I was about as excited as a youngster on Christmas. It would surely be a fine thing to have another white woman close by. Maybe the new family would even have children near the ages of our boys.

I wrapped a loaf of fresh bread in a towel, and we all climbed into the wagon for a visit. We thought maybe they could use some help getting their cabin and barn built. As it turned out, they were an older couple with no children at all. Velma was a nervous little woman and real fussy about things—the kind of person you would expect to find living in a big city, not out here in the middle of nowhere, across the creek from an Indian village. Still a neighbor is a neighbor, and we were glad to have them.

We started doing our wash together in the creek every Wednesday. It gave us a chance to visit while I taught her what I knew about getting along in this wild country.

One Wednesday, not too long after they moved in, Velma and I were doing our laundry down by the creek, chatting and laughing while I kept an eye on my little boys. We were about half done, and had wet laundry laid out on all the rocks and bushes, when I looked up from the shirt I had just wrung out. Two young Indians were splashing toward us through the creek.

They looked to be about sixteen or so—just old enough to think they were tough, and young enough to be obnoxious.

"You get along now," I called to them. "We're doing laundry in this here creek, and we don't want you to mess it up."

They stopped mid-stream and glared at us, their dark eyes flashing and their long hair blowing in the breeze. "You get out of this valley, you white squaws!" the tall, lanky Indian screamed as he kicked water in our direction. "This is our land—not yours!"

His companion, a short, stout Indian with weasel eyes, grinned maliciously and kicked more water at us. Then, he plunged his hoe into the water, riling it into mud and splashing it all over the clean clothes.

I yelled back at them, my own eyes flashing and my hands on my hips, "You quit that now, you hear?" But that only made things worse. The more I yelled, the more muddy water they splashed all over the place.

About the time I got hit in the face with a cascade of mud, I decided I'd had all I was going to take. "Stop that or I'm going to give you a lickin'," I sputtered, thrusting a warning finger in their direction as I wiped mud from my face with my other hand.

"You squaw! You no can fight," the fat, sassy one screamed back at me. And they both moved in on us. More muddy water, churned from the creek, flew in all directions, splattering our clothes and soaking our hair.

That was it; I'd had enough. Before I even stopped to think what I was doing, I charged into the creek—skirts and all—plowing toward them like a mother bear protecting her cub.

Could have caught a trout for dinner in their mouths the way they dropped their jaws. But I wasn't done. I grabbed the hoe away from the short, sassy one and whacked him across the backside with it. Then I let them both have it, swinging that hoe in the air and swatting their backsides every chance I got.

They scrambled toward the other bank, their hands in the air. But I went right after them—chased them out of the water and up the other bank. They took off toward the Indian village, and I just stood there on the bank, my hands sitting on my hips and my breath coming in gulps.

145

It wasn't so easy to get myself back across the creek. I was plumb done in, soaking wet and shaking all over.

Back on the bank, Velma was so upset she hardly made good sense. Tears ran down her cheeks as she wrung her hands and cried. "You've done it now, Caroline! Done us all in for sure!" Her face so red it was almost purple.

I opened my mouth to say something, but she shook her hands at me and paced along the creek bank. "Those Indians are headed straight for their village. They're going to tell the chief what you've done, and we'll have the whole tribe down on our heads! Come and murder us in our beds! Burn our houses down around us! That's what they'll do!"

I stood there staring at her—so weak I could hardly stand. My hair and my dress were soaking wet and covered with mud. Then, I set myself down on a rock and started to laugh. "I think not," I said. "You've got to have some grit, Velma, if you're going to live here in this part of the country."

"You wait and see, Caroline!" she sputtered back, her eyes near to popping out of their sockets. "You just wait and see!"

I picked up the muddy clothes, rounded up my little boys, and took them all home. I was too tired to argue.

Next week I was back at the creek, washing things out again when the same young Indians came back and called to me across the creek. "Shoken's squaw—you mad?"

"No," I laughed, "You go along now, and don't mess up my wash no more!"

It did 'em good, and that's a fact!

"I'm not at all sure that's what the brethren intended when they asked us to teach the Indians to use a hoe," Mosiah laughed when I told him about the episode down by the creek. "But I'm sure they learned a lesson or two they won't soon forget."

Unfortunately, it was not the last time one of the farm implements we gave to the Indians got used as a weapon against us. And the next time, it nearly took my husband's life.

***

Most wash days Little Bird came along. She'd kneel beside me at the creek and scrub silently at the dirt and grass stains in the little boys' clothes while Velma and I worked. Or sometimes she'd tend the baby for me.

Little Bird was growing up. Mosiah baptized her when she turned eight, and I gave her a pretty comb for her hair to help her remember the occasion. When I close my eyes, I can still see her brown eyes dancing with excitement as she cupped the incredible treasure in her hands. Tears sparkled in her eyes as she lifted them to mine for the briefest of moments. Indian children are taught to never look an adult in the eye. Then she whispered her thanks. I don't think the obvious envy of the other Indian children hurt anything, either.

Life was hard for the little Indian girl with the twisted leg. The children made fun of her, and the adults treated her like she didn't exist. Still, she had a sweet, tender spirit. I loved her as if she was my own.

I think she spent as much time at my cabin as she did in the Indian village, and I was glad to have her. As silent as a shadow, she followed my every step and helped me work. With five little boys to take care of, I was busy every minute, and she was a wonderful help. I often wondered what I would have done without her. Little Bird and her sweet mother, Po-e-chi-co, were almost like family to us.

One time when I was busy making soap, Brigham Daniel wandered off. I couldn't find him anywhere. Mosiah took the horse and looked all over for him. My older boys were looking too, but he was nowhere to be found. I was nearly beside myself with worry.

It was Little Bird who found him. I think Indians have a kind of sixth sense for things like that. The little guy had gone off chasing a ground squirrel and got himself lost. When he couldn't find his way home, he had curled up in a deep rock crevice and fallen asleep. Without her help, we might never have found him. When I saw the two of them coming through the meadow hand in hand I was so relieved I didn't know whether to laugh or cry. She was a treasure—yes, she was.

Chapter notes:

1. The story about Caroline and the Indian boys is taken from Caroline's journal.

Chapter Twenty-Two

Grass Valley, Utah Territory
August 1876

The year the Plains Indians killed General Custer and his entire army at the Battle of the Little Bighorn, the whole Indian nation roared liked a lion. Encouraged by their victory and enraged by tales of massacres, a cry for vengeance spread like wildfire. It surged across the plains like a dust storm, leaving a cloud of anger and distrust hanging in the air.

Renegade dog soldiers rode from band to band, stirring up hatred toward the pale faces. They gathered angry young warriors from every tribe, turning them into war parties with murder and revenge in their hearts.

It was August of that year when one of those bands made its way into Grass Valley, stirring up the seething grudges that simmered below the surface of even the most peaceful tribe.

They hit our valley like a hurricane, screaming for war and shooting their guns in all directions. Terrified, the settlers took cover wherever they could find it and sent a rider to Mosiah pleading for his help.

Doing what he felt was his duty, my husband left me and the children while he followed the renegades to the Ute camp.

Our mission was never easy. And as Mosiah had predicted, I had been afraid many times—but never had I felt fear so all-consuming as the terror that gripped my heart that day as I watched Mosiah saddle his horse and ride out. He didn't turn back to meet my eyes. I don't think he wanted me to see the raw emotions written in the worried crevices of his face.

Work is the best medicine, I've found. So I attacked the weeds in my garden with a vengeance. We didn't tell the children what was going on, or where Papa was going—but I could see in their eyes that they understood more than is healthy for a child to know. I tried to keep their hands and minds busy pulling weeds beside me in the garden.

Every few minutes, I stopped to glance in the direction that Mosiah had headed, hoping to see him riding across the field. When I turned back, I saw anxious, little eyes staring at me.

"Papa will be home soon," I assured them, going back to my work with ever-increasing apprehension.

He didn't come home for supper. We ate in silence, and I prepared the children for bed with fumbling fingers.

When we knelt together for family prayer, Isaac broke our silence by pleading with the Lord through tiny trembling lips to bless his Papa and not let the mean Indians kill him.

I didn't need to say anymore. I just hugged my children real tight and cried.

I didn't sleep much that night. Every time I heard a sound, I jumped to attention, pleading with the Lord to let it be my husband returning home. But my twisted insides screamed that it could just as easily be a lurking Indian.

He didn't come home all night. So the next morning, when Little Bird knocked on the door, I made up my mind. The time had come to go after him. Little Bird smiled and nodded when I asked her to stay with the children, delighted with the trust I placed in her.

I wasn't quite sure where to find the Ute camp. They were always moving around, so I had to rely on the Lord to guide my instincts. Mosiah, I knew, would be upset if he had any idea what I was doing. I could almost hear him yelling at me as I rode along.

"Don't do this, Caroline! What if one of those renegade Indians finds you? They might kill the both of us, you know. Then what will happen to our boys?"

I jumped at every cracking twig and every sound in the bush 'til I almost decided to go back. But when I spotted *tepees* in the hollow below me with Mosiah's horse grazing contentedly beside them, I knew I had found what I was looking for.

I rode my mare into the camp, my heart pounding like thunder within me, and my eyes darting around in search of my husband. The Indian women were working in one part of the camp, and the men were gathered in another, the sounds of a heated discussion stirring the air. Curious children ran up to get a closer look at the white intruder, brown fingers finding their way into little mouths as they stared at me with huge, dark eyes.

The door flap from the center *tepee* flew open. An angry-looking brave ducked out and came striding toward me. "You squaw!" he yelled into my face as he grabbed my mare by the bridle. "Why you here?"

I drew myself up tall on my horse, looked him in the eye, and answered back with more courage than I felt. "My husband is here, and I want him to come home and get his breakfast."

"You go now!" he screamed back at me, his eyes narrowing into angry slits and his lips pulled back to show yellow teeth. "Indians kill foolish white man soon. I think maybe kill squaw too!"

If I had learned anything through the years I served with my husband on our mission, it was to never show fear— no matter what. I was afraid now, believe me, but I screamed back at him with a fury to match his own, "I will not go until I see my husband! Get him for me! Now!"

Fury boiled up in his face. He jerked my horse's bridle and slapped her neck with the flat of his hand, making her jump nervously. But I held on with my legs, moving with her, and not allowing my eyes to leave his.

At last, my mare stopped dancing, but the warrior's angry eyes still bore deep into mine, daring me to look away—I did not. Instead, I gritted my teeth and stared back at him, ignoring the pounding heart within me that threatened to escape from my chest.

With an angry jerk of his chin, he spit toward my face, the spittle landing on the front of my dress. Then he whipped around and disappeared back into the *tepee*, returning moments later with Chief Waponey and my husband.

Waponey walked solemnly toward me and said with measured words, "You talk fast. Indians *heap* mad. Maybe kill Shoken." He jerked his head in the direction of a cluster of angry renegades who glared at me through narrowed eyes.

I nodded and Mosiah, with his hands tied behind his back, was allowed to walk up to my horse.

"What in the Sam Hill are you doing here, Caroline?" he whispered through his teeth. "Do you have any idea how dangerous this is? I don't even know if I'm going to make it out of here alive!"

My eyes pooled with tears, and my lips began to tremble. "I was so worried, Mosiah," I whispered. "I had to come and find you."

"Oh, Caroline," he murmured, shaking his head softly. "You really are something, you know that?" A tiny smile momentarily lifted the worried creases around his deep blue eyes. "But you can't do anything here, except put yourself in danger. Now, go on home and take care of the boys. I'll come as soon as I can." He turned without a backward glance and followed Waponey into the *tepee*.

The renegade gave me one more angry look, followed them into the *tepee*, and pulled the flap closed.

I sat frozen on my horse, staring at the *tepee* and trying to catch my breath. At last, I turned my horse around and rode out of the camp while every eye in the band watched silently.

I'm not sure how I got home. I was crying so hard I couldn't even rein my horse. Sure that I would never see my husband alive again, my heart kept telling me I couldn't go on without him. But I had five little boys in a cabin by the creek. So I held on to Lucy's mane and let her carry me across the prairie.

At home, I stumbled through the motions of caring for my family. I was numb with grief—nothing but a walking carcass. I wasn't surprised when he didn't come home that night. The next day blurred in my mind. When at last the afternoon shadows drew long and the light began to fade, what little hope I still held onto died within me. I collapsed onto the bed, sobs racking my body. At last I mustered enough strength to slide from the bed onto my knees, where I pleaded with the Lord for a life that I felt in my heart was already snuffed out.

"Mama! Mama! It's Papa! He's coming!" My little boys' cries broke through my tears and into my distraught consciousness.

I flew out the cabin door and ran into the field. Sure enough, my husband was riding toward us through the pasture.

I stumbled and sobbed my way toward him. He reached down with a strong arm and lifted me up to him. His lips covered my wet face with his kisses as he mingled his fresh tears with my own.

He slid from his horse and wrapped his arms around me. We stood there clinging to each other like there was no tomorrow—laughing and crying and touching each other's faces, just to reassure ourselves that the nightmare was over and we were truly together again.

"Papa! Papa!" The passel of little boys that clung to our clothing and wiggled their way between our legs finally drew our attention. Mosiah bent down to cradle each little face in his hands before they tackled him with their hugs, knocking him off balance until they were all rolling together in the dirt. Mosiah laughed and tickled his sons while they smothered his bewhiskered face with kisses.

I laughed and cried at the sight, wiping happy tears from my face with the back of my hand.

At last he headed to the barn, one little boy under each arm and two more clinging to his pant legs.

I scurried into the cabin, scooped up the baby and a lantern, and followed them. Mosiah's horse beat us all, wandering into the barn of his own accord, eager for his evening oats.

***

Inside the barn, I nestled the baby into the hay, then lit the lantern and hung it on a hook.

"How did you get away from them, Papa?" Isaac asked. "We thought the bad Indians were going to kill you."

"They tried, son. They tried every which way they could think of. But Waponey and his warriors stood guard over me and wouldn't let them do it."

"Did they really?" I breathed in amazement.

"They did, and that's a fact." Mosiah led his horse to a stall and began to remove his tack. "I wouldn't have lasted an hour if it hadn't been for him. And it was no easy task, let me tell you. Flying Arrow and those Indians were mad as hornets and as determined to have my hide as a pack of wolves after a wounded calf."

"I knew they wanted to kill you, Mosiah," I said as I picked up a curry brush and began to work on Samson's chestnut coat. "I could tell by the look in that Indian's eyes. I didn't expect to see you alive again."

"You wouldn't have, and that's for sure. The only reason my body's still in one piece is Waponey."

I gasped and covered my mouth with my hand. "Oh, my goodness, Mosiah! Who were those Indians?"

152

"Flying Arrow is an Arapaho. He was about ten years old when his village at Sand Creek was massacred by Colonel Chivington's army." Mosiah worked Samson's coat with a firm hand, puffs of dust swirling into the air with each flick of his brush. "He escaped by hiding in the bushes while Chivinton's men slaughtered his family."

Glancing quickly at the boys to make sure they weren't listening, Mosiah looked me in the eye and continued under his breath. "He watched while a soldier cut his mother open with a knife and threw her unborn baby into the bushes."

My breath froze in my chest, and I dropped the curry brush into the straw. "Soldiers did that?" I gasped.

"Yes. And she was alive when he started on her. Flying Arrow had to listen to her screams while that devil tortured and killed her." Mosiah stopped working and looked at me, his eyes hard as steel. "After she finally died, he scalped her, and cut off her nose and ears and private parts to show off as war trophies."

"Oh, no! For mercy sake—no!" I murmured as I groped my way to the hay and sat down hard.

Mosiah turned toward the boys, relieved to see they were still busy at play. Then he dropped his brush and walked slowly around the horse to join me in the hay. "She wasn't the only one. Chivington's men killed and mutilated almost a hundred Indians in that village. Most of them women and children. The men were off hunting. There was an American flag and a white flag flying over Chief Black Kettle's lodge to show that they had surrendered and only wanted peace."

He dropped his head into his hands, and I could see his body shaking with silent sobs. Then, he lifted his face to mine, tears running down his cheeks and whispered in broken tones, "I've spent three days listening to Flying Arrow scream at me, reciting every hideous, atrocious killing. When I close my eyes I see babies with their brains bashed out and dismembered bodies strewn all over the ground."

Mosiah leapt to his feet and grabbed his head, his hands clinching his eyes shut against the visions that loomed up before him. "Sometimes he'd rail at me in Arapaho, sometimes in Ute, and sometimes in English. But whatever language he used, the message was the same. There was no missing his meaning."

Mosiah turned to face me, his fists clinched at his sides. "After the soldiers left, he wandered around 'til a Ute band found him and took him in. Is it any wonder that he joined Sitting Bull's band of renegades?"

"So he is looking for recruits then?" I asked.

"Recruits and revenge."

"Are Waponey's warriors going to join them?"

"Some of them might. They're angry and frustrated, and the Indian victory at the Little Bighorn gave them hope. Wanzitz argued to join them, but Waponey stands firmly against it. He says it's a battle they can't win." Mosiah ran his hand through his hair and sat back down beside me.

I looked over at our little boys, amazed at how they always seemed to find some way to amuse themselves. At the moment they were having a wrestling match in the straw.

"When Flying Arrow demanded to know why Waponey would protect me—a despicable white man— Waponey said it was because I was a missionary. A holy man."

"He did?"

"Yes, but then Flying Arrow narrowed his eyes, made a disgusting sound in his throat, and spat right in my face. 'I spit in the face of white holy men who kill women and children!' he screamed."

"What?" I gasped. "You would never do such a thing!"

"I was confused too until Waponey told me that Chivington was a Protestant minister. Doesn't that beat all?" he asked. "I sat there in the dirt feeling like the lowest thing on earth. Couldn't even wipe the spit off my face because my hands were tied behind my back. Just had to sit there and let it run down into my beard."

"Oh, Mosiah," I whispered, reaching up to run my fingers through his faded red hair.

"The funny thing, Caroline, is that I felt like I deserved it."

"Why on earth would you think that?"

"Just for being white. And when he screamed at me about all the terrible ways he planned to kill me—I felt like I deserved that too."

"Oh, Mosiah. No!"

He jumped to his feet, whirled around, and punched the air with his fist. "We call them savages!" he bellowed. "How could there be a more despicable savage anywhere on earth than a minister, a man who has dedicated his life to God, who massacres innocent women and children?"

The silence in the barn was deafening. Even the animals turned to stare.

The little boys hurried over to pull on Mosiah's pant leg. "Who kills women and children, Papa?" Joseph asked.

Mosiah looked down at his sons and sank to one knee. Wrapping his strong arms around them all, he whispered, "Only a terrible man would do such a thing." And four little heads bobbed in agreement.

Settling back into the hay, Mosiah pulled his little boys around him, and I picked up the baby who was beginning to fuss.

"Why did the bad Indians let you go, Papa?" Joseph asked. "Did they get nice?"

"No, they got drunk," Mosiah laughed. "That Waponey is a wily old fox!" he said, giving me a wink. "He sent some of his braves out to find some liquor. I have no idea where they got it, but not long before sunrise, they arrived back with enough whisky to flatten the whole tribe. And that's exactly what happened."

"The bad Indians got drunk?" Isaac asked.

"Sure did. The good Indians too. Everybody but Waponey. He wandered around with a bottle in his hand, laughing and singing—but I noticed that he wasn't drinking very much of it."

"He stayed sober on purpose?"

"Yip. At first, being drunk just made them worse. The renegades got even meaner. But after a while, they all started passing out. Once they were all sleeping good and sound, Waponey cut the rope off my hands and told me to skedaddle. I did!"

"Thank goodness!"

"No, Caroline," he said. "Thank the Lord. It's His protecting hand that's brought me home."

I looked into his eyes and smiled just as a terrible thought slid across my mind. "They'll come looking for you when they sober up."

"They don't know where I am, and Waponey won't tell them."

"And Wanzitz?" I murmured. "What about him?"

"Oh, he'd be more than glad to see me killed and cut up into little pieces," he said. Then with a twinkle in his eye he

155

added, "But he'd protect you with his life, so I think we're all right."

I laughed a little and gave him a playful shove. But, truthfully, I wasn't so sure.

***

My husband lay dead on the floor, the pool of thick black blood spreading out from his still form across the cabin floor. And I screamed. A scream like the wail of a banshee, ripping out from my very core and tearing the air into a million tiny pieces.

Flying Arrow's steel fingers gripped my shoulders like the claws of an eagle, shaking me in his attempts to subdue me. But I fought back with every ounce of my strength. I kicked with my legs, flailed with my arms, and rammed my head against his chest in my desperate attempt to free myself, but to no avail. Flying Arrow's rock-hard body held me firmly against the bed. My hand flew forward to claw his hideous face with my nails, but he caught my hand in his vise-like grip and screamed into my face.

"Caroline, Caroline! Stop it! It's all right, darlin'! It's just a dream!"

My eyes flew open, and one last excruciating scream pierced the air as my husband's blue eyes and bewhiskered face swam into view.

Relief washed through me, and my body went limp. Mosiah pulled me against him, and I sobbed almost as loudly as I had screamed. My gown and my hair dripped with sweat, and every muscle of my body shook from exertion.

"Shhh, darlin'. It was just a dream. Flying Arrow is gone. Waponey says he's headed for Wyoming now." Mosiah held me tight against his chest until my sobs slowly subsided, and we both drifted back to sleep.

Three whole weeks had passed since Mosiah's capture and return home. Time enough to get past the terror and go on with life, but I noticed that my husband still carried his rifle with him everywhere he went.

Chapter notes:

     1. Flying Arrow is a fictional character, representative of the renegade dog soldiers who rode with Sitting Bull. Although fictionalized, the story of renegade Indians coming to Grass Valley, Mosiah's three-day capture, and his escape when the Indians got drunk, as well as Caroline's trip to the camp and her demand that the Indians let him go to get his dinner, is recorded in Caroline's journal.

     2. The Massacre at Sand Creek, where approximately 80 Indians, mostly women and children, were killed and mutilated by Chivington's army, was a real event.

Chapter Twenty-Three

Grass Valley, Utah Territory
1879

"The baby is backwards," Po-e-chi-co whispered to the *wyano* who was helping her deliver my baby. "It will be long and hard." And she was right—it was.

I scrunched my eyes tightly, pushing until I thought my insides would come out and my eyes would pop out of my head. The pain, so intense I felt as if my body was being torn open, reached its peak and then subsided.

One final push, and it was over. Somewhere in the distance I thought I heard a baby cry before I drifted off to sleep.

***

"You will need a new cradleboard." My friend's gentle voice called to me from somewhere far away. With great effort, I opened my eyes. Her smiling face came into focus as she placed the tightly wrapped bundle in my arms.

"I will smoke the doe skin yellow, and we will bead it together. It will be pretty, and she will be happy."

A girl! A little girl! I gazed down at her tiny face with wonder and awe. The baby who looked up at me had masses of thick dark hair, pink cheeks, and a tiny rosebud mouth. Bigger than my boys, she had a wide, round bottom that had undoubtedly been the cause of my distress.

Long delicate fingers wrapped tightly around my own. I couldn't believe she was mine. I did love my passel of boys, believe me, I did. But, oh! A little girl!

Living on the frontier in a rough-hewn, dirt-floored cabin across the creek from an Indian village, I had come to cherish every fine and delicate thing in my life. And they were few and far between, believe me.

"Thank you, my dear *teg-a-boo* (friend). Thank you for your help," I murmured.

Po-e-chi-co smiled down at me and squeezed my hand with her own. My sweet friend was the only soul in the world who knew how desperately I had longed for a daughter.

Soon her helper, Cam-mo, joined her at my side, shaking her head and clucking in sympathy that my hard labor had produced only a worthless girl. But Po-e-chi-co and I shared knowing smiles, and I drifted off to sleep, dreaming of embroidered dresses, ribbons, and bows.

***

"I want to call her Caroline," Mosiah said as I laid her in his arms. "She's going to have hair the color of yours and be almost as pretty."

It took just that long for tiny Caroline to wrap him around her little finger and even less for her to become the sparkle of our lives.

By the time she was four months old, enough settlers had come to Grass Valley to establish the town of Koosharem. Not much when you stack it up against other cities and towns you might know, but Koosharem was a miracle to me. Being a part of a community brought a lot of things that were really important, like regular church services and quilting bees and a general store.

People were even talking about starting a school, and that made me about as pleased as a fox in a hen house. My older children were well past the age for starting school, and it worried me quite a lot. I did what I could to teach them to read and write and do sums, but I was never very good at such things.

Having neighbors wasn't all apple pie and sugar candy though. Sometimes, the new settlers caused at least as many problems for us as they solved. They couldn't seem to understand that the land wasn't just sitting here, free and open, waiting for someone like them to come and grab it up.

It did look that way—but it wasn't so. There were people living here before we came, and this land was just as important to them as it was to us. The more settlers came to Grass Valley, the more problems there were between the whites and the Indians—and my husband was right in the middle of it every time, trying to find a way to keep the peace.

I looked out my window and smiled. Mosiah sat out in the yard astride a barrel, singing at the top of his lungs while he oiled and repaired a harness. He always said a dry harness was an accident just waiting to happen, so he was real conscientious about keeping them cleaned and oiled. I leaned forward and smiled. My little three-year-old, Davie, was busy helping his papa, but it looked as though he was dropping things in the dirt more than anything else.

Mosiah ruffled his small son's mop of sand-colored hair and handed him a rag. "Here you go, tadpole," he chuckled. "You rub that oil in real good with this here rag, and the leather will be nice and soft. Then, Samson will be happy, and we won't have any broken harnesses."

Davie went to work on the harness, his little tongue glued to the corner of his mouth and his brows knit in concentration. My husband threw me a knowing smile and a wink just as two riders dismounted in our yard. They stomped toward him, looking about as ornery as a horse with a bur under his blanket.

Mosiah stood, took a step forward, and extended his hand in greeting. But one of the men ripped off his hat, revealing a full head of blazing red hair and gave the hat an angry shake.

"Dad gum it, Behunin! We've had just about all we can take!" he yelled at the top of his lungs. Then he slapped his hat against his pant leg until dust flew off like he'd stirred up a small tornado. "I woke up this morning, and they were in my fields again—about twenty of those mangy Indian ponies—filling their bellies on my corn. Or I should say what used to be my corn!"

"And last week it was my wheat," a huge man with a voice about as deep as a well bellowed into Mosiah's face. "Near trampled it to the ground before they were done." Without so much as coming up for air, the big man poked his nose into my husband's face and continued letting off steam until his ears flamed red. "You have any idea what this is costing us?"

Mosiah scratched behind his ear, scuffed his toe in the dirt and shook his head as he looked from one man to the other. "I'm real sorry, boys. I was sure hoping this wouldn't

160

happen again." Drawing his brow into a frown, he pulled on his beard a bit and mumbled, "I talked real hard to them last time I was out there—tried to explain that this just can't go on. Seemed like to me they understood and were gonna do something about it."

"If that don't beat all, Behunin, I don't know what does!" The red-headed settler stamped his boot into the ground and yelled back at the top of his lungs, "You can't just go out there and talk perdy to them and expect them to change what they've been doing for years!"

"That's just it, Harvey!" Mosiah yelled back at him, getting pretty red in the face himself. "They've been living like this for years, long before you even heard of this place. They're used to going were they want to go and letting their animals graze wherever they get the itch to. It's going to take some time to change the way they think."

"Well, we ain't got time to wait around for them to figure out that the world has changed since last time they looked. If this don't stop happening, right now, we might as well pack up our families and leave, cause we're all done for. You understand what we're saying?"

"That's a fact, Behunin," the big man answered with a glare, "and we're just wondering whose side you're on."

My hand flew to cover my mouth. I had to hold on tight to the table with both my hands to stop myself from grabbing my broom and taking out after those insolent idiots. *Who do they think they are?*

But my husband had more self-control than I did. He just folded his arms across his chest, rocked back on his heels, and looked each man in the eye. "I'll ride on out there today, boys—see what I can do." Then he turned on his heel and headed for the barn.

Minutes later, after our very rude neighbors had mounted up and rode off, Mosiah emerged from the barn, leading his horse and studying the ground real hard as he walked.

I wiped my hands and hurried to stand in the open doorframe. He looked at me, shook his head, waved, and mounted up. I didn't have to ask where he was going, and I didn't get to hear the equally angry discussion that erupted when he got there, but I sure did hear about it later. My husband was caught between a thorn bush and a prickly pear.

161

Chapter Twenty-Four

Koosharem, Utah Territory
1879

"Can I ride into town with Papa?" Brigham pleaded, looking up from his mush with hopeful eyes. "I didn't get to go last time, so it's my turn."

"You know, Brigham, I think we'll all go today." I answered with a smile, my hands set on my hips. "I have a basket of eggs to sell, and I need sugar and beans."

My announcement was met with a chorus of excited exclamations from the children, who were just finishing their breakfasts. "That is if you can get your chores finished before Papa gets the wagon hitched up," I added.

"Can we get candy, Mama?" Little Davie asked, his eyes peeking at me over his bowl of mush that sat almost eye level with him. He was really too small to sit at the table on a big chair, but he insisted. To him, it was a matter of dignity.

I pursed my lips and looked into his wistful blue eyes. "We'll see," I said. The answer to that question was almost always, no. But today I had a good basket of eggs and thought I just might get enough from them to manage a penny candy for each of the children as well as our necessary items.

That's all it took to send five little boys scurrying to get their chores done while I washed up the dishes and dressed the baby.

An hour later, we all piled into the wagon and headed into town. The sun was shining, the birds were singing, and we were all in high spirits.

"Old Dan Tucker was a fine old man," Mosiah sang in rhythm to the hoof-beats of the team, as he snapped the reins to encourage the horses into a lively trot. "Washed his face in a frying pan, combed his hair with a wagon wheel, died with a toothache in his heel."

"Get out of the way for Old Dan Tucker," we all joined in. "He's too late to get his supper."

162

Before we knew it, we were rounding the bend into Koosharem. That's when the happy hubbub came to an abrupt halt. "What in the world?" Mosiah exclaimed.

There to the side of the road was a new corral filled with twenty or so rather rangy-looking horses. A group of settlers gathered by the gate, apparently in the thick of a rather heated discussion.

Mosiah pulled our team to a halt so fast the boys nearly fell out of the wagon and tiny Caroline began to cry. I looked over at my husband to see his expression go from pure bewilderment to steaming angry in a matter of seconds.

One quick leap, and he was out of the wagon, punching the air with his fists and screaming at the top of his lungs as his long legs ate up the distance between our wagon and the settlers. The children and I climbed out of the wagon and followed cautiously behind him.

"What in tarnation do you think you're doing?" he boomed at the top of his voice. One by one the settlers turned to face him, determined expressions cemented across their faces.

"Have you completely lost your minds?" he yelled as he strode toward them. "Those are Indian ponies."

"Well now, we know that, Mosiah," a settler answered as he hitched up his pants. "And I think you know the reason why we done it too."

Mosiah stopped dead in his tracks and looked the man hard in the eye. Then he shifted his weight from side to side and worked his mouth like he'd eaten something bitter. "What do you think those Indians are going to do when they figure out you have their horses?" he asked. "They're going to think you stole them. You know that."

"We ain't planning on keeping them, Mosiah. We're just going to hold on to them until the Indians pay us for the damages they caused," he shot back.

"Yes, sir," another settler piped up. "It's high time they learn that we ain't going to let them fatten their horses on our grain."

"That's right, Mosiah. We got to learn 'em a lesson," squeaked a little man with a bushy beard.

"Somebody is going to learn a lesson here, that's for sure," Mosiah answered. "But I don't think it's going to be the Indians. They don't have money to pay for damages—you know that—but they'll figure out a way to pay you back. I'd reckon you can count on it."

"We ain't going to stand for this anymore, Mosiah! You hear what we're saying?" broke in the tall man with the fiery red hair who had been out to our cabin a few days earlier. "We've all talked to you about this here problem. And you promised to work it out with the Indians. But I think they've got you buffaloed—so we decided that it's high time we took matters into our own hands."

"I'm working on it, Harvey." Mosiah replied, leaning forward, his fists balled at his sides. "You all know I'm doing the best I can to work this out with the Indians. But it's going to take some time and cooperation."

"You've had all the time you're going to get," the first man yelled back, his face turning red. "And the cooperation we need is from those confounded Indian friends of yours. I think you forgot a long time ago whose side you're supposed to be on."

My husband stared back at him, his eyes bulging out, then he whipped around and marched off about ten paces before he turned back and said with quiet measured words, "You really have no idea, do you, John?"

"Well, I do know this much; those savages ain't getting their horses back until they pay the damages. And that's just what I told those two Indian boys this morning when they came and tried to get their ponies."

My husband's mouth dropped down almost to his boots, and his face changed from red to ash gray. "You surely didn't do that, John. Tell me that you didn't do a stupid thing like that."

"He did. And that's a fact," the small settler with the bushy beard answered. "And you should have seen the look on their faces. They beat it out of here with their tails between their legs. Yes-sir-ee-bob, they did."

"How long ago, John?" Mosiah asked solemnly as he quickly surveyed the women and children milling about.

"Oh, it was likely three hours ago," the big man who seemed to be the ringleader answered nonchalantly. "Now when those Indians come in here asking for their horses, Mosiah, we want you to stick to your guns and tell them they can't have them back until—"

But Mosiah wasn't listening—just thinking real fast. "You men better be getting your families out of here right

164

now," he interrupted. "And plan to be fighting off an attack—because that's what's coming. And we don't have much time either. You boys have your guns with you?"

The grins quickly melted off their faces as each man shook his head. Then they turned to look for their families just in time to hear a woman shriek and point toward the bluffs.

Over the hills they came. The entire war party galloped their horses full-tilt toward us, whooping and hollering as they came. Even at a distance, we could see the glint of the rifles they held high in the air as they rode.

"Run, Caroline!" one of the women screamed at me as she picked up her toddler and headed for the fields. All around us men and women grabbed their children and ran for cover.

My eyes quickly darted about, searching for my own children. Isaac and Joseph had climbed between the corral poles and were lying along the bottom rung of the fence, their arms and legs wrapped tightly around the pole in their effort to remain unnoticed. The three younger boys ran quickly to grab my skirts, and I held Caroline tightly in my arms.

I glanced out at the fields that had so quickly devoured our settler friends and then back at Mosiah. I would not run. I would face this with my husband. One look at his tight jaw and the wide stance of his feet as he watched the war party approach told me that he would not be going anywhere. Bringing my little ones with me, I rushed to his side.

There were about thirty of them, painted for war and wearing nothing but breechcloths. Their hair was knotted on the top of their heads, and they carried not only rifles, but tomahawks and knives.

Wanzitz rode in the forefront, whooping a blood-curdling cry that froze me to the spot. He carried a sickle high above his head, swinging it in all directions as they closed in on us. They circled around us, still riding their horses at a full gallop and screaming out their blood-curdling cries.

I watched the scene as if in a dream—unable to move even a muscle. I couldn't think, scream, or run.

Wanzitz was after Mosiah. He had a glint in his eyes and a sneer across his painted face that left no doubt how deadly serious he was. Again and again he rode toward us, swinging his sickle at my husband's head. Each time I felt certain that it was the end for him—but time after time, Wanzitz miraculously missed.

I was so aghast at Wanzitz's futile attempts to decapitate my husband that I didn't see Chief Waponey gallop his horse straight toward me.

He hit my body full force with the chest of his horse.

I remember pulling tiny Caroline close as my flying body hit the corral fence. I quickly rolled under the fence, saving the baby and myself from the horses' hooves.

I lay there gasping for breath, their insane cries chilling my blood. The pounding of the horses' hooves throbbed through my body as the Indians continued to circle my husband. Through the dust, I watched as he brought his right arm to the square and commanded them, in the name of Jesus Christ, to leave.

With the swiftness of a trap snapping closed, the commotion stopped—the sudden silence screaming almost as loudly as the chaos had done moments before. Each warrior brought his horse to a halt and turned to stare at my husband.

Waponey and Mosiah locked eyes, and I held my breath. A silent battle was fought in a matter of moments. Not a battle of armies and warriors, or bows and arrows, but a battle of wills where the only weapon is courage and the true strength comes from within.

At last, Waponey jerked his chin, lifted his rifle to the sky and with one last blood-curdling cry, he spun his horse and galloped toward the corral gate. In one swift movement, he yanked the gate open. As a flood of ponies poured out onto the open land, Waponey led his war party away from us as fast as they had come.

Wanzitz was the last to go. Obviously reluctant to leave without his trophy, he took one last unsuccessful swipe at my husband's head with his murderous sickle and followed his tribe out into the hills.

Mosiah dropped to his knees. I pushed myself from under the fence, little Caroline still in my arms and ran to his side. With sobs still racking my chest, I fell beside him. Joseph and Isaac scrambled down from the fence and ran toward us, tears cutting furrows through the dust on their faces. We wrapped our arms around each other and our children and wept. As a wind from the east picked up and clouds rolled in, Mosiah began to pray, thanking God for our lives and for His goodness—a prayer so heartfelt and humble it seemed to make the heavens weep.

Lightning flashed and thunder rolled. We climbed into the wagon, pulled blankets about us, and headed for home, not bothering with any of the things we had come there to get.

***

About a week later, Cutler and Jane pulled into our yard, their wagon loaded high with household goods and all eight of their children. "We've been called to settle along the Fremont River," Cutler told us, an eager grin stretching across his face. "Coming here is a little out of our way, but we thought it'd be nice to visit a bit before we head off into no man's land."

"Not exactly no man's land," Mosiah grinned as he slapped his brother on the back. "Seems to me an old friend of yours claims that land as his."

Cutler stuffed his hands into his pockets and rocked back onto his heels. "White Horse? Yes, he's been pretty effective at keeping white folks out of that territory until now."

Mosiah nodded and gave his brother a solemn look. "You sure you're up to taking him on again?"

Children jumped out of the wagon like grasshoppers in dry grass and took off in all directions. I scurried over to take the baby from Jane before Mosiah helped her down. I couldn't miss the look of sheer panic in her eyes when White Horse's name was mentioned. A chill went through me as I remembered the story about Cutler and White Horse during the Black Hawk War.

***

"I told him no, absolutely not, at first," Jane told me as we worked together peeling potatoes for dinner, "but he was so excited about the idea. I guess he finally wore me down."

"What is it about these Behunin men?" I asked, turning to stare into her eyes. "There's something about an untamed land that seems to call to their souls until they can't stand it any longer."

167

"Isn't that the truth!" Jane replied. "And what kind of crazy woman would marry a man like that and follow him out into the boondocks?"

"Only one who's crazy in love," I answered, my hands planted on my hips. And I started to giggle.

Soon, we were both laughing 'til we had to sit down.

At last, I leaned forward and touched her hand with mine. "Don't worry too much about White horse," I told her. "If he wanted to kill Cutler, he would have done it a long time ago. He's had plenty of chances."

"Maybe he's forgotten about the trouble between them," she said hopefully. "It's been a long time."

"An Indian like White Horse doesn't forget the man who almost killed him," I answered. "Take it from me. White Horse made a choice. You don't need to lose sleep worrying about him".

"Even when he finds out that white men are moving in on his territory?"

I looked away and didn't answer. That was another matter, and we both knew it.

***

"They're going to need someone to handle the Indian situation down along the Fremont if this settlement is going to work," I overheard Cutler tell Mosiah. "And you're the logical one to do it."

My hand froze on the barn door, and I stopped dead in my tracks.

Unaware of my presence, the men continued their conversation while they milked and fed the stock.

I had come to call them to dinner, but in those few casual words lay the message I knew would tear my world apart.

"White Horse is as mean and unpredictable as they come," Cutler went on. "Every white man in these parts is scared to death of him. And for real good reason."

"I know. He makes me more than a little nervous myself," I heard Mosiah answer. "Black Hawk knew just what he was doing when he chose him as his lead warrior. That Indian is as wily as he is ruthless. Probably has more white scalps to his name than the rest of the Utes put together."

"There's going to be trouble, Mosiah, when settlers start moving down there," Cutler replied. "They've got to call somebody. And he'd better be good."

I strained my ears to hear more, but for a moment all I could hear was the sound of milk streaming into the bucket. Then I heard my husband's voice state calmly, "They already talked to me, Cutler. Last meeting I went to. Want me to go in the spring. But I haven't told Caroline yet."

Hot rage and cold fear clashed within me, causing my world to swirl out of control. I gripped the barn door with icy fingers as my knees threatened to buckle.

"Will she go?" I heard Cutler ask.

"She'll go."

"No! No, I will not go!" I flung open the barn door with a crash and flew inside, fury blinding my vision. In a flash, I was beside my husband, screaming down at him as he sat dumfounded, looking up at me from the one-legged milking stool.

"I will not go! You hear me? And you can tell the brethren that!" I screamed. "For six years I have stood beside you. Living with the Indians. Scratching for every crumb we eat. And risking our lives every day we live! It's enough—I tell you—it's enough!" I gave the milk bucket a kick and sent it flying—its contents splattering across the barn wall. Molly mooed and kicked out, narrowly missing Cutler who had to jump out of the way. Mosiah toppled off the one-legged stool and looked up at me, a dazed expression on his face.

I didn't wait for an answer. Whipping around, I stormed out of the barn and into the fields as fast as my legs could carry me. I had no idea where I was going, but it didn't matter. I stumbled through the fields in the waning light, sobbing so hard my belly ached. At last I dropped to my knees, the pain in my heart and in my belly more than I could bear. I was four weeks pregnant. My body couldn't take the stress.

As the moon slowly rose above the blue hills, I pulled my knees up to my chest and lay curled in the dirt, sobbing.

Mosiah found me there in the dirt, dropped beside me, and pulled me gently into his arms. "Caroline, darlin'— you know I would never make you do this against your will," he whispered into my ear. "If you feel that strongly about things, I'll take you and the kids back to Richfield and you can stay there while I'm gone. You can get the kids into school. I know how much that means to you."

I pushed my husband away and struggled to my feet. "You would go without me? You would leave our family in Richfield and risk your life on a tribe of crazy Indians while I raise the children alone?"

"Now, darlin'—" Mosiah began. But I didn't wait to hear any more.

I turned and fled back in the direction I had come, Mosiah following behind me like a whipped puppy. I reached the cabin and stormed in, slamming the door behind me, and leaving him to stare at the outside of the door in the dark.

Chapter Twenty-Five

Koosharem, Utah Territory
Spring 1880

I sat at the top of a grassy knoll, my arms wrapped around my folded knees as far as possible, my fingers laced together. Tears streamed down my face as I watched my family from a distance, moving around our tiny cabin. They looked like ants going about the business of a colony.

For pity's sake, why are you crying? I asked myself. *Only a crazy woman would cry about leaving a one-room cabin with a dirt floor.*

My eyes traced the meandering creek that separated us from the Paiute village. Just beyond the willow trees and the dense brush, in a circle of *wikiups*, lived the poorest of the poor. My humble Indian friends.

How can I leave them? I thought. *They're barely learning to stand on their own in a white man's world that has no room for them. Who will help them? How can they get along without us?*

Brown faces swam before my eyes, smiling in the sweet gentle way I had come to trust: Po-e-chi-co, I-oo, No-ni-shee, Shpee-rin. And my Little Bird.

Oh, my Little Bird! My heart ached, and my arms felt empty already. *How will I make it through the day without her beside me?*

I hugged my knees more tightly and sobbed. Truth be told, they would get along well enough without me. Mosiah would still help them now and then. But I, most likely, would never see them again. And I felt sure I could not get along without them.

You were getting too comfortable here in Grass Valley—with a store and a church and friends. How could you have allowed yourself to dream, even a little bit, about that white house with green shutters and a painted picket fence? You should have known better, I scolded myself.

171

But oh! A school! A school will open in Koosharem this fall—and my children won't be going!

I couldn't understand it. Hadn't I done what was asked of me? It had taken every ounce of strength and courage I could muster and then some—but I had done it, hadn't I? And I had trusted in God. But now this! Something inside of me demanded to know why.

"Can't you see us, Lord? Don't you know we're here?" I whispered, feeling hurt, angry, and guilty—all at the same time. "Don't our needs matter at all?"

I knew it was wrong to ask such questions. But I didn't feel chided, just reassured that He was, indeed, aware of our family and our needs. He would watch over and protect us, but there was work for us to do. So, I needed to stand tall and do it.

I planted one hand on each side of myself, feeling the spring grass and the cool, damp earth below it with the palms of my hands and the tips of my fingers. Then, I set my jaw, drew a deep breath of air and shoved myself into a standing position, my hands resting on my protruding belly.

I was afraid. Yes, that was the true fact of the matter—afraid for myself, for my husband, and for my children. But I was a Behunin woman. A Mormon woman. So, like my mother-in-law, Elmina, and my sister-in-law Jane, I would put my hand in God's and step into the unknown. I felt a tiny smile creep across my lips as I lifted my chin and brushed the dirt from my hands. Then, with my skirts swishing about my legs, I strode down the hill toward the little cabin by the creek.

***

Fremont River Valley, Utah Territory
Spring 1880

I had to admit it was lovely. Red sandstone mountains, shaped by the wind into crimson cathedrals, jutted up toward the deep blue sky. The Fremont River, high with spring runoff, surged and plunged. It white capped into rapids in some places and flowed deep and clear in others. Willows and cottonwoods lined its banks. Yucca, coarse grass, and low bushes sank their roots deep into every bit of soil hiding

172

between the sunset-colored boulders. Brilliant flowers bloomed everywhere as if in a hurry to make use of the abundant water and mild temperatures. They seemed to know it would be short lived.

Mosiah pulled the wagon to a stop. "Just look at this, darlin'," he called to me, standing up in the wagon and spreading his arms wide to take in the view before us.

It was a good spot, tucked between the Fremont and the Dirty Devil Rivers like an oasis in the desert. The land before us was level, green, and obviously more fertile than the lifeless sand that dominated the landscape through which we had come.

The children scrambled out of the wagon like ants from under an overturned log. Soon they were jumping and hollering as they explored every rock, bush, and tree with the enthusiasm God gave only to the young. I couldn't help but smile.

Mosiah turned about, his arms spread like the wings of an eagle and his head tilted back, drinking in the fresh spring air. This open, untouched land was where he belonged. And it was enough for me, just to see him happy.

***

Mosiah drew back on the reins and pulled our wagon to a halt in front of a log cabin with potted plants in the window and a row of flowers growing along the path.

I smiled to myself. My sister-in-law never entirely succumbed to the frontier, bringing along small touches of civilization wherever she went.

I noticed a hand at the window pulling back the curtains just as Mosiah called out, "Any Behunins living in this here cabin?"

A moment later the door flew open and red-headed youngsters in seven different sizes poured out. The children's hair varied in hue from blonde with just a touch of gold to deep copper. The colors merged so well with the southern Utah landscape that you might have thought Jane and Cutler found their children underneath the rose-colored boulders in their yard. With their parents at their heels, they surrounded the wagon and began to climb aboard, shrieking greetings to the cousins they hadn't seen for months. By the time Cutler and Jane made it to the wagon, a dozen blue eyes were peering over my shoulder at the newest Behunin: tiny, three-week-old George.

I unfolded the blanket from around him, and the evening sun touched the fluff on his head with its glowing fingers, turning it to gold.

"He has red hair!" they shrieked. Soon they were jumping up and down, causing the wagon to bounce even more than it had traveling the rutty road that brought us there.

"Well now, he's a Behunin, isn't he?" Cutler laughed. With hair and beard a shade or two deeper in color than my husbands, one look at Cutler told you why the Indians called him Red Bull.

"Oh, let me see him," Jane cooed, reaching up for the baby as her husband helped me out of the wagon. "Caroline, he's perfect!" my sister-in-law exclaimed as she touched the sleeping baby's rosy cheek.

Before you could snap your fingers, all the children scrambled from the wagon and began to race about the yard, squealing with happy laughter. It was a sight to see: thirteen small Behunins—fourteen, if you counted the one in my arms. Jane and I looked at each other and laughed, "Look what we've done!"

Mosiah and Cutler left early the next morning taking Cutler's boys Ligie, Will, and Matt, along with Isaac and Joseph, to help build the new cabin.

As hard as it had been for me to leave Koosharem, it would be wonderful to live just fifteen miles downriver from Jane and Cutler.

* * *

I pulled a clothespin out of my mouth, popped it over the white diaper I held on the clothes line, and reached with my free hand for another pin and another diaper. I could hear Jane laughing around the clothespin in her own mouth. It was a race, and we were both pros. We had four little ones in diapers between us, not to mention the ten other children whose behinds we had diapered more times than either of us wanted to count.

By the time we got to the end of the makeshift clothesline, we were both laughing so hard we were all fumble fingers and dropping the clothespins out of our mouths. It was a tie.

Jane settled herself onto a stump in the yard, and I found a barrel. We were both out of breath. "I don't think I've ever had this much fun hanging out the wash," Jane, giggled.

"Well, I'm glad you enjoy it so much," I said with a flare of pretended arrogance. "There will be more where these came from tomorrow, and the next day, and the day after that."

"Please, don't remind me," she groaned. "Seriously though, Caroline, it's so good to have you here. Just makes everything more fun."

"It does, and that's a fact!" I laughed back. "Thanks for letting us stay with you while the men are building the cabin. I really don't want to think about how hard it would have been otherwise. We'd have been living out of the wagon box for weeks while Mosiah built a cabin alone."

"It would have been too hard, Caroline," she said. "You with six children and a brand-new baby. This is what family is for. And you have no idea how thrilled I am to have you living close by. We can help each other out when our husbands are gone—which happens way too often, if you ask me."

"Is Cutler gone prospecting a lot?"

I knew Cutler's big dream was to find gold. Mosiah laughed at his brother's passion, but we worried about the time and resources it took away from their family.

"More than I'd like—and that's true as cats have whiskers." Jane shook her head and laughed. "I keep telling him the only gold he's ever going to find in Utah is on the heads of his own children."

"And what does he say to that?"

"He laughs and says I'm right. But the next day, when the chores are done, he's out in the hills again, looking for specimens." She looked me in the eye. "I truly don't know what to do with him."

"One day, he'll strike it rich, Jane. And it'll all be worth it."

"I don't think so." Jane leaned over to pick up the empty laundry basket and stood, balancing it on her hip. "Cutler doesn't really care about getting rich, you know. It's the excitement of the hunt that he can't stay away from."

"Mosiah says that Brigham Young is discouraging the brethren from prospecting. He says they should spend their time on their occupations and with their families instead."

"We've heard that too. It's not at all like Cutler to go against the prophet's counsel, but he still prospects every chance he gets." Jane smiled at me and shrugged her shoulders. "I love him, Caroline, and he could be doing far worse. I guess I can forgive him for this little thing."

"You're an angel, Jane," I said to her as we walked toward the cabin. "When my husband is gone, it's because he's been called to do it. And I still complain and feel sorry for myself."

"Mosiah isn't just 'gone'," she said, looking me in the eye. "He's risking his life every time he goes."

"Yes," I answered, suddenly aware of the tight ball that seemed to have taken up residence in the pit of my stomach. "And I'm afraid things are going to be even worse here."

***

A couple weeks later, the menfolk were back. They'd thrown up a log cabin and got a good start at clearing the land. Our children bid a sad goodbye to their cousins, and we headed out to start a new life along the Fremont River.

Like our last one, this cabin was a rough-hewn, one room, dirt-floored affair with one small window. We would have a roof over our head. And not much more.

Our place along the Fremont was about as solitary as a lone wolf. Just us and the Indians for miles around. But the children didn't mind; they had each other. That's one of the blessings that came with being a part of a big family. And I have been grateful for it many times.

I did worry about the children's schooling—but when I brought the subject up, Mosiah brushed it off like an unwanted crumb on his shirtsleeve.

"Don't worry about it, Caroline. I never went to school, and I can read and write as well as the next man," he said, dropping a load of firewood beside the hearth. "We'll teach 'em—you and me."

"But, Mosiah, there's more to schooling than reading and writing. What about history and science?"

"Well, darlin'," he answered, throwing a log on the fire and brushing off his hands, "the real science a man needs to know is all around us, in the hills and in the meadows. It's knowing about the plants and animals that share this world with us. It's knowing how God makes things grow, and how they all fit together in His plan." He paused long enough to give the fire a jab with the poker. As sparks flew upward and orange flames danced about the logs, he said "You can read about it in a book, or you can live it. Now, which do you think is better?"

I couldn't argue much with that.

"And history?" he added. "The history that really matters is all found in the scriptures." He reached for the Bible, laid his wide hand across its cover and said, "Right in here is the history of how God created the world, and the history of how He has worked with His children from the days of Adam, right down through the ages. It shows what happens to people when they follow Him, and what happens to them if they don't." He held the scriptures high in his hand, like a lantern in the dark; then, he gently placed them back on the shelf. "That's the history I want my children to know."

So we read the scriptures together every day, each boy taking his turn. If they had a hard time with a word, we'd help them. They got to be real good readers that way and got their religion at the same time. As soon as we finished reading, out they would go, helping their father in the fields, where they'd learn about plants and how they grow, or maybe they'd go fishing and hunting with him, where they'd learn about God's animals.

Mosiah was right, of course, but I still fretted sometimes.

Little Caroline wasn't old enough for school yet, but I truly hoped that things around these parts would be more settled by the time she got to school age. Settled enough to have a school. Things are different for a girl. I wanted her to learn to be a lady, and that was more than a little difficult, raising her out in the middle of nowhere with a whole passel of brothers.

I felt real close to Caroline, and I can't say how grateful I was for her, especially now that we had moved away from Koosharem and the Paiute village. Like a tiny shadow, my daughter began to take Little Bird's place at my side, helping me with everything I did. She was a true joy.

When her brothers left to go fishing, she'd beg to go with them, and I'd have to let her go. But I didn't want her to grow up to be a tomboy. I wanted her to go to school.

177

As soon as we settled in, Mosiah began to work with Chief White Horse and his band. We came with gifts, farm implements, and seed. They accepted our gifts with the same glee their neighbors to the north had done but showed even less interest in farming. Like their leader, this band was haughty, distrustful, and seething with anger toward whites. It was an anger that simmered below the surface, all the time, just waiting to burst into flames.

To make things worse, Wanzitz and a number of the more restless members of Waponey's band had joined with White Horse. Seems they were unhappy with Waponey's attitude. It made me more than a little nervous to have them so close around.

White Horse, himself, was a cunning warrior, but he was a real manipulator too. He'd visit at our cabin with a big smile on his face and eat my home-cooked meals. But his friendship could turn deadly about as fast as I could flip a griddle cake, especially if he had been drinking fire-water. That's what the Indians called the whiskey they bought from money-grubbing traders.

"White Horse, my friend," Mosiah said one day, extending his hand for a hearty shake after the war chief and his party rode into our yard. "I am glad to see you. Come inside, and Caroline will fix you some food."

"We are going hunting," White horse said as he and his warriors sat at my table, shoving biscuits dripping with butter and honey into their mouths at an alarming rate. "And we have come to see our good friend, Shoken."

After filling their stomachs, White horse handed me a large bundle of arrows.

"You keep 'til Indians come back," he said to me. "These good arrows. They shoot right through a man."

I took them from him and nodded. "I'll take care of them for you." I wasn't sure why he wanted me to keep them, but I wasn't going to argue. "You've used these arrows to kill people?" I asked as I placed them in a safe corner of the cabin.

"Ha!" he said with a toss of his head. "One day I shoot white man in back. Arrow go all way through. Man

178

throw up his arms and yell loud! Take hold arrow—pull feathers through him—he fall dead."

"My goodness!" I gasped. "How could you do such a thing?"

He looked at my shocked expression and laughed smugly. "It is nothing," he said.

***

When winter came, I got real sick and ran a fever so high you could have fried an egg on my forehead. Mosiah was nearly beside himself with worry. At last he rode off through the snow to get Cutler to help him give me a priesthood blessing, leaving the children to take care of me while he was gone.

Some of White Horse's Indians came to visit, and when they saw how sick I was, they came back with their medicine man. He came into my house dressed all in ceremonial robes and feathers. "Me make you better," the old medicine man said. And he started jumping around me, shrieking and chanting and shaking his rattles.

The room was spinning, and I couldn't stop shaking. The beat of the drum and his piercing chant spun round and round in my head 'til I couldn't bear any more. At last, I forced myself up on one elbow and screamed with all the strength I had left, "Stop it! You hear me, stop it!"

The medicine man danced over to my side, looked down at my shaking body, and said, "Shoken's squaw, the devil will kill you. I make fire go out of your hands and feet. Then the devil will go out—and you will live."

I surely did feel like a hundred devils were burning inside me, but I knew his magic was not the answer, so I whispered back, "Thank you kindly for trying to help me, but God will decide whether I live or die—not the devil."

He shook his head and left. My children did what they could for me until Mosiah came home. He had been gone for hours, riding through the winter snow to get Cutler. When they came, I was so sick I hardly recognized who they were, but they used their priesthood to administer to me and bless me to get well. I remember the feeling of their hands on my head and the comfort that came into me with their words. My fever broke a few hours later, and I got better real soon.

Chapter notes:

1. Events in Caroline's history are not in chronological order. It is unclear where they are living or what group of Indians they are working with when a particular event took place. I have used the ages and birth places of the children to place events in a logical order.

2. It is unclear whether Waponey and White Horse are two separate Ute chiefs or one and the same. For story purposes, I have treated them as separate: Waponey's tribe inhabiting the area around Fish Lake; and White Horse's band in the area of the Fremont River.

Chapter Twenty-Six

Fremont River Valley, Utah Territory
Fall 1882

My apron bulged with the last fresh vegetables from our garden. I stuffed one more carrot inside and stood to stretch my back, rubbing the sore spot right above my tied apron strings with my one free hand.

We will feast tonight, I thought with satisfaction.

Together with the fresh venison from Mosiah's last hunt, these vegetables would feed our family in a fine manner. Such abundance was rare. Most of the year, our diet became monotonous as I strained to fill so many stomachs from my dwindling food supply. Fortunately, I had learned from the Indians how to gather and cook wild roots and leaves. Along with the meat Mosiah brought home, they filled our stomachs and the children grew. It was a constant battle, and yet with every meal, I thanked the Lord for His goodness. Unlike our friends, the Indians, we never went hungry.

"Company's coming," Mosiah called to me as he strode out of the tall corn, shovel in hand.

I shielded my eyes from the late-morning sun and watched two riders leading heavily packed mules turn into our yard.

"It's Cutler," Mosiah exclaimed. "But who's he got with him?"

I walked to my husband's side, and together we waited for the approaching riders to dismount.

Cutler jumped from his horse, a big grin splitting his face, and gave each of us a bear hug before introducing his companion. "This here is Old Jack," he said, pointing to a buckskin-clad man with a face full of whiskers and more than half of his teeth missing.

"Howdy do, ma'am?" the scrawny fellow offered with an exaggerated bow. He removed a battered hat to reveal a bald head, fringed with stringy, mouse-colored hair.

181

I mumbled, "Glad to meet you, Jack," but didn't offer to shake his grimy hand.

I felt Mosiah stiffen at my side. He'd told me once about a trapper and prospector called Old Jack. The Indians hated him with a passion.

The man I heard about trapped animals in the Indian hunting grounds, leaving stinking, furless bodies to decompose in the sun. And if that wasn't enough, he hid traps along trails, sometimes snaring the Indian's dogs and horses.

Mosiah gave the camping and mining equipment packed on the mules a heavy look and asked hesitantly, "It appears the two of you are planning some kind of expedition. Where are you headed?"

The glint in Cutler's eyes revealed his excitement, barely simmering below the surface like a kettle about to boil. His glance darted between Mosiah and Old Jack.

"Wait 'til I tell you, Mosiah," Cutler crowed. "Just wait 'til I tell you! Old Jack and I are going to make it big this time, aren't we?"

Cutler slapped the prospector on the back and grinned, but Old Jack narrowed his eyes. "Now, Cutler," the old man muttered, "this here is our secret, remember?"

"You don't need to worry none about Mosiah," Cutler answered. "My brother's a missionary. He doesn't get into this mining business. And he's strictly reliable too."

Old Jack eyed Mosiah with a cocked head and opened his mouth to say something, but I jumped in real fast.

"I'll bet you men could use a good meal before you head off to wherever you're going. Why don't you get your animals fed and watered while I fix you some dinner?"

"That would be just wonderful, Caroline!" Cutler quickly exclaimed.

"We'd be mighty obliged to you," Old Jack answered. I think he was as grateful for the shift in the conversation as he was for the offer of food. "Thank you, kindly, ma'am."

I turned toward the cabin. Mosiah gave me a quick smile and led the men into the barn to care for their animals. Before long, he shuffled into the cabin and wandered aimlessly about while I cooked.

"You don't feel good about the idea of Cutler mining with Old Jack, do you?" I asked without looking up from my work.

"No, I don't." Mosiah came to stand behind me, his hands resting on my waist. "And I don't rightly know what I can do about it. Cutler's a grown man. He can do as he pleases. But this expedition has me tied up like a calf on branding day. I'm real worried to have him go."

"Think you can take him aside and tell him what you're feeling?" I asked.

"I sure am going to try," he answered, giving me a quick peck on the cheek. Then he left to call the children in from play. When he came back, the men were with him.

As usual, dinner with eight children under the age of twelve was a rather noisy affair. We ate outside that day on a makeshift table so we would have a little more room.

When the meal was over and Old Jack's belly was filled up, he found a grassy place under a big cottonwood tree and fell asleep, snoring louder than a hibernating bear.

"So tell me about this adventure of yours," Mosiah began as he and Cutler settled into chairs.

Another time I might have found something to do while the men talked, but I was real interested. So I stayed close and tried to listen without being obvious.

"This is the chance I've waited for my whole life, big brother." Cutler leaned forward, his eyes gleaming. "My *whole* life!"

"You know President Young is counseling the brethren not to leave their families to go out prospecting, don't you?" Mosiah asked. Cutler dropped his gaze to the ground, caught off guard for only a second.

"But this is different, Mosiah. It's one of those exceptions to the rule."

"Cutler—" Mosiah began, but his younger brother jumped to his feet and began to pace, pulling on his beard as he talked.

"My harvest is in, Mosiah, and it was a good one. Jane is all right with me leaving. And I won't be gone long." He turned and looked Mosiah straight in the eye. "This is too big to pass up, brother. A chance like this comes once in a lifetime—maybe only once in a hundred lifetimes!"

Mosiah shook his head, but he was laughing a little. "Okay, Cutler. Why don't you tell me about it?"

Encouraged, Cutler sat down and pulled his chair up until he and Mosiah were almost nose-to-nose. "The only reason Old Jack is letting me in on this, is that he needs help. And I'm the only one he trusts."

Cutler waited for a reaction, but when he didn't get one, he went on. "You will not believe what I'm about to tell you, brother, but it is true."

"I'm listening."

"It's like this: one night Old Jack and an Indian friend of his got hold of a bottle of whiskey and began to make good use of it. About the time the bottle was half empty, the old Indian's tongue got real loose, and he let some Indian secrets slip, things the Utes have been hiding and protecting for years."

With a jolt, my husband came to full attention, "Go on."

"Seems there's an ancient gold mine up in the Uinta Mountains," Cutler whispered, his eyes never leaving his brother's face. "A mine with a vein of pure gold."

I noticed that Mosiah's brows knit close together and he crossed his arms over his chest.

"Not only is it filled with gold, what the Indians call 'money rock'," Cutler leaned forward, gripping Mosiah's knee with his tight fingers, "but there's ancient artifacts hidden inside. Treasures, the Indians say, that were put there by 'the old ones', their ancient ancestors—gold and silver masks and gold disks covered with sacred picture writing of some kind. Sort of like those glyphics that were on the gold plates."

I stopped pretending I was busy and drew close. This was incredible!

"They call it *Carre-Shinob*, and they believe that their god, Towats, appeared to their chiefs and told them to protect the mine until the tall hats come. And that's what they've been doing for all these years—protecting the mine and keeping it secret."

Cutler looked at his brother as if expecting to see enthusiastic surprise, but instead, Mosiah stared back at him with eyes filled with deep concern. "Did that Indian tell Old Jack where the mine is?" he asked.

"Old Jack can hold his liquor pretty good. Even though he'd drunk quite a lot himself, he was able to get a real good idea of the mine's whereabouts. He says there's a couple of huge stone formations that stand just outside the mine. The Indians call them the twin bears. They believe Towats put them there to guard the mine—but I think they're going to guide us right to it."

Something about the rock hard set of Mosiah's shoulders and the thin line of his mouth sent an apprehensive shudder down my spine. "If that Indian was drunk, Cutler, you might not want to believe what he—"

"Oh, he was drunk all right! Guess he passed out afterward and slept 'til morning. When he woke up, he couldn't remember a thing that had happened the night before. But, you can bet the Utes would skin him alive if they knew what he told."

Cutler crossed his arms over his chest and waited for his brother's reaction, but I don't think he was quite prepared for the hard look and serious words that followed.

Mosiah leaned forward, placed both of his hands on his brother's shoulders, and said, "Cutler, you've got to listen to me now and listen real good. That gold mine is sacred to the Utes—and for good reason. *Carre-Shinob* means Where the Great Spirit Dwells. They believe that God instructed them to protect that mine with their lives, and that's what they're doing. If you get anywhere near that mine, they will kill you— just like they have done to every person who has ever tried. Don't even think about this, Cutler. Don't even think about it."

"It's real, then? You've heard about it?" Cutler stared at his brother, pure astonishment written all over his face.

"I've heard," Mosiah answered, his eyes never leaving Cutler's. "Chief Tabby told me about it once. Talking about the mine is the greatest show of trust a Ute can give to a white man. He did it because he knew I would honor that trust—and I have."

Mosiah gave Cutler's shoulder a small shake and looked deep into his eyes. "You can't do this, Cutler. It's wrong. You could die. You'd leave Jane a widow and your children fatherless. Leave it alone, Cutler. Leave it alone."

Cutler dropped his head into his hands and sat very still for a long while. I finally realized that his shoulders were shaking. He was sobbing.

At long last he looked up, nodded quickly, and walked out the door.

Mosiah and I couldn't hear the words that passed between Cutler and Old Jack under the cottonwood tree, but we could see the old man hopping around like he was fit to be tied and Cutler's futile attempts to placate him. At last, Old

Jack threw his battered hat into the dirt and stomped on it. Minutes later, he marched to the barn, saddled his horse, and left, leading his heavily laden pack mule behind him.

Cutler watched the old man go, turned, and walked slowly back to the cabin, his hat in his hand. "You're right, Mosiah. I should have known it myself, and I guess I did know it, all along. I just let myself get caught up with the idea of all that gold. I'm feeling pretty ashamed of myself right now. I think I'll go on home to Jane and hope she'll forgive my foolishness."

Mosiah and I both laughed and hugged him, reassuring Cutler that Jane and all the little Behunins would be delighted by his return and that he surely was doing the right thing. From the window, we watched him ride back down the road he had come up only a few hours before, leading his mule packed with all his mining gear behind him.

***

About a week later, Chief White Horse and his warriors rode into our yard. I looked out the window and realized that they were all so drunk they could barely stay on their horses. I shook my head in exasperation. The worst problems always came when the Indians got drunk.

Mosiah was out in the fields, so as soon as I saw the Indians coming, I scurried out into the yard and began to gather up my children. "Isaac," I called out, "go fetch your papa real quick."

White Horse's visits were usually friendly, but in his drunken condition, I didn't know what to expect. The Ute chief climbed off his horse and staggered around our yard. "Where Old Jack?" he yelled at the top of his voice. "Old Jack no good white man. Indians kill him—then he no more make trouble."

What worried me the most was the old sword he had in his hand. Rusty and corroded as it was, I knew it could still do a lot of damage, and White Horse was swinging it around with abandon.

"Get in the house," I screamed at the children as I pushed them toward the door. Just then, Benjamin emerged from the barn and White Horse took out after him, swinging the sword back and forth in the air as he went.

I screamed and distracted him long enough for Benjamin to scamper toward the cabin. The agile youngster darted easily out of danger's way, outmaneuvering the drunken Indian who staggered after him with the sword. As Benjamin dashed into the cabin and slammed the door behind him, White Horse bellowed with fury and swung the sword at the washstand, quickly reducing it to splinters. Then he attacked the cabin, sending wood chips flying in all directions.

"Stop!" I screamed, covering my face with my arm to protect myself from the flying wood chips. My eyes darted about, looking for a weapon of some kind to defend myself, but found nothing. I couldn't believe the Indian chief who had sat at my table just days ago was threatening our lives and destroying our home.

A milk bucket went flying into the air, smashed to pieces by White Horse's sword. But as he began to take apart the wagon, Mosiah came running in from the fields with Isaac close behind.

"Mosiah, watch out!" I screamed.

He stopped where he was, took everything in with a glance, and began to shuffle around in a big circle, facing the drunken Indian.

"What's the trouble here, chief?" he said cautiously. "Why are you busting up my house and scaring my family?"

"Old Jack—dead man!" White Horse said, barring his teeth and swinging the sword back and forth in Mosiah's direction. "Indians kill him. You get Old Jack now!"

Mosiah just kept circling as he avoided White Horse's sword. "Old Jack isn't here. We haven't seen him in a week," my husband answered, trying hard to reason with the Indian. But the war chief was way beyond reason. "Why do you want to kill that old trapper anyway?"

Out of the corner of my eye I saw White Horse's warriors jump from their horses and head for my husband. I screamed, but it was too late. Coming up from behind, they grabbed Mosiah and pinned his arms back. White Horse staggered forward and stuck the point of his sword to Mosiah's chest.

I went faint. I can still remember the taste of fear in my mouth as I watched in horror, unable to stop them.

"You get Old Jack or Indians kill you! Now!"

Mosiah looked him straight in the eye. "White Horse," he said, "You are a great chief to your people. I am your friend and have always told you what is true. I will tell you what is true, now. Old Jack is not here. He left a week ago, and I haven't seen him since."

A hundred years can pass in a few seconds at a time like that. Every moment was a century as I watched to see if my husband would be run through with a rusty, old sword.

I saw the thrust of White Horse's arm, gasped, and screamed—a high, thin screech that started in my toes and ripped out of my throat.

But the chief's sword did not penetrate my husband's body. He let him go—actually shoved him away with a force that sent Mosiah flying on his back into the dirt. Then the Indian chief staggered to his horse and, after several unsuccessful attempts to mount, pulled himself up and rode away with his warriors.

The children came pouring out of the cabin, and Mosiah and I fell into each other's arms, laughing and crying as relief washed over us.

When, at last, our bodies stopped shaking and my heart stopped pounding, the children all had to see the bruise on Papa's chest where Chief White Horse's sword had pressed against his skin.

We were eating breakfast the next morning when White Horse and his warriors rode back into our yard.

Mosiah carefully got his rifle down from the wall and walked into the yard to meet him.

But the Indian chief who climbed deftly down from his horse was a different man than the one who had staggered about our yard the day before.

"Shoken, my friend," the tall Indian said as he pulled himself up to his full height. "You do not need a gun today. I will not kill you."

Over griddle cakes and syrup, Chief White Horse told us how he'd ridden only a little way from our place before he slipped off his horse and fell asleep. Now, the craziness was gone.

Life on the frontier kept a body hoping every minute. And that's the truth of it.

Chapter notes:

      1. Although the story of Cutler's attempt to find Ute gold is fiction, Cutler Behunin was fascinated with prospecting, frequently leaving Jane and the children to go on a prospecting adventure.

      2. The legend of *Carrie Shinob* is a popular Utah legend. The gold mine, said to be guarded by Ute Indian spirits, is also referred to as the Lost Rhoades Mine. It is believed to be located somewhere in the Uinta Mountains.

      3. The story of Chief White horse's drunken attempt on Mosiah's life is taken from Caroline's journal; however her account says it was Chief Waponey rather than White Horse.

Chapter Twenty-Seven

Aldridge, Utah Territory
1884

Little by little, the Fremont Valley began to widen as settlers staked claims, cleared land, put in fences, and dug ditches. The solitary spot we claimed grew into the settlement of Aldridge, and the land around Jane and Cutler's place, near Capitol Reef, mushroomed into the town of Caineville.

Cutler always did have itchy feet it seems, so it wasn't long before he moved his family to a new settlement called Notom. He built their new house out of sandstone that he quarried himself from the white cliffs above the Fremont River.

As the population grew, White Horse became increasingly defensive. Problems between his band and the new settlers festered and seethed. Anger, hanging like a black cloud over our heads, rumbled, flashed, and threatened to explode with the slightest provocation. Through it all, Mosiah stood—a single hand trying to hold back a tidal wave.

As the autumn winds of 1884 blew their chilling breath across the river valley, White Horse and his band made a major raid, stealing cattle from all the settlers along the Fremont River. He herded the animals east into the Henry Mountains. Their intention was to sell the stolen cattle in Colorado, thereby providing for their families through the gaunt winter days to come.

Angry ranchers quickly formed a posse to head off the Indians and the herd before they reached the state line. Like wolves taking courage from the pack, the men worked themselves into a fever pitch and headed out with blood in their eyes.

Cutler eagerly joined the posse, and Mosiah was asked to ride along and negotiate with the Indian chief.

Jane and I, like every other woman whose husband joined the posse, stayed at home, worried, and prayed. It wasn't until the men returned, anxious to tell the story, that we learned the details of the expedition.

In a high valley, deep in the Henry Mountains, the posse spotted the herd and White Horse's band of warriors. As his men loaded their rifles and touched their fingers to the triggers, the sheriff signaled to Mosiah. He would have one chance, and one chance only, to avoid a tragedy which could claim the lives of virtually every brave in the White Horse band.

Banking on his friendship with Chief White Horse and covered by the shining rifles of fifty posse members, Mosiah nudged his horse and began his descent toward the Indian camp.

Coming within hearing distance of the camp he called out to the chief. "White Horse, I am your friend, Mosiah Behunin. The men whose cattle you have taken have surrounded you with many guns. I have come to talk to you."

Like a wave moving through the brush, each man stepped from his hiding place and aimed his gun at the Indians.

A sudden silence stilled the camp, followed by an angry discussion in heated Ute. Within minutes, Chief White Horse jumped on his pony, and, flanked by several of his warriors, rode out to meet Mosiah.

Mosiah raised his hand in greeting but did not smile. "The cattle in this valley do not belong to you. They have been taken from the settlers on the river. This is not a good thing that you have done. I am not happy to see that you have done it. And I do not believe that the Great Spirit is happy either."

White Horse drew himself tall on his horse, flipped his hair into the wind with a toss of his head, and spoke in slow, measured words. "The white man steals land that was our fathers'. We can no longer feed our families because deer and elk are gone from the forests. I do not believe the Great Spirit is happy with the white man for doing this. It is the same."

"No, White Horse, it is not the same. The cattle you have taken belong to the settlers, not you. To take them is not right. This thing you talk about is a hard thing. You and I have had many words about it, but taking cattle from the settlers will not make it right. It will only make more problems for your people."

The chief listened with hard eyes and arms folded across his chest, his face a stone statue, but Mosiah went on, "This is what you must do. Your people can settle on the land, plant crops, and raise animals, as these settlers do; or they can go to the Uinta reservation where much land has been set aside for the Ute nation. This was the treaty. You can hunt in the forests, but you cannot take what does not belong to you."

White Horse did not reply. He merely looked deep into Mosiah's eyes with a hard, cold stare. Then he spat in the dirt, spun his horse on it haunches, and rode back into camp. Very soon, the braves mounted up and rode away, leaving the herd to the posse.

It was a victory, I guess. But my husband was despondent for weeks after that trip.

***

Thanksgiving dawned bright and clear, which was a good thing, because when Jane and Cutler's family got together with ours, eating outside was a necessity.

Together we had eighteen children now. Our youngest, Elijah, was three years old, so we had eight. And Jane and Cutler's baby, Bert, had been born in April, giving them ten. Twenty-two people in all that Thanksgiving Day in '84.

Cutler's wagon pulled to a stop in front of our cabin, and Behunin children poured out of the wagon like milk spilt from a bucket.

Many hands make light work. In no time, a long, improvised table was set up and the feast spread out. The smell of sizzling meat—hot from the spit—fresh berry pies, and warm biscuits hung in the air. Every mouth watered. Cutler's eldest son, Elijah or Ligie, as we usually called him, offered our Thanksgiving prayer.

We passed the steaming dishes up and down the table, and each person filled his plate to overflowing. Cutler looked across the table at his brother with a twinkle in his eye and calmly stated, "Well, I'm sure you won't believe this, but after all these years, I've finally found gold."

My hand stopped in mid-air, the potatoes I had been dishing up falling with a plop onto my plate. "You didn't," I said.

Jane smiled back at me and nodded, "He did, at that."

I caught my breath and covered my mouth with my hand.

Mosiah narrowed his eyes and surveyed his brother, "Um-hmm, and my goose lays golden eggs too. Where did you find this gold, Cutler?"

He waited a minute, allowing the suspense to build. Every fork stopped moving. Then Cutler reached into his pocket and, off-handedly, plopped several gold pieces onto the table. "Under my dinner plate."

Jane and Cutler's youngsters began to giggle like somebody was tickling their toes while the rest of us sat dumb-founded, staring at the gold pieces lying on the table.

"Come on, now, Cutler," Mosiah said. "Where'd you get them?"

Cutler chuckled out loud as he put the gold coins back into his pocket and told his story.

"Well now," Cutler began. "You know how we've been hearing some mighty frightening tales about that Robbers' Roost Gang—the one Butch Cassidy is the head of?"

We all nodded. Cassidy's gang had been stealing cattle from ranches all around us. We were more than a little nervous about it all.

"Well, they were up at our place, not long ago," he said in a matter-of-fact manner.

I gasped, and Jane nodded a knowing glance in my direction.

Cutler buttered a hot biscuit and continued, "I saw them riding toward my place and could tell, right off, who they were. Those boys were about as rough looking as an old boot.

"I had just enough time, before they rode in, to think about what I was going to do. So I decided to treat them kindly—no point in getting their dander up."

"I think that was a good decision," Mosiah nodded as he stabbed a hunk of meat with his fork.

"That's what I figured. So when they rode in and asked for a drink, I sent the kids to fetch them some water. And hay for their horses too." Cutler dished a mountain of mashed potatoes onto his plate and reached for the gravy.

"I was more than a bit surprised, though, by their leader—that Butch Cassidy, we've heard so much about. He sure didn't look like an outlaw to me, and he was about as friendly and polite as anybody I've met."

"I've heard other people say that about him," Mosiah offered. "They say he came from a good Mormon family. Can't help but wonder what went wrong."

"Yes, sir, he was quite likable—had to keep reminding myself who he was. Some of his boys did look real rough, but they were all well-mannered, and they did exactly what Cassidy told them to do.

"I asked Old Butch if they would like some food before they went on their way, and they were purely grateful."

"They stayed for dinner?" I asked Jane, leaning forward to hear her answer.

"Yes, they did," she said. "And they were as polite as any guests we've ever had."

"They even bowed their heads when we said prayer," Jane's boy Hite broke in. "And said 'amen' and everything."

"You'd think they'd never eaten before by the way they devoured my biscuits," Jane laughed as she passed the stuffing.

"Yes, sir," Cutler snickered. "They were real complimentary. Butch told me before he left that if he ever found a woman as pretty as my Jane, he'd marry her right away. And if she could cook biscuits light as a feather and food fit for a king like the meal he'd just ate, he'd never let her go."

Jane blushed and giggled like a girl. "Never thought I'd get a compliment like that from such a man as Butch Cassidy," she said.

"And he wasn't the only one taken in by the Behunin women," Cutler laughed between bites of chicken and corn on the cob. "You should have seen that young one follow our May with his eyes—watching every move she made."

"Oh, Papa, he did not!" May exclaimed, her face turning red and her gaze dropping coyly to her hands in her lap.

"Yes, he did!" all of Cutler's boys said at once. "He even asked if he could help her with the dishes." The boys hooted, earning themselves a well-deserved glare from their sister.

"And guess what he left under her cup?" May's younger sister Nettie piped up. "A solid gold coin!"

"Yes, indeed! And when Jane cleared the table, after they'd gone, she found two more under Cassidy's plate." Cutler laughed and wiped his mouth with his handkerchief,

"And that's how the Behunins struck it rich without even leaving their yard. Now, ain't that something?"

We all laughed. It really was something, and that's a fact.

Cassidy and his gang visited Cutler's family quite regularly after that, always sharing dinner with them and always showing polite respect. On one of his visits, the outlaw carved his name into the white sandstone bricks at the back of the Behunin home. It caused quite a stir. But the coin or two Cassidy's gang left under the plates every time they passed by was the only gold Cutler ever did discover.

Chapter notes:

1. Cutler Behunin's experiences with Butch Cassidy, along with a picture of Cutler's white sandstone house with Cassidy's name carved into the stones, can be found in Ruby Noyes Tippit's *A Song in Her Heart*.

Chapter Twenty-Eight

Aldridge, Utah Territory
Fall 1885

Life on the frontier wasn't for sissies. That's for sure! I heard it said—if you didn't have hair on your chest before you got there, you'd best grow some fast or go back to where you came from. Indians and Indian troubles were a fact of life. And outlaws provided an even more frightening reality.

Most of those ornery rascals weren't anywhere near as nice and polite as Butch Cassidy and his bunch. I had a run-in with a few myself one time when Mosiah was gone to Grass Valley for supplies.

I was just coming in from the barn when a gang of mean-looking polecats rode into our yard. Didn't take much figuring to know which side of the law they were on.

These men didn't ask for food and water—they demanded it. With my husband gone, I surely didn't want to ruffle their feathers, so I fixed them some food real quick, hoping they would get along. But they hung around our place all afternoon, taking themselves a siesta under the cottonwood tree and harassing the children.

I overheard them say that they had killed an Indian in some kind of ruckus. Sounded to me like they were trying to steal Indian ponies.

I was mighty grateful when they finally got on their horses and rode off, but I knew if they had killed an Indian, there would be more trouble coming. And I was right.

The next day, six Indians from White Horse's band rode in. I took one look at their sour expressions and sent the children inside.

I didn't know them all, but Wanzitz was with them, and that made me think things could be difficult. They rode up, jumped off their ponies, and made a beeline toward me with a cantankerous look in their eyes.

"Where Shoken?" asked Pi-ah-ba, a big Indian who had been to our cabin several times.

I didn't want them to know I was alone, but when I couldn't produce Mosiah, they figured it out real quick.

"You see cowboys around here, Shoken's squaw?" Pi-ah-bah demanded.

"Why?" I asked, standing my ground the best I could. "What do you want with them?"

"They kill Indian boy," a young buck answered, his eyes narrowing into slits. "We find them—we kill them."

"If you're talking about the bunch of hooligans that came by here yesterday—they were here all right," I said with my hands on my hips. "But they're gone now, and I don't know where they went."

"You tell us where they go." The big Indian said as he stepped into my face and poked his nose close to mine.

"I told you, I don't know where they went. And whatever they did, it's got nothing to do with me," I shot back at him. With that I turned on my heel, walked back into the cabin, and closed the door.

The second I shut the door, little bodies plowed into me from all directions. Huge tears ran down their faces as they sobbed into my skirts.

"There now, it's all right." I said reaching my arms around them. But the truth be known, I was shaking like a corn stalk in the breeze myself.

Outside, the Indians were getting real wound up, whooping and hollering and shooting their guns in the air.

I turned and saw fourteen-year-old Isaac, white as skimmed milk, standing next to the window, a rifle in his hands. "Isaac," I said as calm as I could, "what are you fix'n to do?"

"If one of those Indians tried to hurt you, Mama," he answered through trembling lips, "I was gonna shoot him."

I walked over, laid my hand on his shoulder and looked deep into his eyes. "You're a brave boy, Isaac," I said. "But the Good Lord almost always shows us a better way to handle things than to kill a man."

I drew him close to me and beckoned the other children to come. "We're in real need of His help right now. So come on over here, and let's ask for it."

We knelt with our arms around each other and prayed hard for the Lord's help. We prayed for His protection and strength; we prayed to know what we should do; and we prayed that He would soften the hearts of the Indians in our yard. But we could hear them screaming outside the whole time we were praying, and we knew that they were up to no good out there.

We ended in amen, and Isaac, Joseph, and I got up to look out the window. It was a sorry sight. The Indians were out in our fields, splitting open melons left and right with their axes and knives and tearing down the green corn.

I watched for a while, my anger mounting with every melon that they split. A whole year of work, gone in a matter of minutes. All because some scoundrel's cowardly deeds had sent the Indians into a dither.

I saw Pi-ah-bah hit the largest pumpkin in our patch with his ax, crack it open, and let out a war whoop as if he'd made some great kill.

Red flashed before my eyes and something snapped inside of me. I grabbed my broom from the corner and marched myself right out the door and into the field where they were busy hacking up my melons.

"Why don't you take that poor pumpkin's scalp while you're at it?" I screamed at Pi-ah-bah, one hand on my hip and the other shaking my broom above my head.

He stopped mid-air, looked up at me, and looked back down at the pumpkin in total disbelief. Then he threw back his head and laughed 'til I thought his teeth would fall out. The other Indians stopped their mischief too, and just stood there looking at me like I was daft.

"Does this make you feel like big, strong warriors?" I screamed as I shook my broom at them, "Chopping up food that's meant to feed those little children in there?"

They looked at each other and back again at me.

"Did we ever treat you this way?" I asked, pointing at Pi-ah-bah. "Don't you remember when you came to my house and I gave you dinner and let you sleep in a bed? Even fixed you a good breakfast before you left?"

Turning, I shook my broom at Wanzitz, "Remember when *you* came to my house? I was young, and scared, but I fed you and let your braves get warm by my fire. Didn't I?" I looked him hard in the eye and spat my words into his face, "How can you be so mean?"

Wanzitz and Pi-ah-bah began to look sheepish. I shook my broom a little and went on.

"My husband has never been anything but kind to you. Teaching you to farm so that you could feed your families. Taking your side when there's trouble between the whites and the Indians. Risking his life for you."

I put my broom down and asked, "Is this the way you pay us back for being your friends these many years?"

Wanzitz and Pi-ah-bah exchanged a hasty glance, and then with a quick jerk of his chin, Wanzitz jumped on his pony and rode off. The others followed his lead, but as they rode out of the yard, a sassy young buck shot my best milk cow with his rifle.

***

We were hoping we had seen the last of them, but we hadn't. The Indians weren't able to find the outlaws who killed the Indian boy. They got so fired-up they decided to take their vengeance out on any whites they could find. And since they knew my husband was gone, they headed back to our place.

They rode in whooping and hollering and made their camp just outside our dooryard; then they started to get themselves all liquored up. They weren't out in the fields hacking up melons or chopping down corn, but they helped themselves to whatever they wanted and were making a real hullabaloo of a racket. Seemed like they were trying to get us to come out of the cabin and have a row with them, but we stayed inside all that first day.

The next day they were still out there making a racket. But we had to feed the stock and milk the other cow, so I took a rifle and my two oldest boys and went out to get it done.

While I milked the cow, Isaac and Joseph watered the stock. We were almost finished when the sassy young buck who shot my milk cow snuck up on us. I looked up just in time to see him jump Isaac and put a knife to his throat.

I didn't know I could move so fast. It took me just a fraction of a second to grab my rifle and point it at that Indian's head. "You let my boy go, or I'll shoot you dead with this here rifle!" I screamed. I didn't need to pretend how brave I was. My maternal instincts had kicked in, and I felt about as fierce as an old mother bear. I was ready to do whatever I had to do to save my son.

The young buck whipped around to face me with one arm wrapped around Isaac's chest. Then with the other hand, he slid the blade of his knife against the boy's throat.

"I kill this boy!" he screamed insanely in my direction. "White man kill Indian boy! Now I kill white boy! All the same!"

I aimed the bead of my rifle right at the Indian's head. But before I could fire, I saw Wanzitz out of the corner of my eye. He was rushing toward us and screaming at the young Indian to leave the boy alone.

With a look of disgust crossing his face, the surly, young Indian pushed Isaac away. I lowered my rifle with trembling hands. I was weak in the knees, and I felt like someone had punched me hard in my stomach.

Wanzitz glowered at me and strode over to the young Indian, giving him a hard kick and a cuff.

The two of them left in the direction of the camp amid a stream of Ute reprimands from the older warrior.

Joseph and Isaac came running to me. Together we made fast tracks for the house. We were a sorry bunch for sure. I had no idea what to do next. More than likely, it would still be several days before Mosiah made it home. And we couldn't leave the stock out there to die of hunger and thirst.

Prayer was all we had. So we prayed. We prayed long and hard. I pleaded with the Lord to help me find a way out of this situation without anybody getting hurt.

"Please, Lord, soften their hearts," I pleaded over and over again.

***

I was rocking in my chair and wringing my hands when little Elijah dropped the almanac into my lap. "Story, Mommy?" he asked, looking up at me with big blue eyes.

"Oh, darlin', this isn't a very fun story," I said, but I opened it anyway. I thought if I pretended to read a little, it might lighten things up, so I thumbed through until I found the day's date. Then I sat up straight real quick.

"Well, I'll be," I stammered. There on the page in front of me was my answer. That very night, my almanac predicted an eclipse of the moon. It was an answer from God—and I knew it—sent in our time of greatest need.

I got up, sliced a loaf of my homemade bread, and spread it with butter and jam. I put it on a plate and walked right out to the Indian camp as calm as you please. "I have come to bring food to our friends," I said to them. "And to tell you that God wants you go away and leave us alone. Tonight He will make the moon go dark, so you will know that this is true."

They looked at me strangely, poked each other, and laughed. I turned and went back into the cabin, and they ate the bread.

That night as the children slept, I sat in my rocker beside the window. I could see their campfire and hear the sound of their laughter as I watched the moon and prayed.

Just as I began to think maybe the almanac had been wrong, a shadow slipped across the moon and darkened all but a tiny crescent. I knew the Indians were watching too, because it became very quiet. A short time later, with the moon shining high in the sky again, I watched six Indians mount their horses and ride away.

***

"How you know about the moon," Pi-ah-bah asked me a few weeks later. Mosiah was home again and the big Indian had returned for a friendly visit. "Great Spirit tell you?"

"Yes," I said. "I prayed to God, who is the Great Spirit, and He helped me to look in the book. The book told me about the moon. Then I knew what to do."

"Pi-ah-bah see book?" he asked. I showed him the almanac, pointed to the page, and read it to him.

He looked at the words in the almanac and back at me, "How you know it say that?"

"Because I can read," I said to him. "If you learn to read, books can tell you things too. I think the Great Spirit would like you to learn. He would like your children to read too. Then He can teach you many things."

"You teach children?" he asked.

"Yes," I said, surprising myself.

***

About a week later, Chief White Horse rode into our yard with three young boys, each about ten years old.

"You teach Indians read white man's book," he said to me and signaled to the boys to dismount. These smart boys. Learn fast. You teach boys—I come back soon."

He rode off, leaving me with three sheepish Indian boys.

It wasn't a very good time for me. I was getting ready to make soap out in the yard. But I put everything aside and did my best to teach them, just as I had done with my own children.

They were smart boys, and they did learn fast. The hardest thing was that I didn't ever know when they were coming. Chief White Horse or some other Indian would just ride into our yard with them and dump them off, expecting me to drop everything and work with them.

And I did.

I came to love those boys; they were bright and eager to learn. In their eyes, I saw the future.

The older braves, especially the ones who had fought in the Black Hawk War, were proud and set in their ways. It was almost impossible for them to change, but these young boys were pliable. I taught them, not only to read, but about the things they would need to know to survive in a white man's world.

Before long, some of the Ute women began to come along. They seemed to understand that the knowledge I gave their children was as important to their survival as the ability to hunt. These women looked to the future instead of clinging to the past.

Like the Paiute *wyanos* I had loved so dearly, these were simple, loving women, confused by the changing world they faced, but willing to adapt. And like the Paiutes, they had a natural way of living close to the spirit. As we taught them about Christ and His gospel, they accepted it with their whole hearts and we were happy to have more baptisms. Then, as always, the spirit strengthened them, and they began to make the hard changes.

Chapter notes:

1. The story of Caroline's confrontation with Ute warriors and how she convinced them to leave by predicting a lunar eclipse is inspired by a similar account related by Caroline in her journal. The time and place of this event are unclear.

Chapter Twenty-Nine

Notom, Utah Territory
Winter 1885

During the winter of 1885, White Horse's struggling band of Utes caught the measles.

At first, it was just the white community that contracted them, and that was bad enough. I think my own children picked them up at church. George and Caroline got them first, and two weeks later, the other children came down with them. Little Elijah scratched at his rash-covered skin 'til it bled. For weeks I got no sleep, caring for one sick, feverish child after another. Eventually, they did get well and were no worse off for the wear.

But it was an entirely different matter with the Indians.

We tried to keep them away from our place. The weather was so cold that the children hadn't been coming to my cabin for school anyway. And once we realized it was the measles, we didn't allow any Indians on our property. We had heard what this disease could do to them. They had no immunity to it.

But by that time, the Indians were interacting with the whites so much that infection was inevitable. And when it came, it hit them like an avalanche. Not just the children—the whole Indian band. They were all so sick they couldn't take care of themselves or each other. I spent hour after hour at the camp, helping in every way I could. Children were dying all around me. It was almost more than I could take, but I couldn't leave.

It had been a lean year, and food was scarce, but now the men were too sick to hunt, and starvation leered down upon the already-decimated Indian band.

"Caroline, we've got to get food for them somehow, or there won't be any Indians left by spring," Mosiah said to me as he stood looking out of the window. He turned toward me and continued, "I'm going to take the wagon and go into the settlements—see if I can get people to give them some food. White Horse says his people have been going from house to house begging, but most people won't answer their door. They know the Indians have the measles. They don't want to take a chance that their own family will get sick."

"That's ridiculous," I answered. "Most white children make it through just fine. It's the Indians this disease kills."

"Nonetheless, that's what's happening," he said as he buttoned up his coat and found his hat. "White Horse thinks they'll listen to me. I don't know, but I'm going to try. White Horse is coming with me."

Two days later he arrived home with the wagon loaded to overflowing with flour, potatoes, and beans. "I decided to go to Notom first and visit Cutler and Jane," my husband said as he hung his hat and coat on a peg by the door.

"You took White Horse to visit Cutler?" I gasped. "And they didn't kill each other?"

"Nope," he laughed. "But you should have seen Cutler's face when I pulled up and he saw who was sitting beside me in the wagon."

"Did White Horse recognize Cutler?"

"Oh, yes. A man doesn't forget somebody who almost killed him."

"So, what did you do?" All the little ears around the table were flapping—thinking they were going to hear a real good story.

"I just introduced them regular-like. I said, 'White Horse, you probably remember my brother Cutler.'"

"And?"

"Well, White Horse just looked real hard at Cutler; then he said, 'Red Bull is your brother?'

"'Yes, sir,' I said, just as calm as you please. Then I explained the Indian situation to Cutler. Cutler looked long and hard at White Horse before he said, 'How about I go along with you to visit my neighbors and see what we can do?'

"Next thing you know, he climbed right up into the wagon next to the chief." Mosiah was laughing pretty hard by this time. "White Horse looked at Cutler real funny and moved over about as far as he could get."

"Well, I'll be!"

Mosiah sat down by the fire and began to pull off his boots. "We rode around to the folks who live near Notom. At each house, Cutler jumped out and went to the door. He'd explain the situation, and they'd almost always give us some food. You can tell by the looks of the wagon, they were mighty generous."

"Did Cutler and White Horse talk about what happened during the war?"

"Not for a long time, but they finally did get around to it," he said as he stretched his hands towards the fire.

"The ride was a mighty quiet one for a long time, but Cutler just kept getting out of the wagon and coming back with more food. I could feel White Horse softening; then he hung his head as if he was ashamed. 'Red Bull,' he finally said, 'I have hated you many years. I have sworn to kill you before I died. But you did not kill me when you could. You fixed my wound. You took me back to my people. Now, you do this so my people will not starve. You are a good man, Red Bull.' And then he cried," Mosiah said softly. "That fierce Indian war chief actually cried."

Mosiah continued, "Then they clasped hands, patted each other's backs, and Cutler told him about Spook. White Horse had to go and see the old dog and give him some pats before he'd leave. It was really something."

The next day Mosiah took the wagon again and visited Aldridge and Caineville. Almost everybody gave him food. I don't think the Indians had ever had so much food for the winter. It was sad to see so many of them die from the measles, but at least they didn't go hungry."

Chapter notes:

1. An account of the measles epidemic of 1885 and Mosiah and Cutler's efforts to help White Horse acquire food for his band is recounted in Ruby Noyes Tippits's history of the Cutler Behunin family, *A Song in Her Heart.*

Chapter Thirty

Cainsville, Utah Territory
January 1886

"Go, Isaac, go!" I screamed, waving my arms above my head and bouncing up and down like a ball on a string.

Beside me, Mosiah jabbed his fist into the air, again and again, as he called out, "Push him, Isaac! Push him! You can do it, boy!"

Around us little Behunins of all ages and sizes jumped up and down and screamed. Some of them were our own children, cheering for Isaac, but some of them were Jane and Cutler's youngsters, cheering for their brother Ligie.

Jane clutched my arm with both of her hands and unconsciously dug her fingers into my flesh as she danced up and down and screamed along with the rest of us.

It was Caineville's first-ever New Year's Day celebration, complete with a potluck dinner, horse races, and relays for the children.

Families from all along the Fremont rode in by wagon to join in the festivities. Wrapped in quilts to insulate them from the chilly January air, they looked like caterpillars, snug in their cocoons.

Fortunately, the weather cooperated. Only a skiff of snow lay on the ground. We dressed warmly and ignored it.

Joseph won the gunny sack race, and Ben and Caroline took third in the three-legged scramble. We laughed, visited, ate too much, and had a generally good time.

The horse race, now in progress, was the culminating event. Three laps around the open field, especially marked for the occasion, and the winner would become the proud owner of the yearling colt corralled in the middle of town.

"Ain't he beautiful, Mama?" my children had exclaimed earlier in the day as they, along with dozens of other children, climbed on the corral fence and reached out to touch the velvety nose of the donated black colt. "I sure do hope Isaac wins him."

Bucky was a fast horse, and Isaac was a good rider, but Cutler's Ligie, riding Red Fury, was equally good and they both worried about Tom Williams from Caineville. He and his big gray gelding named Smokey were favored to win.

Two laps around the field left all but Isaac, Ligie, and Tom in the dust, with Isaac and Ligie neck-in-neck and Tom slightly ahead. It looked to be a close race. Any of the three might win.

But in the blink of an eye, everything went wrong. Ligie's mount seemed to stumble for no apparent reason and went down, throwing his rider high above the red horse's head and slamming him into the ground where he rolled over and over until he lay motionless in the dirt.

The enthusiastic cheers of the crowd turned to gasps as we ran onto the field, almost falling over one another in our efforts to reach the downed boy.

Isaac glanced over his shoulder just in time to see it all happen. He quickly pulled his horse out of the race and rode toward his injured cousin, while Tom Williams rode on to win a barely contested race.

Isaac got to Ligie first, quickly dismounted, and knelt beside the boy who lay in the dirt, moaning and clutching his right side.

Arriving second, Jane dropped beside him, cradling his head in her shaking hands. Skirts and all, she had somehow managed to outrun even the men in her efforts to get to her son.

"I'm all right, Mama," he assured her through clinched teeth, "I just banged up my side real good. I hit mighty hard."

"Yes, you did, son," Mosiah said, smiling through his concern as his skillful hands worked their way over Ligie's body, feeling for broken bones before he allowed the boy to get to up. "I do think you're going to be all right—just bruised and sore."

With everyone's help, Ligie managed to get to his feet. Hunched over and clutching his side, he leaned heavily on his cousin Isaac and hobbled to the sidelines where he could sit for a while.

But physical pain was only part of Ligie's torture that day. The minute we got the poor boy situated on the bench, we turned around to find a couple of men standing behind us with sorry looks on their faces and their hats in their hands.

"Is the boy all right?" one of the men asked, and we assured him that he was fine—just banged up a bit. But something in their eyes told me that we hadn't heard the end of it.

Reaching out to put a hand on Ligie's shoulder, the other man broke the hard news. "I'm sorry to have to tell you this, son, but your horse has a broken leg. Seems he stepped in a gopher hole. I'm sure I don't have to tell you what that means. We'll do it for you if you'd like."

Ligie stared at the men for a minute, his lips trembling. Then he gave them a quick nod. The men returned the nod and disappeared. Ligie dropped his head into his hands, trying hard not to let us see the sobs that racked his aching body, most certainly causing even more pain. We all waited woodenly for the inevitable shot, and we didn't have to wait long. When that rifle fired, Ligie crumpled. Learning to be a man in that rough country was just too hard sometimes.

Ligie sat there on the bench for the better part of an hour, not saying much. At last he pulled himself to his feet and walked about rather gingerly. "I've got to be all right," we overheard him tell Isaac. "I promised Papa that if he'd let me come to this here shindig, I'd head straight out to the sheep camp as soon as it was over. And I've got to keep my word."

Mosiah frowned deeply, and his jaw tightened as he listened to the boys' conversation. I could see my husband's angry feelings toward his absent brother. "Where's Cutler when you need him?" I heard him mutter under his breath.

About an hour later, Jane decided to take her brood home. Mosiah helped Ligie into the wagon. He did seem to be all right—just a little bruised and sore.

"When do you expect Cutler back?" Mosiah asked Jane after he helped her onto the wagon seat.

"Oh, you know Cutler," she laughed. "One never knows for sure. He's gone to Torrey to discuss another prospecting venture with some friends of his."

Mosiah shook his head and nodded toward Ligie. "See to it that he gets some rest. That boy took quite a spill."

Jane smiled and nodded, but I could see tight lines of worry around her usually smiling eyes. My heart went out to her. I knew how hard it was to be alone with the children, especially in times of trouble. I would keep them in my prayers.

***

Snow had been coming down all night, the wind blowing through the chinks of the cabin and disturbing my sleep. By morning, the storm had developed into one of those blizzards you seldom see this far south. The wind howled and blew the snow sideways.

I could hardly make out the barn from the cabin window.

I leaned forward and squinted, trying to figure out what I was seeing moving slowly through the snow.

"Mosiah," I called to my husband, who was busy building a fire in the fireplace, "Something's headed our way. I think it's a horse and rider."

Mosiah wandered over to join me at the window. "Who would be coming through this storm?" he asked.

The wind quieted for a minute, and we got a clear view as a horse with a familiar look about it walked slowly into our yard and stopped. The rider, who seemed too small to be a man, lay motionless against the horse's neck and made no attempt to dismount.

I heard Mosiah catch his breath. In one quick movement, he rushed across the room, flung the door open, and hurried out into the whipping wind with me right behind him.

"Uncle Mosiah," we heard the small rider moan, "Ligie's dead!"

I froze in my tracks as if a sheet of ice had descended upon me.

"He's out there in the snow," the small voice whimpered though excruciating sobs. "You gotta go after him before the wolves get him! You gotta get him out of the snow!"

Mosiah's strong arms pulled the boy from the horse and cradled him against his chest as he hurried toward the cabin.

I followed him, a horrible numbness crawling up my legs and into my heart.

"Isaac!" Mosiah called the moment we hit the door. "Get Matt's horse into the barn and take care of him."

Isaac came running, but when he saw his father carrying his young cousin in his arms, he stopped dead in his tracks and gasped.

"Go!" Mosiah barked, and Isaac went to do as he was told, stopping only a moment to glance back over his shoulder. Something was very wrong.

Mosiah laid the boy on our bed and knelt beside him as I worked to remove his frozen clothing.

"He's dead! Ligie's dead!" Matt kept repeating through his sobs. "And he's in the snow."

"Matt," Mosiah said, shaking the boy slightly in an effort to bring him into some state of coherency. "Tell me what happened."

"Ligie said we had to go. Mama didn't want us to— she's been worried about him since he got hurt—but Ligie said he promised Papa and we had to go."

"To the sheep camp?" Mosiah asked incredulously.

"Yes, but we couldn't go very fast. Ligie kept having to stop and rest."

"You were walking?" Mosiah asked.

Matt nodded. "We always walk. It's not so bad. We always get to the camp before dark, and there's quilts and food and stuff there. But this time was different. After we'd walked a while, Ligie got so bad he couldn't go anymore."

Matt grabbed my husband's shirt with small, icy fingers and cried, "I didn't know what to do, Uncle Mosiah! I just didn't know what to do!"

Mosiah tried to pull the sobbing boy into an embrace. "It's all right, Matt," he soothed. "Just tell me what happened."

But Matt pushed him away and screamed, "It's not all right! It will never be all right! I should have done what he said. Ligie said I should leave him and go to the camp to get quilts, but I didn't dare. It was getting dark and there were wolves. And he was so sick he couldn't get up. I was afraid they'd get him. So I made a fire and I stayed."

"You did the right thing, son," Mosiah assured him, looking deep into Matt's young grief-stricken face. "Nobody could have done any better."

"I was so scared, Uncle Mosiah," he cried through trembling lips. "I just didn't know what to do. I kept the fire going and put my coat over him. I stripped bark from a tree and used the soft stuff under the bark to make him a pillow.

211

But he just kept moaning and crying out. I couldn't think of any way to help him. I prayed and prayed that Papa would come and find us. But he didn't."

My brain staggered to grasp the reality of what this twelve-year-old boy was telling us. But it was too much. Icy shards of disbelief pierced my chest, thrusting their hard, cold way into my heart.

I couldn't breathe.

Through my tears, I forced my hands into motion—carefully removing the frozen clothing from his body. My fingers struggled to untie his snow-encrusted shoelaces and to peel back the stiff, cold stockings from his feet.

They were ghastly white.

Oh, Jane! I kept thinking. *Oh, no! Whatever will you do?*

"When Ligie stopped moaning, I thought he was asleep," Matt whispered. "And I slept a little too."

"You must have been freezing," I murmured. "All night with no coat."

"I didn't care. Ligie needed it more than me. But it didn't help him none. In the morning when I tried to wake him up, he was hard and cold." With that, poor Matt started screaming and crying. His cousins, who had gathered around the bed, stared with huge wide eyes and backed away. The little ones ran to hide.

"He's dead, Uncle Mosiah! He's dead! And lying there in the snow. You gotta go get him before the wolves eat him, Uncle Mosiah. Please!"

"I will, son. Don't you worry. I'll take good care of Ligie. You just get some rest now—relax and get some sleep. But you've got to tell me first—does your mother know?"

Matt nodded. "I covered him up the best I could and left fires burning around him. Then I tried to get home. But it was snowing, and the wind was blowing. And I didn't have a coat. I was crying so hard I couldn't see for the tears. I kept getting lost. It was dark before I made it home. I don't think I would have ever made it if Spook hadn't been with me. He kept showing me the way."

I could hear my children sobbing behind me, and I suddenly became aware that I was biting the back of my hand so hard it hurt.

"Mama turned dead white when I fell through the door. And when I told her about Ligie, she started screaming.

Seemed like she went right out of her mind. She kept crying for me to ride and get you—so you could find Papa and go get Ligie. But they had to shoot Red Fury when he broke his leg, and Papa took Flick. The only horse left was Donny Boy, and he's old and half blind.

"Jane wasn't in her right mind." I whispered under my breath. "She'd never have asked this boy ride out in the night on that old horse if she'd been thinking straight."

Mosiah looked at me and nodded gravely.

"I rode all night to get here. I was so scared, Uncle Mosiah. It was dark and snowing and blowing 'til I didn't know where I was. Donny Boy kept stopping and trying to turn around. And I couldn't see for the snow. Didn't even know if I was headed the right way."

"It's a miracle he got here," I murmured, and Matt turned his watery eyes to look at me.

"I prayed real hard that the Lord would help me find you. I was afraid I'd fall off Donny Boy. Scared I'd die in the snow like Ligie."

"It's a wonder you didn't, boy," Mosiah said softly, his words trembling almost as badly as my hands.

"I closed my eyes and held on tight to Donny's mane. Just kept kicking him whenever he'd stop. When I opened my eyes, I was here."

"The Lord answered your prayer, son; He truly did," Mosiah whispered.

I slumped down into a chair, shaking and sobbing so hard I could hardly catch my breath. *How can something like this happen to a fine boy like Ligie? And what will this do to poor Jane? And Cutler? What will it do to him when he realizes that his son is dead because he took off on some fool prospecting trip?*

I felt my children's arms around me and looked up to see their tear-streaked faces staring down at me with a grief that matched my own.

I got up and hugged them, tight as a mother can hug a child. Tight enough to melt their small bodies into my own heart. *What would I ever do without a single one of them?*

I wiped my tears and gathered more blankets. When I came to the bed, I found Matt asleep. Beside him, my husband sobbed into his hands.

He turned to me with a look of devastation as deep as the ocean. "How can I tell Cutler that his boy has died this awful death because of his own foolishness? How can I do it?"

I took both of his large, work-worn hands into my own and whispered, "With the help of the Lord, you will find a way. Be gentle."

I reached out to touch his shoulder. We clung to each other and wept.

***

Matt's feet were frozen. He had no feeling in them for a while. I put them into buckets of cold molasses, hoping to thaw them out slowly, but when they did begin to warm up, Matt began to scream. The pain got worse and worse. He screamed and howled until he finally passed out from exhaustion.

I took care of him the best I knew how, bandaging his poor feet, and caring for him all through the fever that came next.

Mosiah caught up with Cutler in Fruita. He was on his way home. Guess he all but came apart at the seams, ranting and sobbing and cursing himself for his neglect. My husband didn't have the heart to scold his brother for leaving his family to follow a foolish dream. Cutler already knew.

Together, they found Ligie's body not far from the sheep camp, still wrapped in Matt's coat and covered in snow. Despite their sorrow and tears, the two brothers managed to lift Ligie's hard, cold body into the wagon and take him home to poor Jane, who was so beside herself with grief she appeared half-dead herself.

Mosiah and the boys dug a grave in the stiff, frozen ground, and we buried him on the hill two days later. I tried to be there for Jane as much as I could, but it wasn't easy. She wouldn't smile or talk. Just went through the motions of living. She was like an empty shell.

The skin on Matt's feet blistered into huge pussy sores. I guess it could have been much worse; he could have lost his feet or at least some of his toes. But when his feet began to heal, his toes grew together. Cutler had to cut them apart with his knife.

I wasn't there to see it, and I don't even want to think about how awful that must have been. It was a dark and heartbreaking time for their family. And for ours. We watched and wrung our hands, but we couldn't do much for them.

When spring came, Cutler told us they had decided to move again, this time to Thurber. It was just too hard for Jane to stay there with so many memories.

Weeks after they were gone, I went over to their old place and walked around the white stone house that Jane had loved so much. I traced Butch Cassidy's name still etched into the white sandstone bricks and cried.

––––––––––––––––––

Chapter notes:

1. The events of Elija's (Ligie's) death are related by Ruby Noyes Tippits in her history of the Cutler Behunin family, *A Song in Her Heart.*

Chapter Thirty-One

Hanksville, Utah Territory
Summer 1886

Tiny Mary Jane nuzzled close to me. Her downy head nestled against my breast, and her small, warm body curled against my heart. Another sweet baby girl.

Nine times I had gone into the shadow of death to bring a child into this world. And each time had been a wonder. I never tired of the joy a new life brings. My arms would be awful empty without a soft, warm bundle in them.

I held her close to me as the buckboard jostled along the bumpy road to Hanksville. It wasn't far. Like a mushroom that pops up almost overnight from the forest loam, Hanksville sprang into existence before our very eyes. The land where only Indians once roamed was becoming a thriving community.

Oh, the Indians were still there, but it was different. Those who didn't die in the measles epidemic or leave to join the Utes on the Uinta reservation near Roosevelt had begun to make peace with the white man's way of life.

Our wagon rolled past the Indian farm. Mosiah pulled our horse to a stop and hopped out. In the field, Ute women and children worked with hoes and their bare hands to weed the growing crop. I even saw a brave or two among them—an increasingly common sight these days.

As soon as our wagon pulled to a stop, they came running. Women with laughing eyes and big happy smiles. Children with round bellies and contagious laughs.

The young ones wasted no time climbing into our wagon and throwing their small brown arms around my neck. I laughed and hugged their firm, round bodies as I called out greetings to the friendly Ute women. The older children crowded around us talking and laughing. I smiled into their

216

upturned faces, realizing how many of them had sat at my feet in my little cabin school.

They were very proud of their crops and wanted us to see them. We all climbed out of the wagon and took a look at the rows of plants, growing like hundreds of green soldiers under the warm Fremont sun.

Mosiah was pleased and praised them until every face shone. They shook our hands and patted our backs as we climbed back into our wagon. Then they watched us leave, waving from the side of the road until we were out of sight.

I was still smiling when we pulled into Hanksville. Houses and new shops were popping up all over. And the people seemed different too. Most of the original settlers—the ones who carved this land out of the desert—had moved on, tired of the droughts and the floods.

But the land didn't lay empty for long. New settlers came as soon as the old ones left. All good people of course, but they knew little of the struggles that had opened up this land. And they didn't understand the Indians at all. Didn't treat them much better than the dirt they walked on.

Mosiah pulled the wagon to a stop in front of the general store, and the children hopped out like rabbits let out of a pen.

The older boys went with their father to get seed and nails, but the younger children followed me into the store like ducklings in a row.

A number of customers browsed about the store: women in pretty dresses with petticoats and bonnets, little girls with curls and button-up shoes, boys with barbershop haircuts. I looked about me and became painfully aware of my own tired dress—clean, but faded—not to mention my children's patched clothes and bare feet.

I tried to smile and be friendly but got only blank stares and pursed lips in return. I couldn't help noticing several women gathering their children to their sides and whispering as we came in.

Though I was first in line with my meager purchases, the store clerk helped several other customers before he helped me.

While I waited, six-year-old Georgie wandered toward a slightly older boy who sat on a barrel, licking a peppermint stick. The boy turned the other way until Georgie asked him a question. Then he wrinkled his nose, jumped down from the barrel, and faced the little guy with his hands on his hips.

"You're a Behunin, ain't ya? You smell like an Indian."

"I do not!" Georgie replied. "Anyway, Indians don't smell."

"Do too! They stink to high heaven, and they steal too!" The boy stepped forward and poked his finger into Geogie's chest. "Do you steal too, Indian lover? My Pa says Behunins are Indian lovers, even live with them some times. You look like you live with the Indians. You ain't even got shoes."

"No, I don't live with the Indians. My pa's a missionary to them. Called by Brigham Young, himself."

"He was not. You're just a filthy Indian lover, that's all!" the boy jeered.

That's when Georgie doubled up his fist and took a good swing at the boy. I rushed between shelves and barrels as fast as I could. But by the time I got to the boys, they were rolling around on the floor, fisting it out. It was pretty easy to tell who was most likely to win. Georgie was on top.

I pulled my son off the boy and marched him outside, scolding him all the way. But the looks the other customers gave us as we left could have bored holes in our backs.

***

A school! At long last, a school! After all these years of hoping, wishing, and praying, a school for the children of the settlement opened its doors in the fall of '86.

Thrilled as I was, it wasn't an easy thing to get my children there. They had to walk more than three miles, and they didn't have any shoes. So when the weather was bad, I usually drove them in the wagon. One way or the other, my children went to school every day.

It turned out to be a mixed blessing. The problems I had seen in the general store plagued my children every day at school. After a while, they started to give me a hard time about going, and I couldn't blame them. The boys came home from school with black eyes and bloody noses more times than I'd like to tell. And Caroline cried because the girls called her names and wouldn't play with her. But I never let up. No matter what, I saw to it that my children went every day, and I thanked the Lord for the blessing. Still, it broke my heart.

**

"Fetch the boys and come on down from there," I called to my husband, a picnic basket hanging on my arm. "I've brought you some lunch."

Mosiah climbed down from the bowery that the menfolk of the settlement were building for our upcoming celebration. I smiled as Isaac, Joseph, Brigham, John, and last but not least, my little Davie, followed their father down the ladder and raced across the grass toward the quilt I was spreading out for our lunch. It was the third of July and hot as a firecracker. Mosiah mopped his brow with a red-checkered handkerchief and followed his sons, looking about as worn as last year's britches.

A few of the men had brought their lunch, and some went home to eat. But like us, a number of families spread quilts on the grass and made a picnic of it. We were all mighty excited. The settlement was gearing up for its first Fourth of July celebration. And the bowery was a matter of community pride.

"It's almost done, Mama," Davie called, as he came running toward me, near to tripping over his feet in his excitement. "It's a doosie, don't you think?" He turned around and gazed at the structure, his hands on his hips and pride shining in his eyes. "They're all saying we should have a flag, right up there on the top. Don't you think that would be just fine?"

"It would, indeed," I laughed, smiling at my son's enthusiasm. Davie was mighty proud to be considered old enough to help.

"I sure do wish we had one," he said again as he plopped down on the quilt. "That's what everybody is saying: 'Sure do wish we had a flag.'"

Isaac said the blessing, and I passed out the sandwiches, but Davie couldn't forget about the flag. "Don't you think it would be a fine thing, Papa, if we had a flag?"

"It would. I've heard people say that," Mosiah replied as he grabbed a sandwich and took a bite. "It's a fine idea. But we haven't got one, and it's a bit far to Salt Lake City. So I think we'll have to do without a flag this year."

219

Davie sighed and took a few bites of his sandwich, still looking wistfully at the empty bowery peak.

When every crumb of our picnic was eaten, Mosiah and the boys returned to work on the bowery and I packed up the quilt, the basket, and the younger children. But rather than head for home, as planned, I found myself heading into Hanksville. I did have a little credit at the general store from the eggs I brought in last week—credit I'd planned to use on fabric for school shirts—but maybe if I was real careful, I could work this one extra purchase in.

I stopped in front of the general store and scurried in, Mary Jane in my arms, and Caroline, Georgie, and Elijah trailing along behind. Minutes later we marched back out, Caroline and Georgie each toting a can of paint. I hummed all the way home, planning my little escapade as I went.

As soon as we hit the house, I went into action. First I sent the children to collect the pillow slips from all the beds, and then we tore them apart at the seams. I had no idea where I would get new ones. I decided not to think about that. My fingers flew, and by the time Mosiah got home with the boys, I had transformed the pillow slips into a big rectangle of white fabric.

"What is it, Mama?" they asked me, staring at the huge white cloth draped over the table.

"A flag," I answered, smiling over their heads at Mosiah.

My husband looked at me long and hard and scratched his head, a tiny smile turning up the corners of his mouth. "Caroline, are you sure? Those pillow slips were the only ones we had."

I nodded, and Davie let out a whoop so loud they probably heard it all the way to Hanksville.

***

We worked well into the night on that flag. Isaac and Joseph were real precise, measuring the stripes and using a piece of charcoal to draw the lines. Caroline and I made patterns for the stars. Then we all painted and painted. We had a little bread and milk for supper and kept on working, even after the little ones went to bed.

It was well past midnight when we attached our flag to a pole, and laid it out still wet, in the wagon bed. It would have to dry in the wind.

Mosiah stayed with the sleeping little ones, while the older boys and I drove to the bowery. Isaac and Joseph shimmied up, flag in hand. I was worried about them falling in the dark, but they made it just fine. They hung that flag high over the peak, just like Davie said.

We had barely shut our eyes before it was time to get up and go to the sunrise service. By the time we got there, most of the settlement had already arrived. And the square was buzzing with excitement over the flag that had materialized overnight. "It's a miracle," people said over and over again. Then with the morning sun just peeking over the Henry Mountains and our flag whipping in the breeze, the whole settlement sang, "My Country Tis of Thee." And everybody cried.

We had a chuckwagon breakfast and games and visiting. After that there was a potluck lunch, horse races, and more visiting. It was quite a day. The highlight, of course, was the mysterious flag. All day long people tried to find out who had made it. Davie was near to bursting with the secret, but nobody figured it out.

Chapter notes:

1. Caroline's journal tells about the settlers' scorn for them and about the flag she made and hung in the middle of the night for the Fourth of July celebration. It is unclear, however, what settlement they were living in at the time of the event.

Chapter Thirty-Two

With the children in bed, Mosiah and I snuggled together on the doorstep. The air was finally cool, and the breeze played in our hair. Over our heads, the sky hung dark and velvety, a million stars sparkling like tiny campfires in the night.

"I don't think I've ever seen the children have such a fine time," Mosiah said, smiling down at me. "And it's all because of that flag of yours."

"It was fun, wasn't it?" I smiled back. "Watching their eyes light up whenever someone mentioned our flag? Especially Davie—I feared he was going to burst the seams of his britches." I brushed at my skirts and asked, "Do you think anybody figured it out?"

"No, I don't think so, but they sure enough did try," Mosiah chuckled as he tucked a stray strand of hair behind my ear and stroked my cheek with the back of his hand. "The folks I talked to were dumbstruck that anyone would go to that much trouble to make things special for everyone else and keep it all a secret. I think they were grateful. Wasn't hard to see that some lady had sacrificed her pillow slips."

I wrapped my arms around my knees and hugged them tight, "I'm glad we did it, and I'd do it again in a minute."

"Caroline, you're one of a kind, that's for sure," my husband whispered into my ear, making me giggle, "I'm mighty grateful to be the man you're married to."

I gave his shoulder a playful push. He threw up his hands and laughed as he toppled off the step like a bottle shot off a log. Mosiah sat there for a minute, laughing in the dirt. Then he pulled himself up, brushed himself off, and came after me, all hugs and kisses.

I giggled and tried to get away, thinking it was a good thing the kids were all asleep.

"Mama? What's going on out there?" a little voice asked from the house. It was Caroline.

"Oh nothing, honey. Mama and Papa are just talking, that's all."

"Can I come out and talk too?"

"No, darlin'. You go on back to bed and go to sleep."

Mosiah and I collapsed into each other's arms, fits of laughter wracking our bodies 'til tears ran down both our cheeks. I think there was something in the air that night that made me feel fifteen again.

When we finally composed ourselves, Mosiah swooped me up and whirled me about. "Come on, darlin', dance with me," he laughed.

"Out here in the yard with no music?"

"You bet! Just look at the moon and the stars tonight—you might think they were just a foot or two above our heads. The way they're sparkling so bright, I feel like I could reach up and pick one of those stars, like a daisy out of the meadow, and pin it in your hair. It's a night for lovers. It surely is."

"Mmm," I murmured as I leaned my cheek against his chest and snuggled up, warmed by the tingling sensation that filled my whole being as he held me close and we swayed together in the moonlight. He was right; we didn't need any better music than the sighing of the night breeze in the cottonwood trees.

After a while, I looked up into his eyes and smiled. He wasn't young anymore. I could see crinkles around his eyes and grey streaks in his hair. He had all but worn himself out trying to be a good missionary—and a good husband and father, all at the same time. It hadn't been easy. I knew that.

He'd stood between the settlers and the Indians like a tiny ditch between two wildfires as they raged and roared at each other—armed only with a call from the Lord and the priesthood of God. But he had never faltered. Never wavered. And the territory was a better place because he had been there.

He pulled me close against his chest and breathed into my hair as he whispered, "I love you, darlin'. I truly do! This isn't the life you hoped for when you married me—I know that. There's not one woman in a million who'd do what you've done—follow her man into Indian territory and live the way we've had to live."

My husband stopped dancing and reached down to cradle my face in his hands as he drew my eyes to his. "I told you when we were called that you would have many times to

223

be afraid. And it's surely been much worse than that. We've raise nine children out here on the frontier—and many has been the day when we didn't know if we would live to see the sun come up the next morning."

"That's the very truth of it!" I agreed. "I had no idea what real fear was back then. But surely I do now! It's been hard, and that's a fact. But I feel right good about it. We've done something that nobody else could've done—and it was a good thing."

"Do you think it's been all right for the children?" Mosiah took my hand, and we strolled beneath the cottonwoods and listened to the crickets sing as we talked. "They've missed out on a lot of things that other young'uns have."

"Like schooling?" I asked. "You know how much I worried about that. But once they got into school, they picked it all up real fast." I stopped and looked up at him while I learned against a tree trunk, the moonlight filtering through its branches as the night air whispered and sighed. "They're right fine youngsters, Mosiah—every one of them. They're healthy and strong, and they understanding God and His ways too. They know what it means to serve Him with all your heart. I don't think we could have done better by them. I truly don't."

My husband wrapped his arms around me. Then he pulled me into a strong embrace and kissed me in a way that made me feel he and I were truly one. After a while we wandered hand in hand into the cabin and closed the door behind us.

Chapter Thirty-Three

Aldridge, Utah Territory
October 1887

The saddest day of our mission came almost at its end.

Our harvest was in, and it had been pretty fair. We put away all we could, bottling fruit and drying jerky. It felt good knowing we wouldn't be going hungry that winter. We'd raised hot peppers for the first time, and I'd strung them up on ropes, alongside my sweet onions, to dry in the October sun. They looked right pretty dangling down the sides of our cabin door.

Mosiah sat out front, whittling with his hunting knife on something for the baby while I washed up a few dishes. I could hear him whistling, and it made me feel good. When his whistling stopped, I peeked out the window to see why. Chief White Horse and seven of his braves were riding into our yard.

Mosiah stabbed his knife into the log beside him, got to his feet, and raised his hand in greeting. The warriors returned his gesture and swung down from their horses.

Wanzitz was among them. My stomach tied itself in a knot, just like it did every time I saw him. The grudge he carried against my husband was still heavy on his shoulders. An invisible but ever-present threat hung in the air whenever the two of them locked eyes.

Wanzitz hung back a bit from the others as they exchanged greetings with Mosiah, his eyes narrowing and his chin held high.

"We go to hunt elk," White Horse announced. He asked if Mosiah had seen any.

"Sure did," Mosiah answered with a grin. "Got myself a mighty fine bull just last week," and he nodded toward the large hide he had nailed on the side of the shed to dry.

Like a gaggle of geese, they turned in unison and headed out to the shed to have a look. Mosiah trailed along behind.

I stepped outside and shaded my eyes with my hand as I watched them examine the pelt, measure it with their arms, and nod as Mosiah showed them the head, still sporting a huge, heavy rack.

"You come hunt with us? Show where you find?" White Horse asked when they returned to the door yard. But Mosiah shook his head. "I have plenty already," he explained, "But I'll tell you where I got him." He dropped to one knee and began to draw a map in the dirt as he gave them directions. With one exception, they all nodded, grinned, and then moved toward their horses. Wanzitz, however, seemed less interested in the hunt and more interested in the red peppers hanging at our door.

"What these?" he demanded as he marched to the door, grabbed a large, fiery red pepper, still attached to the rope and turned it in his hand.

I knew we were in trouble the moment I saw that sly smile spread across my husband's face and dance in his eyes.

"Don't you dare," I whispered at his elbow, but he paid no more attention to me than if I was a pesky fly.

"Peppers," he answered with a twinkle. "Food."

I glanced over at Wanzitz. The warrior was powerfully built and a full head taller than my husband. The knot in my stomach swelled up 'til it all but popped out of my throat. "Mosiah, please!" I whispered.

But he merely swung the back of his hand in my direction and shrugged me off.

Mosiah was all but dancing with anticipation. "Would you like one? Here, go ahead," Mosiah snickered as he unfastened the crimson pepper from the rope and handed it to the curious Indian.

Wanzitz took it. I held my breath as he turned it over in his hand several times, inspecting it thoroughly.

"Wanzitz, don't—," I blurted out. But it was too late. As if accepting a challenge, he met my husband's eyes with his own and then sunk his teeth into the pepper, tearing away a huge chunk, seeds and all.

As he began to chew, the triumphant look on his face faded, soon to be replaced by surprise and then horror. His eyes popped huge and red, and his mouth exploded. Bits of crimson flew through the air and sprayed all over my skirt. They peppered Mosiah's beard and dotted the ground.

Mosiah began to shake beside me. "Don't!" I spat at him, but it did no good. Laughter exploded from him in much the same way the pepper had exploded from Wanzitz's mouth. A few feet away from us I heard the braves begin to laugh as well.

Dignity forgotten, Wanzitz began to hop about. He desperately clawed at his mouth in an effort to remove the burning seeds that seared the inside of his mouth and his throat. Grabbing handfuls of dirt, he threw them into his mouth, but nothing did any good. The whites of his eyes burned scarlet, and his face turned as red as the pepper he had chewed. He coughed and retched as his feet beat a tattoo on the ground.

At last his panicked eyes met mine, and I pointed to the well. He took off for it like a coyote with his tail between his legs.

By now, Mosiah was bent over with laughter, tears running down his face and into his beard as he slapped his leg and hooted.

White Horse and his braves were laughing just as hard.

Wanzitz stayed at the well a long time, drinking and spitting and drinking some more. By the time he turned and strode toward us, the laughter was mostly under control, but when his eyes met the eyes of his fellow warriors, he found barely concealed smirks on their faces and their shoulders still shaking with laughter they couldn't quite subdue.

I saw him freeze. Then he pivoted and ran straight at us, his fisted knife glinting in the sun.

"Get in the house!" Mosiah yelled. And I got. But only long enough to grab the butcher knife laying on the table and dash back out.

I saw Mosiah go over backwards just as I rushed outside. His left hand was gripping Wanzitz's knife hand, holding it back with all his strength.

The warrior's face was flushed with rage, his eyes squinted into tight slits and his teeth barred. Despite his strength, I knew Mosiah could not hold him back for long. He was no match for the powerful Indian who now sat astride his body, attempting to drive the knife into his chest.

It took only a fraction of an instant to know what I must do. I had to reach the two men and drive my own knife deep into Wanzitz's back before Mosiah's strength gave out. As he fought and squirmed, I could see his eyes glance over to the knife he had left in the stump. But he had little chance of reaching it.

I screamed. It was a feral sound that tore from my body of its own accord. A wild cry that seemed to emanate from some source other than my own throat. Gathering all my strength, I threw myself toward them, my knife held high.

As if jerked from extreme concentration by the intensity of my cry, Wanzitz's eyes left Mosiah's and darted toward me, an expression of total shock and amazement sweeping across his features. Brief as that fleeting moment was, it gave Mosiah just enough time to curl his fingers around his own knife and thrust it deep into the warrior's heart.

Wanzitz grunted in pain and disbelief. His lips parted, and a stream of blood spurted from between his teeth. His wild eyes met mine, a silent message passing between us. Then they glazed, and his limp body collapsed, his knife biting the dirt just inches from my husband's head.

The world swirled around me, and I sank to my knees, shaking and crying Mosiah's name.

Wanzitz's body moved, and I jumped back in fear as Mosiah rolled from under the big Indian and pushed him over onto his back.

The warrior stared into our faces with wide, vacant eyes. A trickle of blood, red as a pepper, slid down the corner of his mouth and turned black in the dirt.

Huge, gulping sobs convulsed through my shaking body. This man had all but killed my husband—would have if my scream hadn't distracted him. But all I could think of was the majestic warrior who came to my home when I was a young bride, asking for food, and of his tenderness as he knelt beside me and wiped away my tear with his strong finger saying, "You no be afraid, me like you."

White Horse and his men came noiselessly up behind us, lifted Wanzitz between them, and laid him across his horse.

They had seen the whole thing and knew that we had acted in self-defense, but there was a hardness in their eyes as they looked at us and rode silently away.

Mosiah stood like a granite column until the hunting party rode out of sight with Wanzitz's lifeless body across his pony's back, his arms swinging to and fro in a sickening sort of way. Then Mosiah crumpled.

I had never really seen my husband cry before that day. He had shed tears, yes—like when Ligie died. But not like this.

He sat there in the dirt until the sun began to fade in the sky, his knees pulled up against his chest, his hands pulled over his head, and his body shaking with sobs.

I didn't bother him. I knew he had to work it out inside of himself and with the Lord. But for a man who'd spent fourteen years of his life trying to help the Indian people, this was the closest he had ever come to failure.

My husband was quiet as a ghost for days after that, sitting hour upon hour in the yard, staring wordlessly off into the trees.

I tried to tell him it wasn't his fault, that he had done what needed to be done and that it was self-defense.

"Was it?" he asked. "When he came at me with the knife, maybe so. But I did have a choice, and I made that choice when I handed him the pepper."

"You didn't know what it would lead to."

"You did. You asked me to stop. But I didn't listen. Just went right on ahead. I thought it would be . . . Oh, Caroline, what must the Lord think of me now?"

"Have you asked Him?"

"No, I can't face Him. I was on His errand."

"I think it's high time you talk to Him about it. He probably understands better than you think. Give Him the chance to forgive you. And when you're done, maybe you should give White Horse the same chance."

Later that day he wandered off into the trees and was gone a long time. When he came back he was a different man—deeper and humbler, but in some ways, stronger, too.

The next day he saddled his horse to ride to White Horse's camp. I left the young ones in Caroline's care, saddled up, and went with him.

We felt the stillness of the camp the moment we rode into it. Like a forest that hushes with the touch of a human foot, the noisy activity of the Ute camp froze in thin air at our presence.

White Horse greeted us just outside his *tepee* with eyes that seemed sad but not angry. We gave him gifts of food which he accepted graciously. Then he and my husband ducked inside to talk while I sat on the ground by the door.

The walls of a *tepee* are thin and though I couldn't hear all that was said, I heard enough to know that Mosiah apologized deeply, taking blame for Wanzitz's death. The chief sadly accepted his apology and admitted that he too held part of the blame. "It is not a good thing to shame a man," he said. "Laughing at a warrior as strong and brave as Wanzitz should never be done."

Before we mounted up, White Horse and Mosiah clasped each other's forearms and looked deeply in each other's eyes. In them, I saw two strong men from very different worlds reaching out to build a bridge over which their people could cross.

We said very little on the way home, but as our cabin came into view, Mosiah stopped his horse. When I did the same, he smiled sadly into my eyes and said, "Caroline, I think it's time."

I knew he was right.

Chapter notes:

1. Although somewhat enhanced by the author, the episode in which Mosiah gives an Indian a red pepper and, kills the angry Indian in self-defense is taken from Behunin oral history.

Epilogue

Ferron, Utah Territory
1887

Not much more than a month later, Bishop Thurber came to see us. He brought our mission release with him. It was time, and we knew it. But just the same, we floundered like trout out of water. We had been serving on that mission for fourteen of the seventeen years of our marriage. It was all the children knew.

We considered, quite a lot, the idea of staying where we were, tucked between the Dirty Devil and Freemont Rivers, but my heart was set on Richfield. So we packed everything up and retraced our steps, except that we were going back with nine children instead of just the two we left Richfield with.

We weren't truly surprised to find another family living on our old homestead. It had been a long time, and we didn't have any legal claim to it anymore. Still, it was a real hard thing to see. We didn't quite know what to do when we couldn't find land in Richfield we could afford. But we prayed that the Lord would guide us to the place where He wanted us to be. And He did.

We stayed with Jane and Cutler in Thurber for a while. To me, it felt about as good as cozying up next to a fire on a cold winter night to be with their sweet family again. We had truly missed them; and I think they felt the same. That's when Cutler had the idea we might all go to Idaho together and get some land there. So that's what we headed out to do.

The Lord seemed to have other plans for the Behunins though. We only made it as far as Ferron. Good land was reasonably priced there, and best of all, we could be neighbors at last.

Most people don't think of Ferron, Utah as being the Garden of Eden. But for us, it truly was. We bought ourselves a little farm and planted fruit trees, melons, and corn. And we kept bees.

Mosiah made bricks from clay and built us a fine house. It had a kitchen, a parlor, three bedrooms, real wood floors, and a cook stove—at last! I made red-and-white-checkered curtains for the kitchen window, and Mosiah put in a white picket fence all around our yard. On summer evenings, we liked to sit out on the big front porch and watch the sun go down—all purple and orange over the mountains to the west.

My little Sinthia was born in '88 and Robert Perry in '90, giving us eleven children all told.

One late summer afternoon as I sat on the porch husking corn for dinner, a wagon pulled up out front and a young couple got out. Their hair was black and braided, and their skin was dark. But the man was wearing overalls, and the woman wore a regular skirt and blouse.

I couldn't quite make out who they were as they walked up the path to my house until I noticed that the woman's limp. Then I knew.

It was my Little Bird! I ran and hugged her so tight it made her laugh and me cry. My, but it was a fine thing to see her after all those years! She was all grown up into a beautiful young woman.

She was expecting a baby; I could tell. The young man was the chief's son and would be chief himself one day. What a fine looking young man he was! They had come to Ferron to buy ewes and rams for the tribal sheep ranch.

They stayed at our place that night and ate dinner with us. We visited and laughed and talked about old times. Little Bird told me that the Paiutes had their own branch of the Church in Koosheram and that she and Pan-sook hoped to be sealed in the temple soon.

When it was time for them to leave, I held their hands, looked into their handsome young faces, and cried. In that moment, I knew the hard times we had faced didn't mean a thing.

Our mission was the greatest blessing the Lord could have given us. Yes, we did sacrifice. But the good we accomplished and the happiness it brought to us made it all worth it, a hundred times over.

Bibliography

Behunin, Caroline Hill. *Caroline H. Behunin Rreminiscences*, undated unpublished manuscript, from the collection of the Church History Library (Salt Lake City, UT), call number MS 6649.

Behunin, Mosiah Stephen. *Mosiah S. Behunin notebook,* 1875-1881. Unpublished manuscript, from the collection of the Church History Library (Salt Lake City, UT), call number MS 982.

Moss, Fenton E. *The man who named Zion Canyon: the story of Isaac* Behunin /by his great, great grandson Fenton E. Moss. St. George, Utah [?]: Author, 1998.

Our Heritage: A Brief History of the Church of Jesus Christ of Latter-day Saints. Salt Lake City, UT: Church of Jesus Christ of Latter-day Saints, 1996.

Peterson, John Alton. *Utah's Black Hawk War.* Salt Lake City, UT: University of Utah Press, 1998.

Petit, Jan. *Utes: The Mountain People.* Boulder, CO: Johnson Books, 1990.

Riley, Michael.*Golden Legends Fuel Dreams of Rriches* Denver Post (Denver, CO), Nov. 13, 2005.

Tippets, Ruby Noyes. *A Song in Her Heart.* Provo, UT: Brigham Young University Press, 1961.

Tyler, Daniel. *Incidents of Experience.* In Scraps of biography: tenth book of the Faith-promoting series : designed for the instruction and encouragement of young Latter-day Saints, edited by George Q. Cannon, 20-

24. Salt Lake City, UT: Juvenille Instructor Office, 1883.

Acknowledgements

Many people have been instrumental in helping me transform Caroline's story into *I Faced the Wind*. It has been an incredible journey and has left me with a deep appreciation for the faith and selflessness of the men and women whose courage transformed the desert lands of Utah's Dixie into farms, towns, and national monuments.

I would like to thank my amazing editor, Katrina Beckstrand, whose expertise and gentle guidance helped to bring this book to life. Many thanks, also, to my wonderful writing coach, Brenda Bench. I learned so much from you. Many thanks as well to my friend and classmate Marion Steiger, whose comments and edits taught me so much and made *I Faced the Wind* a better book.

I would also like to thank the members of my critique group: Kristin Oliver, Jackie Wood, Marion Steiger, Kathy Wendell, and Heather Darger for their friendship, encouragement and help.

Last, but not least, I would like to thank my husband, Vern Newbold, who is always my first reader and editor. Thank you for your never-ending help and support.

About the Author

Joy Newbold lives in West Jordan, Utah, where she rides horses, raises rabbits, enjoys theater and music, and teaches preschool. She and her husband, Vern, have six children and twenty-two grandchildren. She is the great-great-granddaughter of Caroline and Mosiah Behunin. Even as a child, Joy was fascinated by their remarkable story. Her desire to turn that story into a novel motivated her to become a writer.

Joy's previous works include: *Where the Dragon Soars*, *Ghosts in the Attic: A Young Warlock Faces his Destiny*, and *Shai: The Lamb that Jesus Loved*.

www.ingramcontent.com/pod-product-compliance
Lightning Source LLC
Chambersburg PA
CBHW030254200626
46816CB00002BA/638